PRAISE FOR
UNSPOKEN LOVE

Unspoken Love is a book about many of life's most potent realities. Danielle's writing is intriguing . . . Heaven is in these pages. There is no earthly quality stronger than a parent's love for a child. Such love is traced on every page. The majesty of a personal relationship with the Living God is here. Our God's fingerprints are everywhere in this deeply personal book. . . . Read *Unspoken Love*. Be intrigued. At multiple levels. And watch your soul grow.

— **Stu Weber,**
Lead Pastor Emeritus,
Good Shepherd Community Church
Author of several bestselling books,
including *Spirit Warriors* and *Tender Warrior*

Jesus is vividly seen and experienced by anyone who has the pleasure of knowing Danielle Shryock. This woman has known deep pain and loss, but has found deeper joy through a living relationship with the King. She's a gracious, humble woman of wisdom. I invite you to hear from a heart that will refresh your soul and draw you to Him.

— **Alan Hlavka,**
Pastor at Good Shepherd
Community Church

Danielle Shryock has eyes to see her daughter's disability as a bridge to draw others toward Christ. *Unspoken Love* points us to Jesus and the sanctity of life, and recognizes God is at work in each and every circumstance in our lives.

— **Randy Alcorn,**
Author of *Heaven,*
Safely Home,* and *Deadline

Unspoken Love

Unspoken Love

DANIELLE SHRYOCK

Published by Deep River Books
Sisters, Oregon
www.deepriverbooks.com

ISBN – 13: 9781632694836
Library of Congress: 2018951013

Printed in the USA
Cover design by Robin Black, Inspirio Design

In loving memory of my mom and dad; Major M.G. and Constance Shryock. I could not have asked for better parents, they were my biggest cheerleaders. This book would not have been written without their unending support. Love you, Mom and Dad and miss you very much. Looking forward to our reunion one day in our eternal home.

CHAPTER ONE

Entering the great throne room took Seefas's breath away. Immersed in his favorite sound, countless voices praising his Lord, Seefas stood in awe as he gazed at the beautiful, glassy sea that reflected all the colors in the rainbow. In the very center of the throne room, the most magnificent light radiated from our Lord Jesus Christ. Everyone present couldn't help but fall to their knees in worship.

Angels assembled from every direction on this day in the great throne room to report to their Lord, some to give an account of their work on earth, some to strategize their next plan of action, and some to receive a new assignment. Seefas could hardly contain his excitement: he had heard some angels say that the Lord was going to give out very special assignments today, including ones for children. Now, you wouldn't know by looking at Seefas, a large, daunting angel whom you wouldn't want to face in battle, that children were his favorite assignments. In his last assignment his great strength had been the key to seeing his man succeed. The man had gone into unreached parts of the world to tell people about Jesus; Seefas had been in constant battle during this assignment, and they won many victories for Jesus. Even more hearts were won through the man's martyrdom, and Seefas was given the honor of ushering him into his eternal home. Seeing one of God's men risk everything to further God's kingdom had been very rewarding; the assignment had been a good one. Seefas was eager to receive a child this time, though. Very tenderhearted and incredibly gentle with children, he was anxious to use his easy ability to relate to them again. It had been quite a while, and Seefas's heart leapt with joy at the mere thought of receiving this greatest honor from the Lord, being entrusted with one of His little ones.

Seefas's heart sank a little as he saw what seemed like an endless sea of angels in front of him. He wasn't sure how many new child assignments were being handed out, but other angels seemed to be getting them. He had to remind himself that the Lord always had the perfect person in mind for each of His angels, and there was a reason behind every decision. As the line grew closer, Seefas became increasingly anxious, although he wasn't sure why this time the waiting seemed so intense. He had been up for new assignments before, but never had he felt such a strong desire to be assigned to a child. "Maybe the Lord is putting this desire in my heart and is preparing me for a child that especially needs me." Several angels looked in his direction. Startled that he had made this statement out loud, Seefas flushed a little but continued to ponder.

Captivated by the intensity of the thoughts and feelings swirling inside him, Seefas was shocked to hear the voice of his Lord. "Dear Seefas, let's talk about the mission that's before you." Instantly, Seefas fell to his knees in worship. Rising he said, "Forgive me Lord, I was so caught up in thought I did not realize it was my turn to stand before you."

"My cherished Seefas, it shows me that your heart is ready to receive this very special assignment that I have in store for you. The urgency that you are feeling has been coming from me. I am in the process of knitting together a very special little girl, and she is going to need your strengths in every way. She is one of my most precious creations. In the world's eyes, she will seem incomplete, imperfect; some will say that she should not be given a chance to enter this world. But I tell you, she will have an eternal innocence. She will reflect who I am and have such an impact on the world just by being herself. I look forward to my relationship with her. She will not allow the world to deter her from loving me with all her heart."

"My Lord, I don't understand. How can any human possess such qualities? I have worked with other children before; when they are babies I enjoy playing with them and making them laugh, but as they grow up their innocence disappears, and soon they don't recognize me anymore. What makes this little one so different?"

"Every person that I have placed on earth is fearfully and wonderfully made. Each is made in my image, and is given a free will, to choose to love me or to turn their back on me. When a baby is born, he or she possesses innocence initially but is born with a sin nature. As children start to walk, talk, and imitate the world around them, each must choose how to respond to temptation. But this little creation of mine will be different. She will not be what the world considers 'normal,' for she will be born with a handicap. Everything will come a lot slower for her; walking and talking will not come easily. She will be a happy, content little girl and will not get caught up in the worldly temptations that life throws at her. It should be very exciting for you to see how she's able to impact the world around her. You will need to use all your gifts in working with this little one for she will need your tender heart and your strength. You, Seefas, are the perfect angel for this job."

"Wow! That's a lot to take in. I don't quite understand it all, but I am your servant and I'm here to serve you. I trust you and know that you will reveal all to me in due time. I feel a little hesitant, yet excited all the same. To be with a little child again gives me great delight. When do I get to start this new adventure?"

"As we speak, her mom is about to find out that she's pregnant with this tiny creation. I want you to go now because your little one will need you even through the time in her mother's womb. She is a treasure to behold, and I'm entrusting her to your care. Go now, Seefas, and remember I am with you every step of this little girl's life."

CHAPTER TWO

Cathy woke to the sun streaming into her bedroom, surprised at how peaceful her house seemed at that moment. The Ellertons' cozy nine-hundred-square-foot home was usually alive with excitement. Cathy was routinely awakened by the sound of their fifteen-month-old son, Joshua, yelling for her to free him from his crib so he could play with his Siberian husky, Shawnee. Normally she would also hear her husband, Gene, a software engineer at a company just down the road, in the other room getting ready for work. But silence was all Cathy heard this particular morning.

As she lay in bed wishing for another baby, she suddenly remembered the pregnancy test she'd planned to use that morning. "I guess I forgot since the last hundred times it's turned out negative." Cathy's green eyes momentarily sparkled and her dark brown curls bounced at the thought that she was, after all, only in her late twenties. "It's not like I'm getting too old," she told herself. "We just want a baby soon so the kids will be close in age." They had been trying for a while, though, and she was starting to get discouraged. "I guess I better get the test and get it over with." As she rolled out of bed, she found a note lying on the pillow next to her,

"Sweetheart, I had to go into work early today. Sorry I forgot to tell you last night. Give Joshy hugs and kisses for me. Love you lots! Gene"

Cathy grinned as she walked into the bathroom. She pulled out the pregnancy test, then went to check on Josh as she waited for the results. She poured a glass of orange juice, then sat down and waited for an answer to the question of each morning: "Am I pregnant or not?"

As the timer went off, she made her way to the bathroom. She closed her eyes, took a deep breath and looked at the window of the pregnancy test. She picked it up and looked again, then walked to the kitchen where there was better light, and looked again. "Yahoo!" Unable to contain herself, she started jumping up and down, "It's positive, it's positive."

"Mommy, Mommy, Joshy wants to sing song too."

When Cathy rushed in, he was rubbing his eyes yawning. Scooping him up, she smothered him with kisses. "Sorry Mommy woke you. I'll teach you my song, cute little guy."

A small boy with not much hair, Josh had bright, shining brown eyes and a smile that made you melt. Before long they were both singing Mommy's song, "It's positive, it's positive." Josh thought this was fun and wanted Daddy to sing along too.

"Daddy had to go to work early today, but we can call him on the phone and teach him the words to our song." Cathy dialed Gene at work, and when he answered he heard his wife and son singing this very peculiar song.

"What does 'it's positive' mean . . . are you telling me what I think you're telling me?"

"Honey, the result is positive," Cathy said in her best businesslike voice.

"That's great, Sweetheart! We'll celebrate when I get home."

Although the Ellertons lived in a small house, their backyard was anything but small, with enormous trees and lots of room to run. Cathy and Josh took Shawnee out to play.

"Nap time, my little Buster. When you get up, Daddy should be home."

"O.K. Mommy." Josh was not one to argue when it came to naps; he loved taking them.

While Josh slept, Cathy spent time in prayer, thanking God for her Joshy and the wonderful creation growing inside of her. She had so much she wanted to tell her unborn child that she decided to write her baby a letter.

To my sweet little one, I found out today that you are growing inside me. I was filled with joy and thanked our Heavenly Father for blessing us with such a sweet gift. Your dad and I already love you so much. I want you to know that you are wanted and were conceived out of love.

We are so excited for you to join our family; I'm sure your brother will be as well, once Daddy and I sit down and tell him. My prayer for you, sweet one, is that you will grow up and fall in love with our Lord, Jesus Christ. I pray that you will choose to walk with Him in everything you do. Your dad and I have placed you in the Lord's hands. I promise to be the best mom I can be. On my own I will fail, but with God's help, I can meet that goal. I want you to always feel loved by me and know that you are special.

After Cathy's quiet time, she got dinner in the oven and lay down to nap herself. "Better get my rest, now that I'm carrying you around, sweet one." Cathy was about to fall asleep when there was a knock on the door. It was Sophie Carter, their next-door neighbor.

An attractive lady in her early forties, Sophie had dark red hair and bright blue eyes. When the Ellertons first moved in, Sophie hadn't been too keen on them. They made it known quickly that they were Christians, and Sophie wanted no part of that. She still didn't, but the Ellertons grew on her and she enjoyed their company. Widowed when she was young, Sophie was lonely and often came over to chat with Cathy. She especially loved playing with Josh, as she'd never had children of her own.

"Hi, Sophie, what's up?"

"Cathy, could I come in and visit for a while, or are you busy? I thought maybe I could spend a little time with Josh."

"Uh, yeah, I guess so." Cathy was hesitant because she really wanted that nap, but she hated saying no. "Josh is still down for his nap, but I have some exciting news to share with you."

"Really? What is it?" Sophie loved getting the inside scoop.

"I just found out I'm pregnant. We've been trying for a while so we're very excited." Sophie was happy for her, and they continued to chat until Gene got home.

"Hey, Sweetheart!" Gene gave Cathy a kiss. "Sophie, nice to see you. How have you been?"

"Pretty good, thanks, Gene. I was just on my way out the door. See you later, Cathy."

"Bye, Sophie."

Gene was standing with a grin on his face with his hands behind his back.

"What are you up to, my husband?"

"I got something for you." Gene pulled out a dozen roses.

Cathy gave him a big hug. "When did you get to be the romantic type? Thank you, they're beautiful."

"You are most welcome. I'm very excited about your news. We'll have to start thinking about names. Have you told Josh the good news yet?"

"No, I thought I would wait for you, and we could do it over dinner. I made his favorite meal, pizza casserole, to butter him up a little."

"What did Sophie have to say?"

"Nothing, she was just feeling lonely again. Hey, Josh should be getting up about now. Why don't you go get him, and I'll get dinner on the table."

As Gene was carrying a groggy Josh into the dining room, Cathy couldn't help but smile. Josh was a little carbon copy of his daddy. They both had light brown hair with big brown eyes. Josh was a daddy's boy. "Are you ready for dinner, Sleepyhead? I made your favorite meal."

"Pizza cass-rol?" Josh asked in an inquisitive, yet tired voice.

"You betcha; let's eat."

As they were nearing the end of dinner, Gene broached the subject of babies. "So, Joshy, how would you like to have your own little baby?"

"My baby?"

"Yes, your baby and, well, Mommy's and mine too."

"Yay, a baby, a baby. Where is baby?"

"Well, right now our baby is growing inside of Mommy's tummy. It's still going to be a long time because right now God's making our baby. Special babies take time to make."

"We want a spe- sh -al baby, right?

"Yes, Buster, we want a special baby. What do you say we all go in the backyard and play with Shawnee?"

Cathy chimed in, "That sounds fun, and then it will be bath and bed."

* * *

"Wow, what a day. My pillow feels good right now. What time do you have to work in the morning?"

"Um, Cathy, tomorrow's Saturday. I'm sleeping in."

"Oh, yeah." Cathy said with an embarrassed smile. "All the excitement of the day has me turned around."

"I know. I'm very happy too. I love you, Sweetheart. Good-night." Gene leaned over to give Cathy a kiss.

"I love you, too."

As peace and quiet fell over the Ellertons' home, a deep, gentle voice spoke softly. "Hello, little one, my name is Seefas, and I'm your guardian angel. I'm going to be with you through your journey in your mommy's womb and the new adventure waiting for you on the other side."

CHAPTER THREE

Usually walking into Doctor Tanaka's office gave Cathy and Gene a reassuring feeling. He had been Cathy's OB/GYN since her pregnancy with Josh. His office was warm and welcoming with a painting of Jesus overlooking a mom and her newborn baby. It was a great reminder that Jesus is there overseeing the birth of His children.

Today, Cathy and Gene were anxious. Everything had been going along well with the pregnancy; Cathy felt better in the first eight weeks of this pregnancy than she had with Josh. But when she'd woken up that morning, she had noticed that she was starting to bleed. She'd called Gene and together they decided to see Doctor Tanaka.

"Cathy, the doctor will see you now." It was Nurse Gail, an energetic redhead who loved the Lord and wasn't ashamed to show it.

"Gail, I'm so glad you're here, I need a familiar face right now."

"Cathy, don't worry, you know God's in control. Everything's going to work out for the best. Here's your room; Doctor Tanaka will be right in."

Cathy and Gene had only been there a few minutes when the doctor walked in.

"Mr. and Mrs. Ellerton, so good to see you. How's your little boy doing? Getting big I imagine. What do you say we take a walk over to the ultrasound room and take a peek at that little peanut growing inside of you? I'm sure everything is fine, but that will help alleviate any doubts you are feeling." Doctor Tanaka had a way of putting them at ease. A young doctor with a great sense of humor, he never rushed them out of his office, invariably lent a listening ear when needed, and always had words of encouragement. He also loved the Lord.

"Sounds perfect to us; thanks, Doctor Tanaka," Gene said, taking Cathy's hand as they walked across the hall to the ultrasound room.

"Mrs. Ellerton, go ahead and lie down and, Mr. Ellerton, you can stand over here where you can have a good look at your little one."

"As you can see, at this stage your baby is tiny. But, if you look up in the right-hand corner you can see your little miracle. Looks like it has a little halo; there's your little angel."

Tears welled up in Gene's eyes as he observed his unborn baby. "It is incredible how small we start out, and God continues to knit us together all the way through the pregnancy process."

With teary eyes, Cathy looked at Gene. "You're right. We are definitely miracles; I don't understand how people can go through the process of watching a baby develop and not believe in the Creator of life." Cathy had often struggled with this concept. It had struck her the first time when she was pregnant with Josh.

She then turned her attention to her baby, "God has a special plan for you, little one. You had us a little scared. Isn't it amazing, Gene? That's our baby we're looking at."

"Now you can put your fears aside; your little one looks perfect. Another important thing that we learned today is exactly how far along you are in your pregnancy. This will help us keep a close eye on the progress of this little creation."

Cathy felt herself relax. "Thank you, Doctor Tanaka. This puts my mind at ease. I just don't want anything to happen. I believe that God chose this baby specifically for us."

Cathy and Gene left the doctor's office feeling as though a tremendous weight had been lifted from them. They drove the whole way home singing praise to the Lord and thanking him for their miracle. Although they were unaware of it, Seefas was singing right along with them.

CHAPTER FOUR

Cathy was getting Josh dressed and ready to spend the day with Grandpa Roy, Gene's dad. Gene's mom had divorced Roy when Gene was little. As a single dad he'd raised Gene and his brother Nate and was delighted to still play an active role in both his sons' lives. Roy lived just a couple of blocks from the Ellertons and was a great babysitter. Josh adored him. Today, he was taking Josh to one of his favorite places, a little farm with a train ride that went around the land looking at all the animals.

"Mommy, Grandpa and I love an-mals. But, Joshy miss Mommy, want you come too."

"Buster, Mommy can't come with you this time, remember? I'm meeting Daddy at the doctor's office, and we're finding out if you're going to have a little brother or a sister. I promise to call you on Grandpa's phone and make sure you're the first person to know. Besides, you're going to be having so much fun at the farm you won't have time to miss Mommy."

"Joshy have fun!"

"I know you will, so what do you say we get going? Grandpa's waiting for you."

After Cathy dropped Josh at Grandpa Roy's, she started thinking about her baby. She wondered if she was carrying a boy or a girl. She very much wanted a girl this time. She couldn't believe how fast this pregnancy seemed to be flying by. After that first scare twelve weeks ago with her spotting, the pregnancy seemed to be going perfectly. As she pulled into the parking lot, she saw Gene getting out of his car.

"Hi Honey, great timing. Are you excited to find out what we're having?" Cathy asked Gene as she walked up and greeted him with a kiss.

"Yeah, but I could go either way. Although, it would be fun to have a little girl to spoil."

"Like you don't already spoil our son."

As they walked into the doctor's office, they couldn't help remembering how different they'd felt at eight weeks of pregnancy. This time, they were filled with anticipation. Cathy had been thinking of names for weeks.

As they entered the room they knew so well, Doctor Tanaka was waiting for them.

"Hello, Mr. and Mrs. Ellerton, so good to see you. Are you ready to take a look at your little one?"

"Let's do it!" Cathy said excitedly. Gene and Doctor Tanaka laughed.

"Let's get started by taking a look at this creation growing inside of you. First, I'll take some measurements." They all turned their focus to the screen. "There's the hand; look, your baby's waving 'Hi, Mom and Dad.' Oh! There's a great profile shot; what a striking baby. Then we have a foot, a leg, look there; your baby's sucking its thumb. Here we go, are you ready for the question of the day?"

"Yes!" Cathy and Gene said in unison as they were beginning to get anxious.

"All right, look right . . . there! Do you see anything?"

"No," laughed Gene, "that can only mean one thing . . . we're having a girl!"

"Really, Doctor Tanaka, is he right?"

"Absolutely, a beautiful baby girl."

"I can't believe it; I'm so happy. Little Nicole Rebecca." Overcome with joy, Cathy started to cry.

"Nicole? Sounds perfect," said Gene. "I love it. When did you come up with that?"

"Right now. It just seemed to fit. We better call Joshy and tell him he's having a little sister."

Gene, Cathy, Joshy, Grandpa Roy—everyone, in fact—was excited and happy that day. Though they couldn't see him, Seefas was perhaps the happiest of them all, overwhelmed with emotion at watching God's children rejoicing over the little girl who was going to change their lives in amazing ways. He said a little prayer that their joy would continue, as they were about to enter into the hardest part of the pregnancy. Seefas then directed his attention to Nicole. "Nicole is an ideal name for you, little one; it means victorious heart."

CHAPTER FIVE

Not surprisingly for the U.S. Northwest, it was a drizzly afternoon. The Ellertons loved living in Portland. Having grown up there, Gene would often say, "How many places in this world do you get to experience all the seasons? We're one of the lucky ones." Cathy couldn't argue; her parents were missionaries, so she had lived all over the world. Although she loved her experiences growing up, she was ready to settle down in one place, and she couldn't think of a better place to raise her family than beautiful Oregon.

"So, what do you want to do on this rainy Saturday?" Gene asked Josh, who was getting antsy.

"Joshy want play game." Josh treasured his time with Mom and Dad, and one of his favorite things to do was to play games.

Josh always preferred to play hide and seek with his toys. Cathy let Josh pick out the toys he wanted to hide, and Gene and Cathy closed their eyes and counted to ten while Josh hid the toys. They were having a great time laughing and just enjoying being together when the phone rang.

Cathy got up to answer it. "Hello?"

"Mrs. Ellerton? This is Doctor Tanaka."

"Hi, there. What can I do for you? Is everything okay?"

"Sorry to call you on a Saturday, but I was just reviewing the ultrasound we did a few weeks ago and I noticed that your girl is on the small side. I wondered if you and Mr. Ellerton could come in for another ultrasound so we could take a few more measurements?"

"Is there need for concern?" Cathy asked in a shaky voice.

"No, not at this time. I just want to monitor her development and see if she's made up any ground. Some babies will lag behind and then catch up again. I want to take more measurements as a precautionary measure. If you're free this afternoon, I could get you in so you're not worrying about it all weekend. Does around three o'clock sound good?"

"We'll make it work, thank you, Doctor Tanaka. Good-bye."

"Lord, give them a peace and lift them up as their world is about to change." Watching the relationship between the Ellertons and their son, Seefas knew that they'd pull through this time and be great parents to Nicole.

* * *

"Thanks for coming on such short notice," Doctor Tanaka greeted them as they walked in the door.

"Let's get those measurements." Cathy lay on the table and Doctor Tanaka went to work taking the measurements.

"So, what's it telling you, Doc?" Gene asked apprehensively.

"Your peanut is still about three weeks behind schedule. I've been thanking the Lord for that early ultrasound that we did at eight weeks' gestation. Because of that I know exactly how far along she is. Otherwise, I would probably assume that our calculation of your due date was off. This could be a problem that's just taking place in the womb, called intrauterine growth restriction, which means that she will be born small. But I have to be honest with you, it could also mean that she has Down syndrome or another kind of problem. Many kids with Down have been born with this problem. We will monitor her development closely. Your amniotic fluid is also on the low side, so as a preventive measure, I would like you to drink about twelve full glasses of water a day. Do you have any questions for me?"

Cathy and Gene sat there with blank stares on their faces. Doctor Tanaka had given them a lot of information and they were still trying to process it all.

"So . . . our . . . little girl has Down?" Cathy asked trying to hold back the tears.

"Not necessarily, the problem could strictly be in utero. I just want you to be prepared for the possibility. I know that you both love the Lord. This may sound like a cliché, but He's in control and He knows what's best for your lives. I have met a lot of kids with Down and they are the sweetest children you'd ever come across. Just hold onto the Lord and pray for your precious girl."

Gene and Cathy left the doctor's office with a lot on their minds. There was a discomfited silence as they drove home.

From the backseat, Seefas passionately prayed, "Lord, help them hold onto you. Give them reassurance that Nicole is exactly what they need in their lives, regardless of the outcome. Give them a peace that passes all understanding, bringing them closer to you through this time of uncertainty."

"Sweetheart, you know we shouldn't get worked up over this because everything could just be an in utero problem. We need to remember no matter what the outcome is, God handpicked us to be Nicole's parents, and He will give us the strength we need." Cathy was very thankful for Gene; he always had a way of putting her at ease.

"You're right, Honey, I do feel like our sweet girl is a special gift from the Lord. For some reason, though, I have a feeling that she does not have Down syndrome."

When they got home, they told Roy about their doctor's visit and he said he would get the word out to family and friends to pray.

CHAPTER SIX

Dear Friends and Family, I am writing you to request your prayers for little Nicole Rebecca, my unborn granddaughter, who is now approximately twenty-six weeks' gestation. We learned today that she is about three weeks behind a normal developmental schedule. The doctor believes that the most probable reason for this condition is because she is not receiving enough nutrients through the umbilical cord. This could be due, among other things, to a restriction in the cord or to an impairment in the placenta. This is what happens when the baby has what's called intrauterine growth restriction. The prognosis at this point is good, but there may be cause for concern. We have been informed that Down syndrome is more likely in this kind of pregnancy, and Gene and Cathy are praying through that possibility. They are certainly ready to accept what God provides, but the natural fear is still there. At the moment the plan is to allow Nicole to develop as far as she can while in the womb, but the likelihood is that she will be born early. Just how early depends upon her rate of development from this point forward. It could mean hospitalization for Cathy at some time in the near future, and, of course, may also mean an extended time in the hospital for Nicole. We are reminded again of the delicacy of the developmental process. We are also reminded that God is in charge of this progression. Psalm 139 tells us "For you created my inmost being: you knit me together in my mother's womb." I know that He loves Nicole and is with her at all times. This situation is no surprise to Him. He knows the future of this child and all who are affected by this. Though we do not know what lies ahead, we have absolute confidence that God does and that He will be near to her and will provide as He sees fit. Since we firmly believe in the power of prayer, we would ask for your prayers on behalf of Nicole and Cathy and also for all of the family. We know that God hears our prayers and will bring the appropriate comfort and healing during this time. Thank you, Roy

* * *

"Hey, Roy, I'm sorry I missed you; I was hoping to catch you before you went to work. I wanted to tell you how grateful I am for the letter you sent out about Nicole. We are receiving messages from people all over the world. It's funny how word gets around. The number of people praying for us is blowing me away. If you are free tonight, Gene and I would love to have you over for dinner so we can share with you the many letters that we have received. Give me a call back and let me know."

"Hey, Sweetheart, I'm home." As Gene walked through the door, Cathy gave him a big hug and kiss.

"I can't believe the responses we're getting from your dad's letter. I invited him over so we could share the letters with him."

"I know, he called and told me he'd be coming."

"Daddy, Daddy home." Josh came running out from his room, where he'd been playing. After greeting Daddy, he ran up to Mommy and started talking to her tummy, "Baby, I play with Rab-e, Tee-tu and Pig-a-pee." He loved talking to his baby sister.

"Busterrrr, you are such a good big brother. Were you good for Mommy today?"

"Joshy good boy." He giggled and ran back to his room to finish playing.

"I picked up the mail on the way in. Looks like there are some more responses to Dad's letter. Do you mind if I look through some of these while you get dinner going?"

As Gene finished the letters, Roy arrived and it was time to sit down for dinner. After enjoying a great meal, they spent time playing with Josh before he had to go to bed. Then came one of Seefas' favorite times with the Ellertons, Josh's nightly bedtime ritual: reading a bedtime story, then the Bible, and ending in prayer. Seefas enjoyed seeing God's people raising their families to love the Lord.

After Josh was tucked snuggly in bed, Gene and Cathy sat down with Roy to share the letters they'd received. The three of them took turns reading some of the responses:

"Thanks for the opportunity to let us pray along with you and watch God work."

"Our prayers are with little Nicole."

"I know your heart is burdened and concerned. My thoughts and prayers are with you, especially Nicole. Thank you, my friend, for allowing me the opportunity to pray for your family."

"You can depend on us. We will be praying for this precious little girl and her mommy."

"While having a Down baby would be an adjustment, I know so many people whose lives have been blessed by these special children."

"We're praying that God gives the doctors and nurses wisdom in working with Cathy and Nicole."

The responses kept coming in a similar fashion. Roy, Gene, and Cathy were all in tears as they listened to the letters being read out loud. Seefas too was overcome with emotion watching the family together and seeing the outpouring of prayers and love coming from all over the world. The times of uncertainty pulled people together and pointed them toward Christ.

"You are in our prayers always. Little Nicole is very special to us. She's like a niece, after all her middle name is the same as mine. We will love her and treasure her no matter what." That letter was from Annie Ashby, Cathy's childhood friend. Annie, Eddie, and their kids were like family to the Ellertons.

"Wait a minute, there's more. I almost forgot about the letters that came today." Gene got up to get the mail in the other room. He opened the first letter. "Hey, this is from Sophie. How'd she get the letter?"

"She's back east visiting her parents, so I asked your dad to send her one. I know she's not into 'the Christian scene,' as she puts it, but I thought that it might have an impact on her to be included."

"Dear Gene and Cathy, thanks for the letter. So sorry to hear about your news, I know that you were excited to have a little girl. I'm not sure if you're aware of this or not, but a friend of mine who's a nurse told me you could have an amnio done to see if your baby has Down syndrome. If she does you can always have an a . . . bor . . . tion."

The letter kept going but Gene had to stop. He looked at Cathy and tears were streaming down her face.

"How could she say that? I thought that she was my friend and loved kids. Every baby is a gift from God. How can she suggest that I dispose of my baby, like she's a . . . a . . . an article of clothing?" Cathy was angry. Sophie was suggesting that she have her baby killed. Cathy was so upset that she started to shake. Gene walked over and put his arm around her.

"Sweetheart, it's okay. We love our daughter and we would never have that done. It angers me as well, not so much at Sophie, but at the world. She doesn't know the Lord, so it's easy to get caught up in the world's view. Unfortunately, many people think that if a child's different, there's no need for them. We need to show by example that they are wrong. If our daughter has Down syndrome, we need to show the world that she has value to her life and that she is a special gift from our Lord. This is also a good reminder to keep praying for Sophie. Maybe the Lord's going to use Nicole to reach her heart."

"You're right. I have a feeling that when she's born, Nicole will have a very special purpose on this earth, even if she does not have Down syndrome." Cathy had taken Gene's words to heart and started to calm down.

The night ended with the three of them holding hands and lifting up their prayers to the Lord. Standing right behind Cathy, with his eyes lifted to the Heavens, was Seefas.

CHAPTER SEVEN

Gene and Cathy were back at the doctor's office. Doctor Tanaka had initially said it was likely Nicole would be premature, and Cathy was now in her thirty-sixth week of pregnancy. It had been a long road since they found out about the problems taking place inside the womb. Cathy had to come in weekly for a nonstress test on Nicole to make sure that she was functioning well. She underwent multiple ultrasounds to check measurements and fluid levels. Nicole was hanging in there, but she hadn't made up the ground lost in her development. The Ellertons knew their girl would be born small.

"Good morning, Mr. and Mrs. Ellerton. How are you this morning? Let's take a listen and see how this peanut's doing." Doctor Tanaka pulled out his stethoscope to listen to Nicole's heartbeat. "She sounds great. Praise God, she has made it this far. I don't want to take any chances. I want you to come next Wednesday to the hospital, and we'll do an amnio to see if her lungs are developed. If so, we will induce and bring this little one into the world to meet her family face to face."

"Really?" Cathy said with tears welling up in her eyes.

"Really." Doctor Tanaka couldn't help but chuckle. "Let me go down the hall to see the availability of getting you in for the amnio, and we'll get that scheduled."

Doctor Tanaka had been gone less than a minute when he stuck his head back in. "On second thought, we need to make that Monday. I'll be right back."

Seefas, standing with them and observing all that was going on, looked up to Heaven and said, "Thank you, Lord, for your children who are sensitive to your promptings. Thank you that you know every minute detail of Nicole's life and that everything happens according to your purpose."

"I wonder why he changed it from Wednesday to Monday," Cathy said to her husband.

Gene shrugged. "I'm sure he has his reasons."

Doctor Tanaka came back in. "We're all set. I'll see you guys on Monday."

* * *

Doctor Tanaka greeted them as he entered the room. "Good morning, Mr. and Mrs. Ellerton. Are you ready to see if your girl's ready to enter this world?"

"I'm a little nervous," admitted Cathy, "so now's as good a time as any."

"I'm going to take an ultrasound first to see where a good spot is to inject the needle." He started the ultrasound to look at the amniotic fluid. He had barely started when he stopped. The serious look on his face scared Cathy and Gene.

"Is everything all right?" Gene asked as he took hold of Cathy's hand.

"There is no more fluid left inside the womb. The baby appears to be doing well, but we need to induce right now regardless of the development of her lungs. A baby cannot survive for days without the fluid. We will be monitoring her the whole time, and if we ever feel that she is at risk, we will do an emergency C-section. The good news is that we will not have to do the amnio."

"Basically, you're telling us that if we had come Wednesday, like you had originally said, our baby would not have survived?"

Gene's voice shook. "So, you saved our baby's life by changing our appointment to Monday?"

"Mr. Ellerton, I did not, God did. I have learned the importance of listening to that still, small voice inside of you. When I hear it, I follow it, even if I don't understand it."

"Praise God." Cathy and Gene said in unison.

Seefas was also in that room, thanking God for His provisions and asking for protection for Nicole as she made the journey through the birth canal.

"We will start the Pitocin right away, and I will be checking on you frequently."

"Thank you so much, Doctor Tanaka. We praise God for you all the time." After the doctor left, Cathy added, "We better call Mom, Dad, and Roy and let them know what's going on." Cathy's parents had arrived from Florida, they were planning on staying for a month to help. Josh was excited that his Papa and Granda were there to hang out with him.

* * *

About 12:45 Tuesday morning, they called the families to give them an update, then the nurse told Gene and Cathy to get some sleep. She said that Cathy was only dilated to a three and needed to be at ten before starting the pushing process. A half-hour later. "Gene! I need to go to the bathroom, and I can't get up because of my epidural. What do I do?" Cathy was panicked.

"Sweetheart, it's okay. Let's push the call button and get a nurse in here."

"Yes," said a nurse on the other end of the intercom, "Can I help you?"

"My wife needs to go to the bathroom, and she's not sure what to do."

"Well, your nurse just went on break, so be patient, and I'll send her in as soon as she gets back."

Cathy breaks in, "I need to go to the bathroom now! I can't hold it. Send someone now."

"All right, Mrs. Ellerton, I'll be in to check it out."

Minutes later, which seemed like hours to Cathy, the nurse walked in.

"I have to go to the bathroom. Do I just go here or what?"

"I will just have you go where you are, but before you do, let me check something." The nurse checked to see how far dilated Cathy was at that point and then said in a rather panicked voice, "Wait, don't go. The feeling that you're experiencing is not having to go to the bathroom, but is your baby trying to come out. I can see her head. Whatever you do, don't push."

"I can't hold her in; she's coming."

"You can't give in to the urge to push. I have to get the doctor here first."

"Hurry!" Cathy was panting and in obvious pain. "Honey, I can't do this. She's coming."

"Sweetheart, take deep breaths. You can do this."

This went on for over an hour.

"Little Nicole, just wait, sweet one, I know you're in a hurry to start your journey. Hold on until the doctor gets here. It's important that you wait." Seefas was talking to Nicole, trying to encourage her. "Lord, please keep her in there until the right time. I know that you are sovereign and in control. Thank you for being concerned with all things related to your children."

The doctor stuck his head in.

"Doctor, hurry, get in here, I can't wait any longer."

"I need to get my scrubs on Mrs. Ellerton; I'll be right back."

"Ohhh! I can't do this any longer. Honey . . ."

"I'm right here. The doctor will be right back. Just a minute more."

Doctor Tanaka came back into the room. "All right, let's do it. Give me a push. Okay, one more."

Cathy heard the sound of a baby crying. "Never mind, don't push. Your baby's here. Mr. Ellerton, quickly come over and cut the cord."

Gene quickly walked over and froze for a moment. Nicole was white as a ghost, very skinny, and had enormous eyes. She looked like a little alien. As the doctor encouraged him to hurry, they wrapped Nicole up, stuck her in her daddy's arms, and told him to run. Gene didn't know where he was running to, but he followed the team of nurses. Unbeknown to him, Seefas was also following very close behind. All Cathy could do was watch helplessly.

"Doctor Tanaka, I want to be with my baby. Is she okay? Why did they hustle her out of here without giving me a chance to hold her?"

"Your baby was born with the cord firmly wrapped around her neck. That is why she was so white; her circulation was being cut off. They took her to the ICU so that they could get her checked out and keep her warm. She's going to be all right. God was watching over that little one."

"When can I see her?"

"Unfortunately, it's going to be a couple of hours. You need to stay lying down until your epidural wears off. I'm finished here, so I'll go check on the baby and give you an update. Also, your dad is waiting outside to see you." Cathy's mom had stayed at the house with Josh, but her dad had made it to the hospital in time.

"Thank you. Oh, Doctor Tanaka, does my baby have Down syndrome?"

"I'll let you know. You can come in now, Mr. Saterlee."

* * *

Gene followed the nurses to the ICU, where a team of doctors waited for them. One grabbed Nicole from him, placed her in an isolette, and began hooking her up to machines.

"Is she going to be all right?" Gene felt like he should be doing more. The doctors could only respond to his question by acknowledging him with a nod. Gene felt bad that Cathy couldn't be there with Nicole, but he was glad that he could. Once she was all hooked up, he sat next to her and held her tiny hand. Minutes later, Doctor Tanaka arrived, accompanied by the on-call pediatrician, Doctor Birkin.

They examined Nicole, then Gene and the doctors left to go update Cathy. Seefas seized the opportunity to talk with Nicole. He couldn't believe that the time finally had come to meet his little one. "Hi, sweet Nicole, we finally meet face to face. I'm your guardian angel, Seefas. I'm going to be with you your whole life. We'll get to know each other very well. God has great things in store for you." Seefas's and Nicole's eyes met; it was the start of a great new friendship.

* * *

"Hi, Dad. I'm so glad you're here. Were you able to see Nicole?"

"I just saw her as Gene ran by. I thought you might want some company."

"Thank you, Dad." Cathy started to cry. "They won't let me see her yet. Doctor Tanaka said he would let me know how she is as soon as he's examined her. I'm glad Gene can be with her, but, I don't want her to think her mommy doesn't care."

"Honey, I'm sure she knows her mommy loves her, and it won't be too much longer."

Doctor Tanaka, Doctor Birkin and Gene walked in.

"I wanted to have you all together when I gave you an update on Nicole. First of all, she does not have Down syndrome. But, she is a very special little girl, and God has had His hand on her the whole time."

Cathy believed this to be true even if Nicole would have had Down.

He continued, "She weighs three pounds, thirteen ounces, and is sixteen inches long. She will need to remain in the isolette for a few hours so we can make sure she can maintain her body temperature." He turned his attention to the doctor standing next to him. "This is Doctor Birkin, the on-call pediatrician here. Since OB/GYN's are only the baby's doctors until they are born, he will be overseeing Nicole's case from here on out."

"Thank you so much, Doctor Tanaka. How much longer until I can see Nicole?"

"Well, we're done here. I think you've waited long enough. I'd like you to go in a wheelchair, but now seems like a good time."

Cathy was filled with anticipation as Gene wheeled her to the nursery to meet her daughter for the first time.

Nicole was in a room all by herself, and she looked so tiny and frail. She had gotten some color back, so she no longer looked like an alien. Cathy wheeled over to her, put her hand through the hole in the side of the isolette and said, "Hi, Sweetie, I'm Mommy." Overcome with emotion after the long wait to meet her daughter face to face, Cathy burst into tears.

"Nicole is such a big name for such a tiny person. I think we'll call you Nikki." Gene nodded in agreement. "God brought you through a hard road, but now you're here, safe with us. Welcome, my sweet girl."

When the nurse walked in, Cathy asked when she'd be able to nurse Nikki and just hold her. After Josh had been born, the first thing she got to do was hold him. She felt so cheated this time. They had lost ground to make up. The nurse said now would be great and helped Cathy get Nikki out of the isolette.

"Look how tiny she is, Honey." Nikki nursed right away, which amazed both Gene and Cathy. "She's our sweet girl. I can't wait for Josh to come in the morning to meet his new sister."

After Nikki finished nursing, Gene held her for a little while, and then they took turns going back to the room to get some sleep. Cathy planned to stay at the hospital with Nikki as long as she had to be there. At this point, they didn't know how long that would be.

* * *

When morning came, Papa and Granda brought Josh to meet his sister. Josh was wearing the shirt Grandpa Roy had bought him that said, "I'm the big brother." He instantly connected with his sister and wanted to hold her hand the whole time he was at the hospital. After they had been there a couple of hours, Daddy explained that he would be home later that day, but Mommy was going to stay with his sister.

"When Mommy and Sissy come home?" Josh wanted to know because he was not too excited about going home without them.

"We're not sure how long Sissy has to stay yet. In a couple of days, Mommy's going to be going back and forth between home and the hospital so Sissy won't feel alone, and she can spend time with you."

"Joshy don't want Sissy be scared." Josh understood and was already taking on the protective big brother role.

After many visitors they were ready to get some rest. Before they could, Doctor Birkin updated them on some things.

"Mr. and Mrs. Ellerton, Nicole is finally out of the woods." This was news to the Ellertons, as they didn't even know she had been in the woods.

Gene asked, "What do you mean by that?"

"When they're born this small and the vital signs are as low as Nicole's were, there's always some concern. I would like to run a series of tests as a precaution to find out why she had intrauterine growth restriction; this information will come in handy if you decide to have any more children."

"How long are you anticipating keeping her in the hospital?" Cathy wanted to know.

"That's hard to say right now. It will depend on how well she eats and if she's able to hold her own body temperature. It could be a couple of weeks. We just don't know. I'll be checking on her daily."

"Thanks, Doctor Birkin."

Nikki surprised them all by continuing to nurse well, and she was out of the isolette after only a few hours. Even though she was so small, she did well maintaining her body temperature and the Ellertons were able to bring her home six days later.

CHAPTER EIGHT

It was great having Nikki home. She was now two weeks old, and Josh loved being with her. When she slept in her bassinet, Josh would lay next to it. He wanted to be with her at all times, and she seemed to like having him near. They also had several visits from family and friends over the next couple of weeks. Although because of Nikki's small and seemingly fragile size, Cathy tended to be on the protective side, she loved the visits.

On one particular day, everything seemed routine. Gene was at work, Nikki was asleep in her bassinet, and Josh had fallen asleep next to her on the floor. Cathy was getting her housework done when she got a phone call from Doctor Birkin.

"Hi, Mrs. Ellerton, am I catching you at a bad time?"

"No, not at all, just getting some housework done. What can I do for you, Doctor Birkin?"

"I got the results back from the series of tests that we ran and wanted to go over them with you. Is your husband there with you?"

"No, he's at work. What did the tests reveal? Did you figure out what's going on? Was it an in-the-womb problem?" Cathy kept firing questions at the doctor.

"Mrs. Ellerton, the problem that Nikki has is a chromosomal problem. The short arm of the fourth chromosome has a deletion."

"I don't understand. What do you mean? Nikki has a short arm?" Cathy was very confused.

"A chromosomal problem is what kids with Down syndrome have . . . "

"I thought you cleared her of having Down?"

"Nicole does not have Down. It is a different kind of chromosome problem. It is a problem that took place in the fourth chromosome. The medical name for it is Wolf-Hirschhorn syndrome. It is extremely rare. I want you to make an appointment with a Doctor Kaplan, over at Oregon Health and Science University. She is a geneticist and will be able to explain the whole thing better to you. Could I have your husband's phone number? I want to call and explain all this to him and have him come home right away. You shouldn't be alone right now."

When Cathy got off the phone, she felt like her whole world had just fallen apart. "How could this be, Lord? I thought everything was fine. When the doctor announced at the hospital that she didn't have Down, I never dreamed that it would be something else. . . ." Cathy couldn't talk anymore. Her words turned into sobs. She heard Nikki stir, and she walked over to pick her up. She held Nikki close and continued to cry.

A few minutes later Gene got home. His eyes moist with tears, he whispered, "We'll get through this, with the Lord's help." Josh woke up and didn't understand what was going on, but he went to snuggle with Daddy. The family sat there in silence for what seemed like hours.

"Oh, Lord, lift up this family. They are hurting so much. Right now they're not able to see the wonderful things that are ahead of them. Help them not lose focus. They have fallen in love with their daughter and that has not changed."

* * *

Gene, Cathy, and Nikki were sitting in Doctor Kaplan's office waiting for her to come in. On the walls was a plethora of information on chromosomes. Gene spent his time waiting, reading the information.

"Good morning, Mr. and Mrs. Ellerton, I'm Doctor Kaplan." She was an elderly lady with gray hair and glasses and the look of someone who possessed a great deal of knowledge. "So, this is Nicole?" Nikki was now three weeks old. She hadn't gained too much weight since birth; she was only about three and a half pounds.

"Yes, and I'm Gene and this is my wife, Cathy."

"There is not a lot of information on Wolf-Hirschhorn. I ran her test about five times to make sure that I wasn't mistaken. On this chart, you can see that her chromosomes are made up of tiny bands that are not neatly in order. So, I had to take every band and piece it together. Each chromosome is made up of a long and short arm. Nicole is missing the tip of the short arm in the fourth chromosome. In the tip, there are about one hundred and fifty genes. Any questions so far?"

Cathy had lots of questions, but she knew that Gene was knowledgeable in this sort of thing. He was fascinated with medical technology, so she decided to let him explain to her later. She said, "Not at this time; please continue."

"What I read here is that if Nicole makes it one year, her life expectancy is unknown. You'll have to take it day by day." At this Gene and Cathy teared up. Cathy held onto Nikki tighter.

On the way home, Gene explained things better, then said, "We need to find out more information; I'll get on the Internet when we get home. There has to be more out there than what she's telling us."

Cathy, still crying, said, "Our daughter may not live a year. Gene, I can't accept that. God could heal her; nothing is too big for him. After all he's the creator of chromosomes."

They drove in silence the rest of the way home, except for sweet gurgles coming out of their little girl in the back. Nikki was enjoying playing with Seefas.

Gene found out a lot more about Wolf-Hirschhorn. A support group sent him a great deal of information, including case studies of kids born with this syndrome. At the time of Nikki's birth, researches were only aware of a couple hundred other kids with the syndrome.

The main thing he'd found out was that kids with this syndrome vary greatly. There was nothing he and Cathy could look at to say, "Oh, this is what Nikki will do." When kids with Wolf-Hirschhorn die young, he discovered, it is due to physical problems at birth. So, while life expectancy was unknown, their initial impression that most live less than a year was not entirely true. This brought tears of joy to the Ellertons' eyes. As they continued to sift through the information Gene was gathering, a widely varied picture emerged. Some kids with this disorder are able to accomplish more than others; some walk and talk, while others don't. The list of possible physical problems was lengthy; it included hearing loss, eye problems, heart difficulties, and seizures. Nikki's doctors advised Gene and Cathy to start having these things checked out.

The first thing on their list was a hearing screening. Cathy had just gotten off the phone with the scheduler when there was a knock on their door.

"Sophie, good to see you. Come in. We've missed you. How's your mom doing?" Sophie had been gone for a few months visiting her parents in Michigan, where her mom was having health problems.

"She's doing pretty well. She was starting to get around better, so I felt comfortable leaving her."

"Glad to hear it. We've been praying for her." Sophie winced when Cathy said this. She still didn't feel comfortable with "the whole Christian thing."

"So, where's that new baby of yours? I'm excited to see her."

"Since she should be waking up from her nap about now, I'll go check on her." Cathy went to the back room, where Nikki had been sleeping. When Cathy looked in on her she was smiling, as though she was playing with someone. This baffled Cathy a bit, but it was no mystery to Seefas; he and Nikki were having a great time.

"Hi, sweet girl. How long have you been awake?" Cathy picked Nikki up and peeked in on Josh, who was still fast asleep.

"Sophie, meet Nikki." Cathy walked over and handed Nikki to Sophie. "I assume you want to hold her."

"You assumed right. She's so tiny. She's beautiful, just like her mommy." Nikki had big, bright eyes, a tiny nose, rose bud lips, a fair complexion, and light brown hair with a couple of curls on top. It was obvious that her hair would be curly like her mom's. The only thing of her dad's that she seemed to have was his eye color.

"Thanks, Sophie. Well, a lot has happened since you've been gone. When Nikki was born the doctor informed us that she did not have Down syndrome. We were so relieved." Sophie nodded in agreement, and Cathy continued. "A couple of weeks later we got a call from the doctor. He had run several tests and informed us that Nikki had a different disorder." Cathy still had a hard time talking about this without tearing up. "She has what's called Wolf-Hirschhorn syndrome. It's a rare disorder and ironically, in many cases they can have more severe problems than kids with Down. We've just started getting Nikki checked for possible physical problems. She may never walk or talk and we're just not sure what. . ."

"Um, Cathy, I gotta go. I just remembered that my mom's going to be calling. See you later." She handed Nikki to Cathy and was gone without another word.

"What do you suppose that was all about?" Nikki looked up at her mom with shining eyes and gave her a little smile. "I love you so much, Sweetie."

"Dear Lord, please bring healing to my girl. I know that nothing is impossible for you. I want to be able to talk with my little girl and experience things that moms and daughters do together."

As Cathy was praying, Seefas was saying a prayer of his own. "Lord, help Cathy to accept what is and to soak in the joy that Nikki is going to bring to her."

* * *

When Gene got home from work, Cathy was in the living room playing with Josh, and Nikki was in her car seat watching.

"Hi, Honey. I just had the weirdest encounter with Sophie." Cathy told Gene about the conversation, and they were both puzzled by it. "How was work?"

"Great. I had a life-changing talk with Ryan. I've been witnessing to him for over a year and haven't gotten anywhere. Then today, I start talking about our situation with Nikki and telling him that God's in control. I told him that I've just accepted

Nikki and that there's a purpose to all that's happening. We talked for about an hour on our lunch break and then at the end of our conversation, he says, 'I know one reason why it's happened. I've had blinders on my eyes. In the past, every time you've talked to me about Christ, I've tuned out. But, today after hearing your story, it's all become clear. I want what you and your wife have.' Then we prayed and he accepted Christ. He told me to give Nikki a kiss for him and tell her thanks." Gene was so excited. There was nothing like leading someone to the Lord. Gene walked over, picked Nikki up and gave her a kiss. "Thank you, Nikki."

Cathy was stunned. They had been praying for Ryan for over a year. "I can't believe the impact our daughter had without even being there. Think about the impact she'll have when God heals her."

"Sweetheart, God's going to heal her. But you need to accept that it might not happen until she's in Heaven with Him. Don't try to make her someone she's not."

"Gene, you need to have faith and believe. God's going to heal her here. I know it." Cathy got emotional every time they talked about it. She didn't understand how Gene could just accept the disorder and be happy about it. Cathy loved her daughter very much, but she kept thinking about all the things that she wanted for her daughter, and they wouldn't happen unless she was healed. "Dinner's in the oven, I'm going to lie down until it's ready."

"Thank you, Lord, for Gene's perspective. Help him to continue to be the example that his wife needs. And I praise you, Lord, that another child came to you today. I wish I could have been in Heaven as you celebrated another soul sealing eternity with you." Seefas loved the parties the angels gave when one of

God's creations received him. He was always astonished that people on earth didn't hear the singing that took place; it was by far the most joyous occasion.

CHAPTER NINE

Cathy had felt so blessed to have her parents with her, but the day came when they had to go back to their ministry in Florida. They said they would continue to pray for everyone and wanted to hear the results of all the doctor appointments as soon as possible.

Over the next couple of months, the Ellertons had Nikki checked out by doctors. They had a scare with the hearing doctor, who thought that Nikki was deaf. But Cathy was convinced that the Lord healed her because at the next visit she passed with flying colors. Cathy was so thankful; she didn't want her daughter to miss out on things like music, which was such a wonderful gift, and hearing people's voices. At the cardiologist, they discovered that Nikki had a small hole, called an ASD, in her heart, but the doctor said the chances were that it would close on its own. Everything checked out at the eye doctor; there were no concerns there. Seizures were always a possibility down the road, but so far they hadn't seen any sign of those.

Cathy was grateful that there were no big health scares right now, but she still prayed that the Lord would heal Nikki completely from this disorder. One afternoon when both kids were down for a nap, Cathy pulled out her Bible and looked up Scriptures on healing. She was surprised how many there were. She read of people just reaching out and touching Jesus and instant healing took place. There was one incident when a parent approached Jesus on behalf of his little girl and she was healed. "Maybe Jesus will answer my prayer on behalf of my girl."

* * *

The kids had both woken up happy from their naps. Cathy got some projects done around the house while Josh played nicely with his sister. He loved to show her all his toys and tell her the names of each one of them. Nikki would respond with little coos. She was a couple of months old now but had no head control, so when Josh wanted Sissy to play with him, Cathy put her in her car seat so that she could watch.

"Mommy, someone at door." Josh got so excited about visitors, always hoping it would be someone to play with him.

"Sophie, hi. How are you? I've been a little worried about you since the last time you were here." Cathy hadn't seen Sophie since the day she'd walked out abruptly after Cathy's update on Nikki. Baffled, Cathy had tried unsuccessfully to call Sophie.

"Oh, I'm all right, I've just been busy. I was wondering if I might spend some time with Josh today. It's been awhile since we've had some good playtime." Sophie ignored Cathy's comments. Josh was excited as he loved playing with Sophie.

"Joshy want to play! Can Sissy play too?"

"Well, Joshy, I was thinking that maybe just you and I could spend time together. How about that?" Josh looked a little disappointed, then brightened up. "Okay, Joshy play with you."

Cathy was a little puzzled, but decided to let it go. "That's fine. Nikki's physical therapist is going to be here any minute.

Cathy straightened up the house before the physical therapist arrived. Their doctor had suggested contacting the county's early intervention program. A therapist would come to the house and do therapy with Nikki for free. The Ellertons felt like they had nothing to lose in giving this a try.

Nikki was now four months old and only weighed six pounds, eleven ounces. She was a content baby who loved to smile and laugh.

Josh heard the doorbell from his room and raced out to get the door before his mom could. He waited for his mom because he knew he couldn't open the door unless his mom or dad was next to him.

Cathy opened the door. "Hi, please come in. My name is Cathy, this is my son Josh, and this is our little Nikki."

Josh said a quick hello and ran back to his room to play with Sophie.

Lisa laughed. "Hi, nice to meet all of you. I'm Lisa. I'll be Nikki's physical therapist until she's three. I wasn't prepared for her to be so small. She's a doll. Can I hold her? You call her Nikki, not Nicole?"

"Mostly; we felt like Nicole was too big a name for such a tiny girl. And, of course, you can hold her."

"Hey, Nikki, I'm Lisa. We're going to be seeing a lot of each other." Lisa worked with Nikki for about an hour, doing stretches and playing with her. "Cathy, we'll be doing more and more as she gets older. Right now stretching is important, so she doesn't get too tight. This is something that you can work on with her."

"I'd be glad to do that."

"How are you and your husband handling the whole situation? I know it's tough when you have a special-needs child."

"We have great support from family, friends, and our church. God has been faithful in giving us the strength that we need to get through this. Nikki makes it easy. She is such a content, happy little girl. God has already healed her of a hearing loss, and I believe he can heal her completely. We take it one day at a time."

"I had heard that she had a hearing loss. But I'm not so sure I believe in miracles. Wasn't it just something simple, like having fluid in the ears?"

"She did have fluid in the ears, but earlier when they had checked for that, she did not. God sometimes works in the simple ways, so that people can fathom it." Cathy talked with Lisa for a while. It was clear that Lisa didn't have a relationship with the Lord. Cathy prayed that Nikki could have a direct impact in changing that. "Lisa, it was very nice meeting you. I think Nikki liked you too."

"Nice meeting you too. We don't always come across parents who are so supportive. I'll enjoy working with you and I'm looking forward to working with Nikki. I'll see you next week."

After Lisa left, Cathy got Josh and Nikki ready to go for a walk to a nearby school so Josh could play, something they tried to do often before it got too cold. She asked Sophie if she wanted to join them.

"Please, Sophie. I love to go to park to play."

"That sounds like a lot of fun. I'd love to join you."

Sophie often joined them on their jaunts to the park. Sophie still didn't want to interact with Nikki. But Cathy had kept Sophie updated on Nikki's progress, even though she didn't seem interested. At one point in their previous conversations, Sophie had mentioned that her husband had believed in all that "wacky Christian stuff," but she wanted nothing to do with it. Cathy didn't press her further at the time, but she was interested in learning more about that part of Sophie's life. Cathy thought it might help her understand Sophie.

As they walked, Cathy thought this might be a good opportunity. "So, Sophie, how did your husband come to know the Lord?"

Sophie was shocked by Cathy's question and hesitant to answer, but she knew she had accidentally opened that door and would have to answer it eventually. "Um, well, it was about a year after we were married. One of the guys from work invited him to this thing called Promise Keepers. It's this thing for men only, and they talk a lot about marriages and about God. Needless to say, Kevin was hooked. He came home and said that it changed his life. He wanted me to, how did he say it, um, receive the gift of Christ too. It scared me; all of a sudden, he wasn't the same man that I had married." Sophie got real quiet, as if in deep thought. "Anyway, I don't want to talk about it anymore."

When they got to the park, several people instantly came up to admire Nikki. It happened almost everywhere they went; people just seemed drawn to her. This always made Sophie uncomfortable, and she'd excused herself quickly.

"Hey, Josh, what do you say you and I go play on that swing set?"

"Yay! Let go Sop-ee."

While Cathy and Nikki watched, Cathy realized that Sophie had some deep pain going on inside. She wanted to be able to help, but she didn't know how. "Lord, give me the wisdom to know how to help Sophie. I pray that her walls break down and she sees that true healing, even emotional healing comes from you."

Seefas was deep in thought as well. "Lord, what's it going to take to impact someone like Sophie? She is so hardened. Josh is very special to her, but she wants nothing to do with Nikki.

How can a person have so much love for one child and turn her back on another? It's like she sees Nikki as being insignificant, ever since she found out about Nikki's disorder. Nikki seems dead to her. Use the Ellertons to reach this woman, somehow!"

CHAPTER TEN

One evening Gene got a call from the president of a Wolf-Hirschhorn support group, asking if they could meet sometime. He lived in Gresham, which wasn't far from the Ellertons, and had a boy in his twenties with this syndrome. They decided to meet at the Ellertons' church that weekend.

After the meeting, Cathy was discouraged. Although she knew kids with Wolf-Hirschhorn can vary greatly in what they're able to do physically, it threw her off meeting this boy. He didn't walk, talk, or even have any head control. Cathy went into a slump and got really depressed. She felt like she had been dealt another blow; the reality that her daughter might never hold her head up was too much for her to handle.

Gene wasn't sure how to help his wife. Everything he said seemed to make it worse. So, as a distraction, he decided that they'd take a trip to Washington State, where Cheryl Bradley, Cathy's sister, lived. Cheryl was the oldest of the six kids in the Saterlee family; Cathy and Cheryl had developed a close relationship over the past couple of years. She and her husband, Dean, had four kids. They were missionaries in Guatemala and were home for a year on furlough. Dean, who had a passion for music, was loving being able to intern for a year as music pastor at a church in Bremerton. The Ellertons had talked about going to visit them and had never gotten around to it. Gene felt like this was the perfect opportunity. He gave Cheryl a call and arranged the whole thing, Cathy jumped at the chance to get away.

* * *

"Cathy, we need to be at church early because I have to work in the nursery the first hour. Why don't we take Josh with us because I'm working in his class? You, Gene, and Nikki can come for the second service."

"Thanks, Cheryl. That way I can get Nikki fed and not have to worry about that at church." Cathy hadn't been able to stop thinking about the boy that they had met with Nikki's syndrome, she couldn't seem to get out of the slump she was in. Everyone was doing his or her best to help her out of her funk.

When they got to church they met Cheryl in the nursery and she showed them where Nikki would be. When they were signing Nikki into her class, the nursery worker struck up a conversation with them. "I heard when your daughter was born she only weighed three pounds, thirteen ounces."

"Yeah, that's right." Cathy found it a little unusual to begin a conversation like that, but she shrugged it off.

"I adopted a little boy from India, and he weighed about the same. In fact when he was eight months old, he only weighed eight pounds!"

"You're kidding. Nikki's eight months and weighs eight pounds."

"I was told that he might never walk or talk. He does both now; it was slow, but it came. Praise God."

* * *

Back at the Bradley home, Cathy couldn't stop talking about the lady she met. "Don't you find it odd that the exact thing I was depressed about, this lady hit on? Maybe a coincidence, but I don't think so. I think God sent that lady to encourage me. I believe He was telling me Nikki will walk and talk one day."

"Sweetheart, I agree with you. But, you need to keep in mind, it's in God's timing. He might simply be telling you that life here is short, and time with him is forever. In Heaven Nikki will run and sit down with us to converse. She will be perfect. I'm not trying to take anything away from today. Nikki will walk and talk, and it just might be here on earth."

The Ellertons enjoyed the rest of their time with the Bradleys. The two sisters embraced and said they needed to take advantage of being so close in proximity before the Bradleys went back to Guatemala. On the way home, Cathy thanked Gene for taking them there. It was just what the doctor ordered. Then Cathy, Josh, and Nikki all fell asleep, and Gene spent time listening to praise music.

Seefas thanked the Lord for the woman who talked to Cathy that day. He knew that Cathy needed something to move her forward, and God always knew the right way to do it. "Only you know for sure when our little Nikki will walk and talk. But what I'm learning in spending time with this extraordinary girl is that it doesn't matter if it happens here on earth. When you first gave me this assignment, I felt sorry for her. She doesn't need our sympathy, she brings joy to everyone she meets. I pray that the Ellertons will eventually be able to grasp the full meaning of this. I'm still not sure how she'll be able to reach people like Sophie, but I'm looking forward to continuing to watch you work."

It had been a couple of months since their visit with the Bradleys in Washington, but Cathy thought often about that trip and the conversation she had with the woman at the nursery.

Josh interrupted her thinking. He was screaming in Nikki's room. "Mommy, Mommy. Come. Come." Cathy ran to the nursery and saw Nikki in her crib, her head was tilted to the side, drool was coming out of her mouth, and she was twitching. Cathy panicked not knowing what to do. What was wrong with her little girl? She didn't know if she could pick her up, and she simply froze.

"Mommy!" Josh started to cry, and Cathy snapped out of it.

"It's going to be all right, Buster. I need to call Daddy. Can you bring Mommy the phone?" Cathy didn't want to leave Nikki's side since she didn't know what was wrong, and she wanted to make sure that Nikki didn't stop breathing. Cathy called Gene, grateful he worked just down the road; he was home within minutes. On his way, he'd called his dad and they both got there around the same time.

"Joshy, you need to stay with Grandpa. We need to take Sissy to the doctor. Pray for Sissy, and we'll call you as soon as we can. Everything's going to be okay. Thanks, Roy. We'll call as soon as we know more."

Cathy cried and held Nikki all the way to the hospital. They didn't know if it was safe to put her in her car seat the way she was twitching. When they got to the emergency room, the nurse rushed Nikki in. Gene and Cathy followed behind feeling helpless. Everything seemed crazy to Cathy as the doctors and nurses went to work on Nikki, hooking her up to this and that. All she wanted to know was whether her daughter was going to be all right.

"Your daughter had a grand mal seizure and from the sound of it, it lasted around an hour and a half. We want to life-flight her to Emmanuel Children's Hospital, where they're more equipped in dealing with young ones."

"Are you kidding me? Life flight, is that really necessary?" Gene was confused. "You stopped her seizure. Is she in a life-threatening situation?"

"I don't believe it's life-threatening. We just need to get her over there."

"Then take her by ambulance and that way my wife can ride over with her." Gene was adamant about it, so the doctor gave in.

In the ambulance, they wouldn't let Cathy sit in the back with her daughter. Cathy cried because she didn't want Nikki to feel alone and scared. However, Nikki wasn't alone; Seefas was holding her hand the whole way.

When they got to Emmanuel, the ambulance drivers wheeled Nikki to a children's ward with Cathy following closely behind. At the door, the driver told Cathy she couldn't go any further.

Cathy was furious. "I'm going with my daughter," she stated loudly.

"Sorry, ma'am. It's against hospital policy. The doctor will be out as soon as he can to talk with you." Then, just like that, they were gone with her daughter. Cathy hated this feeling of helplessness. But, of course, Seefas was with Nikki. He wished he could tell Cathy that he'd be with Nikki and not to worry.

"Was that your little girl?" Cathy was so absorbed in her thoughts she didn't notice the couple sitting there.

"Yes. She's only ten months old, and they wouldn't let me go in there with her. I feel powerless!"

"We understand. Our son's in there. He has cancer, and he's only seven. Although we've been here weeks, they only let us in when shift changes are over."

"I'm so sorry."

"Thank you. Whenever we feel like we can't handle it, our Tommy says, 'Jesus is here, right beside me, holding my hand. Don't be sad.' Leave it to a seven year old to bring you back to the right perspective. We know God is in control. When we don't understand, we just have to trust in him and pray. I'm sure that Jesus has someone in there holding your little girl's hand too."

"Thank you for those words." Cathy was overcome with emotion. "My husband and I are also Christians. We'll pray for you."

"Thank you. Do you mind if we pray with you right now for your little girl?" This brought tears to Cathy's eyes. Even though their son may be dying, they wanted to pray for her and Nikki. When they were done praying, Cathy thanked them and felt a bit better. It blew her away how God seemed to give strength when needed. Cathy would never forget this couple and she would pray for Tommy. Cathy never heard from that couple again, but she thanked God for placing them in her path. By the time Gene showed up, the couple had already gone in to be with their son. Cathy told him what happened, and Gene thanked God for bringing that support to his wife. Then they waited together for the doctor to come out.

"Mr. and Mrs. Ellerton?"

"Yes. How is she, doctor?"

"Well, Mr. Ellerton, your daughter had a grand mal seizure that lasted for quite a while. It's going to be some time before we know if it caused any brain damage. She's stable right now. We have her hooked up to an IV, and we want her to stay here a few days so we can monitor her before sending her home."

Cathy was getting anxious. "Can we see her now? She's going to be hungry, and I need to nurse her."

"Yes, you can go in now. But, Mrs. Ellerton, you will not be able to feed her at least for a couple of days. We want her to be solely on IV until we know she's not going to have any more seizures."

"Can we stay the night with her?"

"Yes, one of you can. We have a chair that reclines in her room for your use."

When Gene and Cathy went into Nikki's room, she seemed so small hooked up to all the IVs. She was sleeping peacefully, so they just prayed over her and watched her for a while. When Nikki woke up, Cathy held her hand and stroked her hair. "I love you, Sweetie!"

* * *

After Cathy got Josh tucked snuggly in bed, she went into Nikki's nursery. She walked around and touched all of Nikki's stuff and started to cry. She hated coming home and having to leave Nikki at the hospital. Cathy took one of Nikki's little dolls and fell asleep in the rocking chair holding on to it.

Cathy woke up early and Josh was still asleep. She took a shower, pumped breast milk to take to the hospital, and had a moving quiet time. She was reading a passage in the book of Daniel about his trust in God, regardless of the outcome. He didn't stop praying to God and was thrown in the lion's den. He knew the consequences if he kept praying, yet he remained faithful to the Lord and God protected him. "Dear Lord Jesus, help me to trust you and know you're in control, regardless of the outcome with Nikki. Give me the strength that I need to be strong for her and for Joshy."

Nikki was doing well; no more seizures had occurred. Later in the day, Nikki started to cry and seemed hungry. This was devastating to Cathy, as Nikki rarely ever cried. She was the most content baby Cathy had ever known. She felt like such a bad mommy because they wouldn't let her nurse Nikki. The nurse told her that most likely in the morning, she'd be able to nurse. As Cathy rocked Nikki and sang praise songs to her, she seemed to calm down and soon fell asleep.

All day long at the hospital, Cathy got one phone call after another, telling her that they were praying for Nikki. One of the pastors from their church came and prayed with them. The thing that really struck Cathy was how many people cared about them and were lifting them up in prayer. Cathy could feel the prayers. Her attitude had really turned around since the day before. She felt God's presence in that room, and she knew that what the couple had said about Jesus sending someone to hold Nikki's hand was true. She was right; Seefas hadn't left Nikki's side since her seizure.

The Ellertons met a new doctor who would be in Nikki's life for a long time. Doctor Casarin, a neurologist, prescribed medication to help prevent Nikki's seizures. He wanted to see her in a month to check her blood levels to see if the medication was at the right dose. When Nikki was released three days later, everyone was glad to be home as a family again. Josh really missed his little sister, and she missed him too.

CHAPTER ELEVEN

It was birthday month. Josh was going to be three and Nikki was going to be one. Where did the time go in this life-changing year for the Ellertons? Nikki hadn't had any more seizure episodes, since that scare a couple of months ago. As Cathy was filling out the birthday invitations for her kids, she spent some time reflecting.

When Nikki was first born and diagnosed with Wolf-Hirschhorn syndrome, she didn't want to accept it. When she had first found out that she was pregnant with a girl, the entire so-called normal mother-daughter things went through her mind. She dreamed what their relationship would be like. The news that her daughter was different was hard for Cathy to swallow. Cathy knew that the God she served was powerful and the creator of the whole universe and that He cared intimately for the Ellerton family. She believed that He could heal her daughter and make her whole. She hadn't been ready to accept that God's answer could be no or not yet.

Now, as she sat there filling out the invitations, she realized how far she had come in a year. One day, her daughter would be healed, but it might be when she meets her maker face to face in Heaven. God had answered the prayers of her husband. He had given Cathy a peace and true acceptance of their daughter. Once that happened, Cathy was able to experience the pleasure of being Nikki's mom. Cathy didn't want her to be someone else. She was the happiest little girl, who brought a smile to everyone's face. People were drawn to her wherever they went. The impact she had on people was remarkable. Cathy knew that she loved her daughter, and nothing was ever going to change that.

Cathy finished the invitations, and the kids were still down for their naps, so she decided to get a few things done around the house. Sophie knocked at the door. Cathy invited her in and told her that Josh was still sleeping, but she was welcome to come in and chat. After talking awhile, Cathy decided to dig a little more into what made Sophie so cynical when it came to Christianity.

"Sophie, you previously said when your husband became a Christian he changed and wasn't the man you married. Was it a good or bad change?"

Sophie was uncomfortable talking about this, but, for some reason, Cathy put her at ease. "It wasn't a bad change; in fact he treated me better than he ever had. But, it scared me. I didn't understand the transformation in him. When he started looking for a church that he wanted us to attend, I was hesitant at first but decided to give it a shot."

"Did he find a church?"

"Yes, we started going to a nondenominational church in Beaverton. Kevin loved it. He started getting involved in the men's Bible study group, and he wanted us to join a study as a couple. We eventually joined a study, but I was still skeptical. In time, I accepted the changes in Kevin. I liked the new Kevin, but I was fine the way I was. Kevin said he would just keep praying for me. We got closer and our relationship was better than ever. Then Kevin got sick."

Sophie's voice softened and she seemed sad. She didn't want to talk about it anymore, and Cathy decided not to push. Cathy was glad because, on the one hand, she was slowly beginning to understand Sophie, but on the other, it was getting more complicated. What made Sophie go from accepting who her husband had become to being a skeptic?

Josh and Nikki woke up and Sophie seemed relieved. She spent time playing in the backyard with Josh and Shawnee. When it was getting close to the time Gene would be home, Sophie said she had to go, Cathy invited her to come back soon.

* * *

"Hey, Sweetheart. I'm home. Where are my little ones?"

"Daddy . . ." Josh came running out, Cathy and Nikki close behind. They had been in Josh's room playing. Gene swept up Josh in his arms and gave him a big bear hug.

Cathy smiled, enjoying the interaction between father and son. "Hi, Honey. How was work?"

"Good. How was your day at home?" Cathy explained about her conversation with Sophie. They both decided they needed to have her over more often and continue to pray for her.

* * *

The day of the party came. Josh was excited and loved getting to share his birthday with his sister. They had only invited family and close friends, but their small house was full. The bulk of the party was outside. They had invited Sophie to join them and also felt it appropriate to invite Gene's coworker, Ryan, and his family. Soon after Ryan became a Christian, his wife had made a commitment and then his kids followed suit. They gave much of the credit to Nikki. It was a fun time, and everyone seemed to get along well.

"Mommy, it's time to open presents. Right?"

"If you say so, Buster. I'll go get them." Cathy got everything set up. When she was separating Josh and Nikki's presents, she noticed that Sophie had only gotten a present for Josh but not Nikki. This made Cathy sad. She wondered how long it would take for Sophie to accept Nikki. Every time Sophie came over, Nikki would coo, screech, and get excited. Sophie would just walk past, like she wasn't even there. When that happened, Cathy would always say a little prayer that Sophie would one day come to love Nikki too.

"All right, everyone, gather around. It's present time. Josh, do you want to open your presents first?"

"No, Mommy. Sissy go first and Joshy will help her open her presents." It was very sweet watching Josh help his sister. Nikki was sitting in her car seat and Josh would put the present on her lap, open it up, and show her what it was. He did this for every present. Cathy was watching Sophie. Today was different. Usually Sophie would find something else to do when Nikki was involved, but now she seemed to be moved watching Josh with his sister. Cathy thanked Jesus, feeling this was a step in the right direction.

"My turn, Daddy. Take a picture of me." All the attention then turned to Josh. While he was opening his presents, Cathy noticed that Nikki was laughing and cooing.

Nikki was playing with Seefas. "Well, happy birthday, little Nikki. This is a big day for you. You are now a one year old. You've accomplished a lot already in your young life. Ryan and his family coming to know Jesus is a direct result of hearing about you, and so many others have been drawn to Him because of you. "

"See-fs." Seefas laughed out loud. Was it his imagination, or did Nikki just try and say his name?

"Now, Miss Nicole, did you just say my name?"

"See-fs!" Nikki laughed and cooed. Now, Seefas knew that to everyone else listening to Nikki, it sounded like babble. But he could understand what her babble meant. "Thank you, Lord. Will I actually someday be able to carry on conversations with this little girl?" The thought thrilled him.

After the guests were gone and the children were in bed, Gene and Cathy reviewed the day. Cathy shared what she observed about Sophie regarding Nikki. Gene agreed that it was a step in the right direction.

"Honey, I was also watching Nikki when Josh was opening his presents. Call me crazy, but I'm convinced that she was playing with her angel." Cathy had observed this on many occasions; the more it happened, the more sure she was.

"That would be cool. Maybe one day she'll be able to tell us. Goodnight, Sweetheart!"

CHAPTER TWELVE

The Ellertons were on their way to Florida. Cathy's youngest sister, Cassie, was getting married. The Ellertons had never met Mike Guilles, the groom. The family had not been together since Gene and Cathy's wedding five years earlier. Her parents, Grant and May, had an extra apartment, so all six kids and their families were staying at their place.

The Ellertons were among the last to arrive and were greeted by Cheryl and her family; Chad, the Saterlees' oldest son, a military officer, and his family. Cathy's brother Charlie, who was still single, had been adopted by Grant and May when they were missionaries in the Philippines along with Cassie. Craig, who was just a few years older than Cathy, and his family would arrive soon. While Cassie and Mike finished wedding details, May started dinner and Grant finalized plans for the evening.

Everyone enjoyed dinner, being together, and meeting Mike. Grant planned a devotional and Dean played his guitar and led a time of worship. Cathy loved praising God with her family, and Nikki enjoyed it too. Grant asked everyone to gather around to pray for Nikki.

"As we have all separately invested time in prayer for Nikki, I thought that it would be good for all of us now to pray over her together." As an inspiring time of prayer followed, Nikki seemed to have her eyes fixed on Heaven, as if she understood. Seefas was there, joining in with the whole Saterlee family as they came together before the Lord. Seefas knew when two or more were gathered together in prayer, mighty things happened. He wasn't sure what God had in store next, but he believed that it would be entered into with strength and peace for the adventure ahead.

"Thanks, everyone, for praying. As you know, I had a hard first year accepting my daughter's syndrome. I wanted her to be someone she's not. But I fell in love with who my girl is. I believe that she is among one of God's most precious creations. We have encountered people who think that Nikki doesn't have any rights because she's different from what the world considers normal. It makes us so sad because they are missing out on a very special gift. Nikki has so much to offer, she has a peace about her that's hard to comprehend. I tell Gene often that I think Nikki's closer to Jesus than I ever will be here on earth. I don't know what's ahead, but your prayers have given me confidence that we can handle whatever it may be."

The family enjoyed their time together over the next few days. Mike was a photographer, so they took a family picture. Who knew when they'd all be together again, so they needed to capture the moment. The wedding was wonderful. Cassie looked beautiful. Josh was the ring bearer and two of Craig's girls were the flower girls. They all looked adorable. Cathy loved being with her family and the time went by way too fast.

* * *

Gene got home from work and found Cathy in tears. Nikki was asleep and Josh was playing in his room. The house was a mess, Cathy was still in pajamas, and dinner wasn't ready. Gene was concerned; this was all unusual for Cathy.

"Sweetheart, what's wrong? Are you sick?"

"Oh, Honey, I don't understand. Today was terrible. From the minute Nikki got up this morning, she's been fussing. The only time she has stopped is when I was holding her or she was asleep." Cathy couldn't figure it out.

"Did you take her temperature? Is she running a fever? This is so out of character for her. Something must be going on." Gene was very concerned. He had only heard his little girl fuss maybe once, if that.

"Yes, I took her temperature. If she has one, it's only a low-grade fever."

"Maybe she's teething."

"She's gotten a tooth before and didn't act like this. I don't know what's wrong!"

"Did you call the nurse?"

"I made an appointment for her first thing in the morning."

When Nikki woke up and continued to cry, Gene was just as baffled as Cathy. Gene decided to take the next morning off to go with Cathy to Nikki's appointment.

* * *

The Ellertons felt comfortable taking Nikki to their family doctor, Doctor Williams, because he knew his limitations. Whenever he had a question about something, he was quick to refer Gene and Cathy to a specialist in that area. Today, though, he was stumped.

"I can't find anything wrong with Nicole. I want to draw some blood and have several things checked out to be on the safe side. Keep an eye on her and bring her back if she gets worse."

"Thanks, Doctor Williams. We would appreciate hearing back from you as soon as you get the results. It's just not like Nikki to be acting this way, so it's starting to worry us."

"I understand, Mrs. Ellerton. I'll let you know as soon as I can."

Gene and Cathy left still feeling discouraged. The next few days Nikki seemed to get worse instead of better. She started not wanting to nurse, and it was a struggle to get food down her. Cathy was disheartened. While she fed Nikki, she would pray every bite that Nikki would eat.

After one feeding, Cathy put Nikki in her car seat and took her into Josh's room to watch him play. Cathy was hoping that it would help settle Nikki down, and Cathy needed a break.

After a few minutes, Josh came running into the living room. "Mommy, I'm showing Nikki my toys and she won't look. Please come tell her to look at them."

Cathy walked into Josh's room and Nikki was staring at the ceiling with a glaze in her eyes. Cathy tried to get her attention, but Nikki wasn't even blinking. This lasted for a couple of minutes, and it worried Cathy. When Nikki came out of it, she started fussing. Cathy called Gene and he said to keep an eye on her. To Cathy's growing concern, it happened again and several more times that day.

When Gene got home, they contacted the on-call doctor. He said that it sounded like Nikki was having miniseizures and to contact her neurologist. After calling Doctor Casarin's answering service, he called back within half an hour. He confirmed that Nikki had seizures. He didn't feel it was an emergency, but he wanted to see her in the morning.

"Honey, this is so discouraging. She was doing great. A fussy baby has replaced our happy baby. I thought we were out of the woods with her seizures since it's been four months since that first one." Cathy was so tired; she wasn't used to her daughter being so demanding. The only time that Nikki would settle

down was when Cathy held her, and she still wasn't eating .
Cathy wasn't able to get things done around the house, and she
felt like Josh was being neglected.

Gene hugged her. "I know it's hard. I don't like seeing her
like this either. However, we should be grateful that her seizures
aren't like the first one. Let's see what Doctor Casarin says in the
morning."

Gene set up Nikki's portable crib in their room so they
could monitor her through the night. Nikki finally drifted off,
and they were able to get some sleep. About half an hour later,
Nikki woke up again, whimpering. The Ellertons didn't hear
her, but Seefas was right there by her side. "Miss Nicole, I know
you don't feel well, but hang on. They'll get it figured out. It's
going to get better."

"See. . . " Nikki tried to say his name, but she was in a lot of
pain and couldn't get it out.

"Shhh, it's okay. Don't try to talk. Just go back to sleep, I'll
be right here by your side." Nikki did go back to sleep, and it
was the best night's sleep Cathy and Gene had been able to get
in several days.

CHAPTER THIRTEEN

The Ellertons took Nikki to see Doctor Casarin. He had blood work drawn and found that Nikki's medicine levels were too low. He increased the medication and put Nikki on an additional medicine to help control her seizures. He wasn't sure why she was having them all of a sudden, but he said that when kids have seizure disorders, they could show up in all kinds of different ways. He said to call any time if they had questions, and he'd always be available to call back.

Doctor Casarin was true to his word when the Ellertons called him multiple times over the next few weeks. Nikki's seizures seemed to get worse; sometimes she'd have them every fifteen minutes. Doctor Casarin then gave the Ellertons an additional medication to help stop her seizures from coming so frequently.

They received a call from Doctor Williams, reporting that all the tests he ran came back negative. He couldn't find anything wrong with Nikki. The Ellertons were getting more discouraged. Their daughter wasn't the same happy girl she used to be. Cathy thought maybe this is how kids with Wolf-Hirschhorn became. Maybe being fussy is more the norm for them because nobody could explain what was wrong with her daughter.

* * *

One day while Gene was at work, Cathy was rocking Nikki to keep her calm, and Josh was having a hard time. He loved his little sister, but he couldn't understand why she cried all the time and why Mommy couldn't play with him. Cathy felt bad for him and didn't know how to make it better. Her daughter needed her. Then she had an idea. They hadn't seen Sophie in a while, so maybe she would enjoy coming over to play with Josh. Cathy wasn't sure if she could talk her into it. After the kids' birthday party, Sophie was coming quite frequently to visit and even seemed to slowly be warming up to Nikki. Well, she wouldn't exactly talk to her or play with her, but she told Josh one time that his sister could watch them play. Cathy had taken it as a step in the right direction. Then after Nikki started fussing and having seizures, Sophie became distant again. She never came around, even when Cathy invited her.

She decided to give Sophie a call because Josh really missed her. When she called, Sophie tried to refuse, but Cathy was persistent. Josh really needed some special time, and she knew he would love having her come. Cathy also told her that Nikki's therapist, Lisa, was coming over, and Josh could use the distraction to have someone there for him. Sophie finally gave in and said she'd be right over.

Minutes later Sophie arrived. "Sophie, thanks for coming. Josh has been bouncing up and down since I told him you were on your way."

"Well, I missed him. Where is the little guy?"

"Joshy, Sophie's here."

Josh came running from his room. "Sophie! You want to come in my room and play dinosaurs with me?" A new favorite game, Josh loved playing with his dinosaurs, especially when someone played with him.

When Lisa arrived, she said she felt that it was important for Nikki to have her therapy session, even if she wasn't feeling well. Lisa worked mostly on stretching with Nikki. "How are you guys holding up since Nikki's been sick? I know before she started feeling bad, you said part of what made it so easy was that Nikki was such a happy girl. Now things have changed. Are you as confident that your God's still there for you?" Lisa was skeptical when it came to the Ellertons' faith. Cathy had shared with Lisa how several people had come to know the Lord because of Nikki. Cathy could tell that Lisa was just humoring her when she would make comments like, "That's great."

"Well, Lisa, I'm not going to lie and say it's easy; it's not. It's been hard watching Nikki change so dramatically and to know there's obviously something wrong with her. It's also discouraging to keep taking her to the doctor hearing that they can't find anything wrong. We're just confused, wondering why all this is happening. But am I confident that God's here for me? Absolutely. One example I can give you is that since this all started, Nikki doesn't want to eat. I dread her eating time. What used to take thirty minutes now takes over an hour and a half. I only get through it with God's help. When I'm trying with no success to get a bite down Nikki, I pray and she opens up. No joke. It's like God opens her mouth for me. When this all started, I had no energy to get work done around the house. Now it's just as bad, or worse, than before, but God's given me the energy that I need. I still don't understand why it's happening, and I do have bad days. But I can rest in the fact that He's in control and there's a reason. I just can't see it yet." Before they knew it, Lisa's time was up.

Cathy didn't know if it was her imagination, but she felt that Lisa was listening this time, without rolling her eyes. Although Cathy didn't realize it, Sophie had been listening from Josh's room as well.

Seefas had seen all this happening and prayed that Cathy might be able to get through to these two women. They both seemed to want nothing to do with the Lord, but Seefas noticed something different in Lisa today. Maybe she would come around sooner than he thought. With Sophie, he wasn't sure. Something had happened to really harden her heart, and he knew it would take a miracle to soften it up. He rested in the fact that God knew exactly what was troubling her and what the final outcome would be.

Later that night when Gene was home, they were talking about their trip to California. They were going to spend Christmas with Grandpa Ellerton, Roy's dad, and Roy's sister's family. Roy, Nate, Lynn, and their daughter Hailey were also planning to take the trip to California because Grandpa Ellerton was ninety-one and hadn't been doing that well physically.

* * *

The Ellertons decided to gather at Gene and Cathy's for an early Christmas. Before everyone arrived, Gene and Cathy's family opened stockings, and Josh and Nikki's big presents were sitting out. It felt very much like Christmas morning. Then the whole clan had brunch together, opened presents, and talked about the upcoming trip. Roy questioned whether Gene and Cathy wanted to go with Nikki still not herself. Gene felt that since it had been going on for about five months now and the doctors still couldn't figure anything out, it would be all right to go. As they said their goodbyes at the end of the day, they all looked forward to meeting at Grandpa Ellerton's in a couple of days.

The next evening while Cathy was packing for California, Gene was feeding Nikki. They had started giving her water in a bottle because she kept throwing up her milk. Cathy had stopped nursing Nikki when she got sick, and the water seemed to be working until that night. Nikki had a couple of ounces before she lost it all. Gene was so concerned that he contacted the on-call doctor, who told him to keep a close eye on her and bring her in the next morning. As he told Cathy what the doctor said, he suddenly exclaimed, "Sweetheart, forget that. There is something terribly wrong with Nikki, and she is very cold. We need to take her to emergency, now."

"Do you really think that's necessary? The doctor said just to keep an eye on her."

"I don't know why, but I have a feeling that we need to go now. I'll call my dad."

"Honey, you're scaring me. Do you think she'll be all right?" Cathy was very worried about her little girl and started to cry.

"Sweetheart, I don't know. But we need to go. Please hurry. This time we need to go straight to Emmanuel."

On the way to the hospital, they didn't say much. Both were praying and worried about their daughter. Seefas, on the other hand, was talking to Nikki. "Hold on, Miss Nicole, you're going to be all right. Just hold on. Oh, dear Lord, please don't let her life end now. There's still so much that she can accomplish. Please don't call her home at this time."

When they got to the emergency room, before they could say a word the nurse grabbed Nikki from Cathy and said they needed to admit her right away. She knew something was wrong.

Frightened, Gene and Cathy followed helplessly behind. The nurse took her to a room and a doctor was there within minutes. He took her temperature and looked worried. "Nicole's temperature is dangerously low. We need to get her upstairs to the children's ward immediately. To save time, can you tell me how old she is and how much she weighs?"

"She is eighteen months old and weighs about ten and a half pounds," Gene answered. Cathy was too shaken and couldn't speak. She just kept saying a silent prayer that God would spare the life of her daughter.

"All right, you two can follow us upstairs, but you'll need to wait in the waiting room. A doctor will be out as soon as possible to fill you in on her condition."

Watching Nikki go behind those forbidden doors brought back memories of the last time they were there. Gene started to pray, "Lord, last time we were here, we know you sent someone in with her when we weren't able to go. Please send someone again. And please, let her make it, let us take her home with us once again."

* * *

"Miss Nicole, I'm here with you. Hold on, Sweet One. Your mommy and daddy are here, too; they just can't come in here yet. Don't give up. You're a fighter and I know you can beat this thing. Give her the strength, dear Lord."

* * *

Time went by slowly for Gene and Cathy. They were worried about their daughter. After a while a doctor came out to see them. "Mr. and Mrs. Ellerton?"

"Yes, that's us." Gene said. Cathy was still unable to get any words out, for fear that she would break down.

"Your daughter is very sick. At this point, I don't know what's causing her problem. We will run lots of tests. It appears that her kidneys aren't working effectively, but the reason is unclear to us."

"What are her chances, Doctor?"

"Mr. Ellerton, right now, I'm sorry to say there's probably a fifty-fifty chance of her pulling through. We're doing everything possible, and I will keep you updated frequently on her progress. There is a room down at the end of the hall that will give you more privacy. You can wait there."

"When will we get to see her?"

"As soon as all the tests are run."

Cathy finally joined in on the conversation, in a shaky voice. "Doctor, I want to be with her during this time. She needs me." Cathy was persistent, and it was clear that she wasn't going to take no for an answer.

"All right, but just one of you."

"Go ahead, Sweetheart. I'll call our family and friends to give them updates. I love you." Gene knew that emotionally, Cathy needed to be the one to go with their daughter, even though he wanted to be there too.

They wheeled Nikki to X-ray, and Cathy held her hand the whole time. In the X-ray room, they asked Cathy if there was any chance she was pregnant. Cathy answered, "I don't believe so, but I guess there's always that chance." They got Cathy a lead apron, Cathy had no problem with that. Once all the tests were run, they went back to Nikki's room and Gene joined them.

"I made some calls, and there's going to be a lot of prayer going out for our girl." There were two chairs in Nikki's room, and the Ellertons felt this was a good time to get some sleep as they planned to spend the night. Roy had said he would stay the night with Josh and not to worry.

CHAPTER FOURTEEN

It was Christmas day, and Nikki had been in the hospital for a few days. At first things were touch and go. The doctors were having a hard time pinpointing the problem with Nikki's kidneys. Cathy did some research on her own; she pulled out the case studies on kids with Wolf-Hirschhorn and checked everything she could find that related to the kidneys. Taking everything to the doctor, he specifically checked each thing and found that Nikki had kidney reflux; the urine that came from the kidneys was being shot back up into the kidneys, causing an infection. As a result, Nikki started having seizures and was put on medication. Then the medication became toxic, which was the cause of her vomiting. The doctor was convinced that this was a direct result from kidney reflux.

They started treating her reflux by putting her on a prophylactic to stop the infection. After the medicine got into Nikki's system, she had a complete turnaround. The doctor said, "It is a miracle she's still alive." He wanted her to remain at the hospital for a few more days for observation.

The Ellertons were relieved and thanked the Lord that their daughter was going to be all right. They knew that God had saved her life. They were also thankful for that early Christmas with Gene's family.

They wanted to do something special for the other families spending Christmas at the hospital. They decided to buy a cake with 'Happy Birthday, Jesus' written on it and put it at the nurse's station for everyone at the hospital to share. The nurses were grateful for the gesture and told the Ellertons to take a break, that Nikki would be well taken care of.

Josh had been staying with Annie and Eddie Ashby since Roy had left for California when it became clear that Nikki was going to be all right. Earlier that day, Annie had invited the Ellertons to join them for Christmas brunch at a hotel in the Clackamas area. They were thankful for the distraction, except that Cathy felt bad going without Nikki.

The Ellertons took Josh to visit Nikki after the brunch. He had been missing his sister. When they arrived at Nikki's room, they were amazed to find it full of presents. Each present had a note attached to it. Nikki's nurse explained that the other families in the hospital were touched by the Ellertons generosity in thinking of others while their own daughter was spending Christmas day in the hospital. The nurse told them that the families had asked if Nikki had any siblings, as they wanted to buy something for both Josh and Nikki. This made Josh's Christmas. He was ecstatic and tore into his gifts as well as Nikki's. He placed each of her gifts nicely around her crib. This whole scene brought tears to Gene and Cathy. They started opening the cards, most of them generic thank yous for the cake. One card was from a single dad who had lost his wife when their baby was two. His daughter was now seven and in the hospital on Christmas day. She had a cold that turned into pneumonia, and she was admitted to the hospital. He was angry at first. His wife had died around this time five years earlier, and since then he tried to make Christmas special for his daughter. The letter went on to explain that his wife was a Christian and had tried to tell him about Jesus. When his wife died, he became angry with Jesus for taking her away and hardened his heart. He said that he couldn't explain it, but when he saw the cake that said, 'Happy Birthday, Jesus,' he burst into tears. He asked the nurse about the people who bought this cake and discovered that they had almost lost their daughter a couple of days earlier. The love that he saw in this gesture reminded him of when his wife would tell him about Jesus. He thought of the story of God sending his son to die on the cross for sinners, like him. That was all it took, a cake, and he said he got down on his hands and knees right there and asked Jesus into his heart. He wanted to meet the Ellertons face to face and thank them. His name was Jim Drake and his daughter's name was Emily.

As Gene read this letter out loud, Cathy started to cry. "Gene, this could be the whole reason Nikki was sick, and who knows how many other seeds might have been planted because of a cake? I wonder if Jim and Emily are still here."

"I'll find out if they're still around."

A few minutes later, Gene returned with a man following close behind. "Sweetheart, meet Jim." Jim was an attractive man in his forties. He had blue eyes, dark brown hair, and an excited look on his face.

"Nice to meet you, Jim. I'm Cathy, this is our son Josh, and this is our little girl, Nikki."

"Nice to meet you all too. I wonder if the reason Emily got sick last night was so we could come here and meet you. I've been thanking Jesus for sending you here to me, so that my blinders could be taken off and I could ask Jesus to come live in me."

"We feel honored to meet you. God is good. I learned today that doing simple things, like buying a cake, could be a life-changing experience for someone else. Seeing your excitement and knowing you will one day be with Jesus in Heaven made

Nikki's illness worth it. I know if she could talk, she would agree with me." They talked for over an hour. Before Jim checked out with Emily, he brought her to meet them. She thanked them for making her daddy smile again. They exchanged numbers and promised to keep in touch.

Seefas was observing the whole scene and thanked Jesus for the ways that He works. "Lord, I have to confess that I questioned why Nikki had to be here. I didn't understand why, after everything was going so well with Cathy's change in attitude and Sophie slowly starting to warm up to Nikki, this all had to happen. You are sovereign. You know everything. Everything you do, or allow, is turned for your glory."

The Ellertons brought Nikki home on New Year's Eve. They couldn't think of a better way to start the New Year.

* * *

Nikki, happy again and seizure-free, had been home for about a month. Things were going well. Cathy was so thankful to have Nikki's illness behind them. But she thanked God for that time because they had become good friends with Jim Drake and his daughter, Emily. It was awesome to see Jim's excitement for the Lord. Jim had introduced them to several of his friends, and they testified to the dramatic change in him. He now had a mission field of his own.

Josh was glad to have his happy and content little sister back. Cathy had been feeling nauseous and lacked energy. Gene asked her if she had taken a pregnancy test. Cathy said that hadn't even crossed her mind. They wanted another baby, but Cathy had been preoccupied with other matters.

When she bought a pregnancy test, the results were positive. She called Gene at work, "Honey, God has the perfect little baby picked out for us because it's not our timing, it's His. What I'm trying to say is, I'm pregnant."

Gene was excited. "Maybe it's time to think about getting a bigger house."

"Are you serious? Don't mess with me, you know I've been wanting a bigger house."

"I'm serious. I've given it a lot of thought, and we'll start looking into it. Have you told Josh and Nikki the good news yet?"

"Of course not, that's something we can do together. Maybe I'll make pizza casserole again."

Cathy got off the phone and remembered that Lisa was coming to do therapy with Nikki. She hadn't been there since Nikki had been in the hospital. The last several months Nikki had been so fussy, it was hard for Lisa to accomplish much. She heard Lisa at the door.

"Hi, Lisa. Come in."

"Thanks, Cathy, it's good to see you. And there's that sweet girl. Wow! She looks great." Not only was there a smile on Nikki's face, but Lisa noticed she had grown. Her hair had gotten longer, and beautiful curls now encircled her face. She looked like a stunning little doll. "You're gorgeous, Nikki. Are you ready to work hard?"

Nikki just giggled, as if to say, "Let's do it." Lisa worked with Nikki for about an hour, and Nikki responded in positive ways. Her head control was really coming along and Lisa said they could start thinking about rolling. Cathy was thrilled to see her daughter's progress. Lisa remarked how different Nikki was now; she had a gleam in her eye and seemed to be trying to communicate with her. When Lisa finished, Cathy told her the details of Nikki's hospital scare and what had happened with Jim. Lisa had a look in her eyes that Cathy hadn't seen before.

"Um, Cathy, do you think it might be okay if, um, I come with you sometime to church?" Lisa seemed nervous, but Cathy was thrilled.

"Of course. How about this weekend?"

"I guess that will work."

"Why don't you meet us here, and we'll go together." After finalizing the details, it was time for Lisa to go. Cathy had wanted to tell Lisa that she was pregnant, but she hadn't told the kids yet, so she decided to wait.

When Gene got home, Cathy told him about Lisa. Gene thought it was great how God seemed to be working all around them. "Our little girl is a great tool for sharing the gospel. She's touched more lives in her short life than I have in my entire life. She's a blessing. Are you ready to tell our sweet girl and her terrific brother about our news?"

"You bet. Josh, come in the living room, please. It's just about dinner time." When Josh came in, Cathy was sitting on the couch and Gene was holding Nikki in his rocking chair.

"Hey, Buster, why don't you join your mom over there on the couch. Sweetheart, do you want to share the good news or should I?"

"You may have the honor, my dear!"

"Well, Josh and Nikki, we are excited to tell you that you are going to have a new baby brother or sister." Gene shared this with such excitement that Nikki laughed and Josh jumped up and down.

The rest of the evening was wonderful. They ate dinner, played a game as a family, and had their devotional time.

"Time for bed."

"Aw, Mom." Josh was having so much fun, he didn't want it to end. After they got the kids tucked in, Gene and Cathy spent some one-on-one time. In the other room, they could hear Nikki's sweet little coos.

"So, Miss Nicole, are you excited about having another brother or sister?"

"Yes, See-fs! Nikki love brother Josh. I love other brother too."

"Well, you know you could have a sister this time?"

Nikki giggled.

"It's good to see you happy and feeling better. That was exciting today, that Lisa wants to come to church with you."

"Nikki pray for Lisa."

CHAPTER FIFTEEN

"Mommy, Sophie's at the door. Can I open it?" Cathy was surprised. They hadn't seen much of Sophie, and Cathy was looking forward to sharing with her about Nikki.

"Hold on Buster, I'll be right there. Then you can open it." Cathy let Josh open the door, and he attacked Sophie with a bear hug. Nikki seemed excited too and squealed with delight.

"Good to see you too, Joshy. I'm not coming at a bad time, am I? I just missed Buster here, and thought I'd pay him a visit." Sophie, once again, paid little attention to Nikki.

"It's a great time. We were just hanging out, and everyone's up from their naps. We haven't seen you in a while. Did you go back to visit your parents again?"

"No, I've just been putting in extra hours at work. They've been shorthanded, so I said I'd fill in." When Sophie's husband died, he left her with a lot of money, and Sophie didn't need to work, but she'd decided to work at a grocery store as a cashier to keep from getting bored.

"I have been excited to share with you what happened when Nikki was in the hospital. And, I almost forgot, I haven't told you yet, we're having another baby."

"Congratulations." Sophie seemed sincerely excited for them, but she looked concerned. "Aren't you afraid that you may have another child with problems? But, I guess this time you can get that amnio done and go ahead and abort your baby if you need to." Sophie said this so matter of factly that it took Cathy by surprise.

* * *

"Lord, give Cathy the words and confidence as she has this conversation with Sophie. Open Sophie's eyes and heart to receive the message that she will hear. Speak through Cathy." As the conversation continued, Seefas was praying on Cathy's behalf.

* * *

"Sophie, I love my little girl immeasurably. She is a special gift from God and she has taught me so much more than I could have imagined. When I'm letting problems get to me, I look at her and see such contentment in everything. I want to be more like that. I have to admit, it would be hard to have another child with Nikki's syndrome because of the possible health concerns, but I would never, never have an abortion. Every child is a gift from God, and He has a special purpose for each of us. Who am I to decide not to let His creation live?"

"Cathy, I didn't mean to upset you. You do know that they're not really babies until they're born."

"Sophie, that's where the world is wrong. Do you know how many ultrasounds I had before Nikki was born? More than I can count. Every one that I had, I saw my baby. One time, she was sucking her thumb, another she was playing with her toes, once it even looked like she was waving hi. She wasn't born yet, but she was definitely an active little baby." Cathy was passionate about this subject, and Sophie looked like she was listening.

"I'm sorry. I didn't mean to offend you. I guess I've never given it much thought. I hear what women say about their freedom of choice being taken away, and, well, I guess I've never really thought about the fact that there could be a baby involved. I'm sorry." Sophie genuinely seemed to feel bad about what she'd said.

"That's all right, Sophie. I know what the world says and most people don't give it much thought. It really hits at a personal level when people say that if a child's different, they don't have a right to enter this world. If people with this opinion would only take the time to get to know someone like Nikki, I believe their opinion would change."

"Aren't you afraid of getting hurt?"

"What do you mean, getting hurt?"

"What if you had lost Nikki a couple of months ago, when she got sick? How would you deal with losing someone you love? Isn't it hard to get close to her, when you could lose her at a young age?"

"Oh, Sophie. We're all going to die someday. Life here on earth is short. If we were always worrying about losing someone, we would never experience the joy that comes in relationships. If I had lost Nikki when she got sick, yes, it would have been very hard. But, at least I would have had the privilege of having her in my life, and my life is so much richer because of her. What a tragedy it would have been if I'd never taken the time to know this jewel of a girl. That would have been the true loss." When Cathy said this, Nikki giggled with delight, and, for a moment, Cathy thought she saw tears in Sophie's eyes. Cathy softened a bit because the thought came to her that Sophie might be talking about her own life, in losing her husband.

"Cathy, do you really believe that?"

"Yes, I do. Sophie, I'm sorry if I've upset you in any way, but my daughter is one of the best things that's ever happened to me, and I guess I'm a little passionate about the subject. Everything I've said though, I truly believe."

"You've given me a lot to think about. And, to be honest, it's bringing back some painful memories of losing my husband."

"Do you want to talk about it?"

"Not right now, thanks, Cathy. Maybe one day, I'll be ready to talk about it, and maybe one day, I'll take the chance to get to know Nikki, but I'm not ready. Sorry." Sophie was quiet for a while and then said, "Do you mind if I take Josh to the zoo tomorrow? I'm off and I haven't spent much time with him."

"That would be great. I'm sure he'd love it." During Cathy and Sophie's conversation, Josh had become bored and was playing in his room; Sophie went in to say good-bye. Cathy wasn't sure how she got sidetracked from telling Sophie about Nikki's stay in the hospital and hoped she wasn't too hard on her. Cathy thought maybe the timing wasn't right to tell her about Jim and Emily, but one day she'd like to tell Sophie that story.

After Sophie left, Cathy started on dinner. Josh was still playing in his room, and she could hear Nikki playing in the living room, most likely with her angel, she thought.

After playing for a while, Nikki asked Seefas, "My mommy loves me, huh?"

"She loves you very much."

"Jesus loves Nikki too?"

"Yes, Sweet Nikki, He does. Why do you ask?"

"I feel lucky to have Mommy and Jesus love me. I love them too. Jesus loves Sophie too. Huh?"

"Yes, very much!"

"I wish Sophie had someone like Mommy to love her. Can we ask Jesus to have someone love her?"

"Miss Nicole, that is a wonderful idea. You can ask Jesus anything. We will keep praying for Sophie, that she will first fall in love with Jesus, and then maybe another kind of love will come her way."

* * *

Silence had fallen over the Ellerton house. Cathy couldn't hear anything coming from Nikki's room, which meant she was truly asleep. Cathy often heard Nikki giggling and cooing before she drifted off to sleep. She could also hear soft snores coming from Josh's room and loud snores from the man she loved. Cathy, however, stayed awake thinking about her unborn child. She was excited about another child for several reasons. Cathy loved kids. She understood that the more stimulation Nikki had the better, and what better way than to have another baby around? She also wanted Josh to have a playmate, even though he loved his sister very much.

"Lord, I have to confess, I'm scared. I love my daughter but I don't think I could handle having two children with a disorder. I'm also scared to have a girl. The last thing I want to do is start comparing Nikki with a sister. I'm afraid that it will make me think about the way Nikki would have been. I want Nikki to always have a special place in our family. What better way than to be the only girl, our little princess? It just seems that a boy would be the best fit for us. Josh could have a brother to roughhouse with, and Nikki could have two strong brothers to look out for her and protect her. I know Lord that you know best. You already have this all figured out. If you choose to give me another girl, I know it will be all right. Please give me peace, whichever way you have decided." Then Cathy drifted off to sleep.

The next morning Cathy got Josh ready to go to the zoo with Sophie. Josh was excited. Sophie picked him up and said they'd be gone most of the day. After they left, Cathy decided to take Nikki to the store to buy some baby things she needed. Nikki had fun at the store, enjoying moving about in her stroller and taking in all the sights around her. She was the best shopping companion Cathy had. When they finished, Cathy called Gene to see if he wanted to join them for lunch.

Cathy and Nikki picked Gene up and they went to Olive Garden, one of their favorite restaurants. As they walked in the door, a girl who worked there approached them. "How's Nikki doing?" This took Gene and Cathy by surprise because they did not recognize this girl.

"She's doing well. Thanks for asking." Cathy tried to respond as if she remembered this girl.

"I love having you guys come in, and I'm going to have them put you in my section. See you in a few minutes."

"Do you know who that was, Cathy?"

"I'm not sure. I don't recognize her, but she definitely knew who Nikki was; she even knew her name."

After they were seated, the girl came to their table, excited to be their server.

"I'm sorry, but I can't remember where we know you from." Cathy tried to say this in the nicest way possible.

"That's okay; it's just from here that I remember you guys. I was your server one time, and well, your little girl made an impression on me. I think about Nikki often. I've told all my friends about her. I'm Val." She was a young woman, probably in her early twenties.

"Nice to meet you, Val. I'm Cathy and this is my husband Gene."

"This is going to sound strange, but I was wondering if I could ever babysit for you guys. You also have a little boy, if I'm remembering correctly. I understand if you say no. I wouldn't trust my kids to a stranger either. It's just that I would love a chance to get to know Nikki better. She's a very special little girl."

"Why don't you let me and my husband talk about it. But that's very sweet." Then Val took their order and was gone.

"It amazes me the impact Nikki has on people everywhere we go. I don't know, Cathy, about having her babysit."

"I agree, but what do you think about inviting her over for dinner sometime? I like her and that way we can get to know more about her." Gene agreed, and they enjoyed the rest of their meal. When they were paying their bill, Cathy asked Val if she would like to come over for dinner sometime. Val excitedly agreed and thanked them for the offer.

On the way back to Gene's office, they talked about Val and wondered how God was going to use Nikki this time.

* * *

"Hey, Buster, how was the zoo?"

"It was great, Mommy. Next time you and Sissy need to come too."

"That would be fun. Sophie, how was it for you?"

"It was fun. The whole time, though, Josh kept saying Sissy would love this. He also said, maybe Jim and Emily could come next time. Who are they?" Cathy welcomed the opportunity to talk about their friends, especially with Sophie.

"We met them when Nikki was in the hospital." Cathy went on to tell her about how they met and about Jim's life. "Maybe sometime you could meet them." Sophie just sat there taking it all in. She was amazed how similar her story was to Jim's, except she didn't have any kids. Tears welled up in her eyes as it brought back her own memories of Kevin's death.

"Maybe sometime," Sophie responded.

"I'm sorry, Sophie, I don't mean to keep bringing back memories of losing Kevin. You've never told me how he died. Do you mind sharing that with me?"

"Kevin just started getting weak. He would be working around the house and not have the energy to finish. At first we thought he was coming down with a cold, and we didn't think much of it. Later, he started getting worse and would pass out doing anything physical. One day, while he was playing basketball, he collapsed. His heart rate was slow, and they rushed him to the hospital." Sophie stopped. Tears were filling her eyes.

"You don't have to go on."

"That's okay, I think I can. I got a phone call telling me that Kevin had been rushed to the hospital. I hurried over and the doctor told me that Kevin's heart was giving out, and they would have to do a transplant or he would die. They didn't have time to find a heart because Kevin died forty-eight hours later." Sophie was crying now and couldn't go on. Cathy walked over and put her arm around Sophie.

"I'm sorry to make you talk about it. I had no idea."

"I know, Cathy. I'm glad I told you. I want you to know. Thanks for being my friend." Cathy felt like this was the first time that she and Sophie had connected in more than a neighborly way. Before, Sophie's focus had always been on Josh. Now, possibly there would be a true friendship between herself and Sophie.

* * *

"Lord, thank you for today. It seems like Sophie's walls are slowly being broken down. I pray that she will be able to open up more to Cathy. And, who is Val? And how is Nikki going to change her life? You were right, Lord, when you said, that it will be exciting to see how Nikki's able to impact the world around her. Thank you for giving me this assignment."

CHAPTER SIXTEEN

On the way home from church, Lisa talked nonstop about the service. "I've never been to a church like that before. Do you always just sing and share with one another?" That weekend at church, they had a worship service in which they sang and shared how God had touched their lives. Gene had shared a little on how God had blessed them through their daughter and the many ways He had used her to win people for Him.

"Usually, we sing and our pastor gives a sermon. Once in a while they will have a service like the one today."

"Cathy, I've always thought of Christianity as a bunch of rules you had to follow. But, in hearing you talk about Nikki and seeing what I experienced today, something struck me in a different way. I think I want that in my life. Can you tell me how to do that?" Right there in the car, in front of Gene and the kids, Lisa gave her life to Jesus. Lisa couldn't wait to tell her family about Jesus.

* * *

Seefas again looked up to Heaven and wished he could be part of the celebration for another of God's creations receiving Him. He looked at Nikki and she was smiling.

* * *

Cathy got a phone call from her parents who said they were planning on moving to Oregon. They were hoping to be there before Cathy's baby was born. When she got off the phone, she shared the news and brought up the subject of putting their house on the market.

Gene told her that Ryan had given him a name of a realtor, and they had an appointment next week.

Cathy was thrilled. "So, where are we going to move? I was thinking Gresham's a great area and it's closer to church. You know, we've talked about Josh going to school there." The Ellertons' church had a school that went through eighth grade.

"I like Gresham, too. We'll start looking into it."

"Oh, no! What about Sophie?"

"What do you mean?"

"I don't want her to feel we're abandoning her."

"Sweetheart, people move. She'll understand." Gene didn't understand Cathy's concerns, but Cathy felt she was finally establishing a true friendship with Sophie and didn't want to do anything to jeopardize that.

Cathy thought about that. "I'll just have to make it clear that I still want her in our lives." Cathy felt a little better. She knew with three kids she wanted a bigger house. They couldn't live their lives around Sophie. Besides Cathy knew that God was in control.

The next morning Cathy was going in for her six-month appointment, and she would finally learn if she was having a boy or a girl. Last time with Nikki she'd so wanted a girl, and this time she really wanted a boy. Cathy was quiet while they waited to be seen at Doctor Tanaka's office.

"What's the matter, Sweetheart? Why are you so quiet?"

"Gene, I'm scared. This is the time with Nikki that we found out something was wrong. What if it happens again?"

"I don't think it will, but even if it does, God knows best. He'll help us, whatever the outcome."

"Good morning, Mr. and Mrs. Ellerton." Doctor Tanaka walked into the room. "Any preference to what you're going to have?"

"Gene could go either way, but I'm hoping that God chose a boy for us. I guess we're about to find out." Doctor Tanaka went to work taking all the measurements and checking the baby thoroughly. Sometimes it took awhile for babies to get in the right position to see their gender.

"While I'm waiting for your little one to change positions, I've been checking out the measurements. Your baby is right on schedule and not lagging behind at all." At this Gene leaned down and gave Cathy a kiss.

"Thank you, Lord." Gene said, looking up to Heaven. Cathy, speechless, was overcome with joy.

"I'm still going to monitor this pregnancy closely, but things look good so far. Hey, it looks like your little one decided to cooperate. Are you ready to find out what you're having?"

"Let's do it." Gene started to chuckle. "Sweetheart looks like God agreed with you. If I'm not mistaken doctor, we're having a boy."

Now Doctor Tanaka started to laugh. "Not too hard to tell with those boys, is it?"

"Are you serious?" Cathy couldn't stop grinning.

"Have you picked a name out yet?"

"Yes, we have. Zachary Joseph."

"No kidding? Zachary is my son's name. Good choice." While they talked, Doctor Tanaka wanted to know how Nikki was doing. He said he always prayed for her. The Ellertons really appreciated his kindness.

Arriving home, they told Josh and Nikki that they were going to have a baby brother. They both seemed excited, especially Josh. He couldn't believe he got to have a sister and a brother.

"Your realtor called. He has someone interested in your house and wants you to give him a call."

"Great. Thanks, Dad, and thanks for watching the kids."

"Always a pleasure." After Roy left, Cathy and Gene had mixed feelings about a potential buyer for their home. It wasn't that they didn't want to move, but they just hadn't found the house they wanted. Cathy also wanted to tell Sophie before she saw the for-sale sign. She was due back next week after a quick trip to see her parents.

"Well, Sweetheart, the right house is out there somewhere. I'm just praying that we find a place before this house sells. I don't want to live in an apartment."

"I'm with you. This is the part about moving I don't like."

* * *

"So, Miss Nicole, how do you feel about having another brother?"

"Seefas, Nikki's very excited. I love Josh and I love Zacky too." Her mom would put her up to her tummy and she would coo and smile while talking to the baby. It seemed like they already had a connection.

Seefas was always on full alert in protecting Nikki, but getting to know her was his favorite part.

"Good-night, Seefas."

"Good-night. I'll be watching over you all night long."

* * *

"Josh and Nikki, Daddy's going to be home any minute and shortly after that Val's going to be here. I want you both to be on your best behavior." Nikki giggled at her mom. It always amazed Cathy how much Nikki seemed to understand.

"All right, Mommy. You can count on me." Josh was very curious about this Val person his mommy and daddy talked about, and he was sure he was going to like her.

"Joshy, can you help me pick your toys up in the living room and take them to your room?" Cathy already had dinner in the oven and was trying to get the house straightened up.

"Hello, Daddy's home." Gene always greeted the kids that way, even if they were standing right there. He would give Nikki kisses and Josh would jump into his arms.

"Hey, what about me?" Cathy teased as she walked over to give Gene a kiss. "How was work?"

"Great. What time is our guest coming?"

"In about half an hour." The next thirty minutes flew by and Val was finally there. Josh had been waiting impatiently all day.

"Val, I'm so glad that you could come."

"Thank you, Mrs. Ellerton."

"Please, call me Cathy. Are you hungry? Dinner's ready to be served." During dinner Val asked a lot of questions about Nikki. She wanted to know about her disorder and anything they could tell her. After dinner they played a game together, Val had Nikki on her team. She was really taken with Nikki and Josh. She was wonderful with the kids. The family had their nightly devotions, and Val seemed a little uncomfortable. When it was the kid's bedtime, Josh went grudgingly because he was having so much fun with Val.

"Val, you're welcome to stay a little longer. We've talked a lot about our family, but we don't know much about yours. Can you tell us about your family?"

"There's not much to tell, Cathy. I have lived on my own since I was sixteen. My dad died when I was in junior high, and my mom went off the deep end. She started drinking and couldn't hold a job. My older brother was sixteen when it happened, and he split. As the youngest, it was just my mom and me. I was pretty much raising myself, so when I turned sixteen, I thought I'd follow in my brother's footsteps. I don't communicate with my mom very much. On holidays, I give her a call to say hi."

"I'm sorry to hear that. It must have been hard."

"It was at first, but I guess I was forced to grow up fast. I see my brother on occasion, but he hangs out at bars most of the time, just like my mom. Some of my friends are my anchors. Without them, I think I would have ended up at the bars too."

"You seem to have pulled it together pretty well. When we see you at Olive Garden, you seem to have a perpetual smile on your face."

"Cathy, it's mostly an act, except when I see Nikki come in."

"What is it about her that draws you?" Cathy was curious.

"She's so petite, and it's obvious that's she's older than her size indicates. She has the sweetest look, and her eyes seem to twinkle. Even when she falls asleep while you guys eat, it is such a peaceful sleep." Nikki still ate baby food, so the Ellertons always fed her before they went out. It wasn't unusual for her to take a short nap in her car seat, as she could sleep anywhere. "I always wondered what makes her so content. Do you guys have any idea?"

"We've talked a lot about that and our guess is that she doesn't let the worries of this world cloud her perception of things. I'm convinced that she can see her angel. There are times when she's playing with someone, but I can't see anyone there. She teaches me so much. When I let simple things bother me, I look at her and see the contentment. It makes me stop and reevaluate the situation, and it usually turns my mood around." Cathy always got a little teary eyed when she talked about her daughter. Gene excused himself for he felt that Val might open up more if he wasn't there.

"Wow, her angel? That's cool. It always seems like something's missing in my life. What do you think is Nikki's secret?"

"Jesus is her secret. I believe Nikki has a special relationship with Him. It's incredible for me to see that, although she doesn't talk, other than coo and giggle, the impact she has is unbelievable."

"Do you really believe in Jesus? My mom always told me that He's just a made up story. After my dad died, a friend of mine invited me to church. All the stories I heard about Jesus seemed so exciting to me. I would go home and tell my mom, and she would say, 'They're brainwashing you; Jesus isn't real.' I figured she's my mom, I guess she knows, so I stopped going with my friend."

"Val, Jesus is real. It says so in the Bible, and I've experienced Him in my life. In the Bible it says that He loves us so much, He died for us. He longs for everyone to come to Him."

"What do you mean when you say, you've experienced him in your own life?"

Cathy recounted all the times in Nikki's life when she had felt Jesus there with her: when Nikki was in the hospital, when it was hard to feed her and God opened her mouth, the healing of Nikki's hearing, and through Cathy's whole pregnancy.

"Val, you can experience Him too. All you have to do is ask Him for forgiveness of your sins, believe He died for you, and ask Him to come live in your heart. It's a free gift. All you have to do is accept it."

"It's so hard to believe that. No one has ever accepted me just the way I am. My mom always told me I wasn't good enough, that I had to do better. I tried to make the pain of losing my dad go away, but nothing I did was good enough."

"You're right, Val. Nothing we do is good enough. That's why God sent His Son to die for us. He took all our sins upon Himself. He was the ultimate sacrifice. We are all sinners, and we will always fall short, but Jesus died in our place, and we can ask Him for forgiveness, and He will forgive us. Nothing we do is too great for Him to forgive. It's not what we've done, but what He's done."

"Cathy, can you help me receive that in my life? I want to experience Nikki's kind of contentment." They prayed, and another life was won for Jesus. Seefas stood beside them, rejoicing.

Cathy went to bed that night with a smile on her face. She felt like she always got the pleasure of leading someone to the Lord, when Nikki had done all the work; it didn't seem fair somehow. But Nikki also experienced the joy; Cathy just didn't know it.

"Seefas, now Val loves Jesus just like Lisa."

"You're right. Jesus continues to use you, little one. It's awesome to be a part of that."

CHAPTER SEVENTEEN

Cathy's parents had just moved to Oregon. They were staying at a house in Sandy, in a basement apartment set up for missionaries.

Today Cathy and her mom were going house hunting while her dad watched the kids. They went to see some new houses being built in Gresham, and Cathy immediately fell in love with the area. There were large trees to the left and right of them, and, as they turned into the subdivision, there was a breathtaking view of Mount Hood.

"It's beautiful here, Mom, and the neighborhood seems great. I hope the houses turn out to be just as nice." New houses were being built all the way down the street and in a cul-de-sac. Cathy felt a cul-de-sac would be a perfect place to raise kids. One house was different from the rest; it was wider and seemed to have more character. It was framed, but the interior was not finished. As they looked through the house, Cathy loved it! There was even a bonus room above the garage. It seemed enormous compared to their existing house.

"This is the one, Mom; it's perfect. I hope Gene agrees. Do you see anything you'd be interested in?" Grant and May wanted to get a place near Cathy.

"Sweetheart, Dad and I don't need anything this big. I was thinking a one-story would be nice. Why don't we drive around some of the adjoining neighborhoods and see what's there?" They drove into the next neighborhood and found many houses for sale. The houses were about five years old and in nice condition. As they turned the corner May saw an interesting house and asked Cathy to pull over so she could get a flyer. The flyer said there was a pond in the back yard. May was excited. "Dad and I are getting older, and the less yard work the better. I think Dad will love this house, and it's within walking distance if you buy the one you like. We'll just leave it in the Lord's hands to see if this is the best place for all of us."

When they got back to the Ellertons', Papa was playing with Josh and Nikki in the backyard with Shawnee. Nikki was sitting in her swing. Gene and Cathy had added a special swing on their swing set for her that she really enjoyed.

"Did my kids treat you right, Dad?"

"We had a lot of fun. They keep me hopping. We need to do this more often."

"Well, if you and Gene like the houses we want to buy, you can do it all the time. They're within walking distance of each other."

"I'm sure I'll like whatever Mom picked out; she's always done well in that area." They chatted for a little longer before Grant and May had to leave. Cathy suggested to the kids that they walk down to Sophie's and see if she was home from Michigan.

Josh had been asking when she was coming home. Cathy got Nikki loaded in her stroller, and they set off for the short walk, three houses down. When they got there, Josh wanted to ring the doorbell. He rang it a couple of times, and they were about to turn around, when, finally, Sophie came to the door.

"Hi, Sophie. Hope you don't mind us stopping by. We didn't know when you were getting back from Michigan."

"I've been home about a week now," Sophie said in a monotone voice.

"Why didn't you come by and let us know you were back? We've missed you."

"I guess I didn't have the time." Cathy could tell by her tone that something was wrong.

"Is everything all right? How's your mom doing?"

"She's fine."

"Sophie, Sophie, we're going to move into a bigger house. Mommy and Granda went looking at one today." As Josh was saying this Cathy realized that Sophie didn't know they were planning to move and she suspected this was what was bothering her.

"Yeah, I saw the sign in your yard."

"Sophie, I wanted to tell you myself, but you were in Michigan, and it all happened quickly. But that doesn't mean we don't want you in our lives. At first, I told Gene it was hard to make the decision to move because of you. Then Gene pointed out that friends don't always live next door to each other, and yet they remain friends."

"I'm your friend?" Sophie seemed surprised.

"Sophie, of course you are. You are a very dear friend, we are very grateful to have you in our lives."

"I figured it was just because of Josh you put up with me." Cathy couldn't believe that Sophie felt this way, but then she thought about it; it was usually Sophie who came to their house instead of vice versa.

"Sophie, I'm sorry I've made you feel that way. I know I don't get over here very often, but it's not because I don't enjoy your company. I just get into my routine at home and don't venture out much. I apologize. Yes, Josh does love you, but so do the rest of us." Nikki cooed when Cathy said this.

"You don't know how much that means to me." Sophie's mood lightened. "So, where will you be moving?"

"I found a house in Gresham that's only about twenty minutes from here. We'd have you over all the time, and you could just drop in on us like you do here. It will be great. Just wait and see."

"Sounds good. I've always liked the Gresham area. I think I'll take you up on your offer. " Sophie and Cathy laughed and everything felt like it was going to be all right.

"Josh and Nikki's birthdays are coming up, and we'd love for you to come to their party again. Most likely we'll still be in this house. I'll give you more details as the time gets closer."

Sophie and Josh spent a little time playing with her brand new kitten. Then Cathy said they had to go and fix dinner before Gene got home.

* * *

That night, Cathy told Gene about the houses that she and her mom found. He seemed genuinely interested and said he'd run by there on his lunch break the next day.

"I got a call today at work from our realtor, and the couple he thought was a sure thing put an offer on another house. We'll just have to pray that the timing works out, finding a house for us and selling this one. How long until the house you saw today will be finished?"

"I'm not sure. We'll have to call and find out. It looks like they still have quite a bit to do." Cathy then went on to explain her conversation with Sophie and said it ended on a positive note.

* * *

"Nikki, did you have fun at Sophie's house today?"

"It was fun, Seefas. But I keep praying that she will like me one day. I really like her. It's fun watching Josh play with her though."

"You are very gracious; it's not always easy being ignored. She just doesn't know how to relate to you."

"I know. But, I have a feeling she'll come around."

The kids' birthdays came up fast, Josh was now four and Nikki was two. It had been a busy year, and it was fascinating comparing last year's guest list to this one. Each new name had its own unique story; there were Jim and Emily, Lisa and their newest friend, Val. Cathy's parents were there this year too. Of course, the same people from last year would be there as well.

"Isn't it amazing the impact Nikki's had on people in her short two years of life? It never ceases to amaze me."

"I know, Cathy; Ryan still goes on at work about how God used her to reach his family. They're all involved at their church and his kids love going!"

"I'm looking forward to Jim and Emily being here. I think Jim could really be the one to help Sophie; as their stories are so similar, he would understand her."

"Cathy, don't go trying to play matchmaker."

"I'm not. I'm just saying she needs someone to talk to who could understand her. But, you know, they would make a cute couple. I hadn't thought of that."

"Yeah, right."

"Mom, when are people going to get here? I'm ready to start this party." Josh came bouncing out from his room.

"Anytime now, Buster." Just as Cathy said that, the first guests arrived. Soon, it was a full house—literally. The Ellertons were thankful for the beautiful weather so people could be outdoors, as they still hadn't moved and it would have been a tight squeeze in their small house. Their big backyard, however, easily accommodated all their guests. It was a bustling place, filled with laughter and chatter. The kids were having lots of fun playing on Josh's play structure. Nikki loved the stimulation of all the activity taking place around her. The grown-ups were talking, and Gene was busy barbecuing the meat.

As Cathy sat there soaking it all in, she noticed that Jim and Sophie both seemed to be unoccupied, so she jumped at the opportunity to introduce them. "Sophie, come with me. I want you to meet someone." She pulled her over to where Jim was standing. "Jim, I want you to meet Sophie."

"Sophie, nice to meet you. Cathy only says wonderful things about you. I'm Jim Drake."

"I've heard your name mentioned quite often. I think the first time was when I had Josh at the zoo and he said that, 'Jim and Emily need to come with us next time.' So, I asked Cathy about you."

"I love that kid. He brightens up my day. He has mentioned you often too."

Jim and Sophie seemed to be hitting it off, so Cathy excused herself, leaving them alone to talk, and went to visit with Val, who hadn't left Nikki's side most of the party.

"Hey, Val, are you having fun?"

"Nikki has been keeping me utterly entertained. I love her little coos and giggles. I wish I could understand what was going on in that head of hers."

"I think that all the time. I can't wait to sit down with her in Heaven and have some long, in-depth conversations. So, have you gotten to know anyone today?"

"Actually, Jill and I went to the same high school. I didn't really know her then, but it's been fun getting to know her now. She invited me to go with her to the college group at her church; I'm going to give it a try and see if I like it. I've wanted to find a church ever since I accepted Christ into my life. Jill just went in to use the bathroom; she's been hanging out with me and Nikki." Jill was Ryan's oldest daughter. Cathy was thrilled that Val was able to meet a Christian gal her age. She hadn't even thought of getting those two connected.

* * *

"Lord, you are amazing, the way you weave together people's lives. All these connections taking place today are not happening by accident. You knew exactly what each of them needed before they even entered the Ellertons' lives." Seefas loved watching the interactions taking place, and he loved the way Nikki soaked it all in. He laughed when he thought of the way she had been communicating with Val and Jill, like she was hanging out with friends. He loved to see Nikki enjoying her birthday.

* * *

Josh once again insisted on helping his sister open her presents before his own. He laughed and she giggled. It was fun seeing them interact. Jim and Sophie hung out together the rest of the party, and Val and Jill were glued together as well. Cathy was pleased as she thought about the day. When everyone had gone and the kids were tucked soundly in bed, Cathy and Gene talked over the day as they crawled into bed.

"So, Sweetheart, today was a great success. Good job."

"I couldn't have done it without my wonderful husband. You know that, right?"

"Well, that is true." They both laughed.

"Did you see how Jim and Sophie spent most of the day together?"

"You didn't by any chance have anything to do with that, did you?"

"I just introduced them. There's no harm in that, is there?"

"No, I suppose not. Ryan was excited that Jill found a new friend, as she has been having a hard time feeling connected in her college group. He's thrilled that Val's going to start going with her because he thinks that's all Jill needs to gain confidence and start reaching out to other people."

"It's perfect for Val too. I don't think she has any other Christian friends."

"She has us."

"True, but we're not in our early twenties. Val seemed to beam around Jill. Val commented to me at one point that Jill's different from any friend she's ever had. I think God did well today. Oooh!"

"What's wrong?"

"Nothing, the baby just started kicking. Here, feel right here. I think he's been asleep most of the day, and it's his wake time now. I love feeling him move around. Even though this is my third pregnancy, it's still amazing to me. Well, Zachary's waking up, but I need to go to sleep. I love you, Honey."

"Goodnight, Sweetheart."

CHAPTER EIGHTEEN

Lying in the hospital bed holding her brand new baby, Cathy couldn't help but smile. She was remembering that when Nikki was born, she didn't get to see her for hours. This time, they had wrapped up Zachary and handed him right to his mom. Zachary hadn't opened his eyes until he heard his mom's voice, a moment that touched Cathy's heart and one she knew she'd remember forever.

"Hey, baby Zacky, I'm Mommy, and this guy is your daddy."

"Hi, Zachary, nice to finally see you face to face. Your daddy loves you very much. Your brother and sister are going to be here in the morning to meet you." Gene was a proud dad. He and Cathy couldn't believe how much Zack looked like Josh as a baby. Even his weight and measurements were the same as Josh's had been.

"He's such a beautiful baby. He's perfect. Look at how big his hands and feet are; they're huge. You're going to be a big boy one day, aren't you?" Cathy kept gushing over her new baby. She couldn't help wondering how Nikki was going to respond to him. She knew Josh was excited about having a new brother, but she wasn't sure Nikki understood that a new member of their family was going to come live with them. It would be interesting to see her reaction with him. Cathy nursed Zachary and he drifted off to sleep.

Morning came quickly. Papa and Granda were due to arrive any minute with Josh and Nikki to meet the newest member of the family. Josh was the first to peek his head into the room.

"Mommy!" Josh ran over to give his mom a kiss. "Where's my new brother?"

"He's sleeping in his bassinet. It's almost time for him to wake up and eat, and then you can hold him. Would you like that?"

"Yes." Josh was quick to reply. Then Papa and Granda came in, pushing Nikki in her stroller.

"Josh asked which room was yours and took off running," Papa said as he got Nikki out of her stroller and handed her to her mommy.

"I can see he was excited. How about you, Sweet Girl? Are you excited to have a new baby brother?" Nikki giggled as if she understood. Cathy laughed, "I think she's excited too."

Zachary woke up ready to eat. After feeding him, Cathy let Josh hold him, then she held Nikki and Zachary at the same time to introduce them to each other. Papa took some pictures of the new Ellerton family, and it was a joyous occasion. That is, until Granda said, "It's time to go." Josh was not happy. Cathy assured him that she and Zack would be home tomorrow and he had to make sure his room was nice and clean for his brother because they were going to share a room. Josh brightened at the idea and wanted to make sure his room was all ready for Zack.

"See you tomorrow, Zacky. You get to share a room with me. I'm your big brother." Cathy gave Josh and Nikki kisses and said she'd see them the next day. When they left, Cathy was relieved at how well Nikki seemed to respond to Zachary and realized she needn't have worried.

* * *

A few days after bringing Zachary home from the hospital, Cathy began to think about their housing situation. The house that Cathy wanted to buy in Gresham was going to be finished in a month, and they still hadn't sold their existing home. The builder said he was willing to work with them a little, but his hands were tied; if they didn't have a buyer by the time the house was completed, he'd have to look for a new buyer. This upset Cathy, not only because she loved the house, but also because her parents had purchased the house her mom found nearby and were already moved in. Knowing she needed to leave it in the Lord's hands, she spent some time praying about it.

Cathy spent the rest of the day just enjoying her children. She put Zachary under Nikki's play gym with her, and Nikki seemed delighted. Zachary, on the other hand, only being a few days old, just fell asleep with a contented look on his face. Cathy was convinced he liked being with his sister. Not wanting to be left out, Josh lay down by the play gym on the same side as his brother. They were all very excited about having Zachary there.

When Gene got home from work, he had some exciting news. "Sweetheart, we need to get the house straightened up and go out for dinner."

"Why?"

"Because the realtor just called and some clients of his drove by our house. They want to see it in one hour."

"Are you kidding? I was just praying about that today, thinking about our time frame and all."

"Don't get your hopes up. Lots of people have looked at our house, with no takers."

"I know. I decided today that I need to put it in God's hands. I guess I better keep it in His hands."

About ten minutes after they returned home from dinner, their realtor called.

"Gene, they loved the house. They're meeting with me tomorrow to make an offer. I'll call you afterward, and we'll go from there. All right? Have a good night." When Gene got off the phone, he shared the news with Cathy. They were thrilled.

* * *

"Miss Nicole, what do you think about your baby brother? Do you like having him around?"

"Yes, very much. I loved having Mommy put him next to me under my play gym. He's so small, and he sleeps a lot, doesn't he?"

"That's what babies do, sleep a lot. But he'll start staying awake longer as he gets older, and you'll be able to interact with him more."

"Mommy was pretty worried about our house today, but, she remembered to put it in the Lord's hands. I know that He will work it all out, won't He, Seefas?"

* * *

Everything with the house moved fast and it was already moving day. Gene had a group of guys coming to help.

Cathy and the kids were going to Sophie's while Gene and the men did the hard work. "Thanks for letting us hang out while Gene moves. We were afraid the kids would get in the way."

"No problem, always glad to have you. You know, you're still going to have to come over once in a while after you move."

"Is that an open invitation?" Cathy said with a grin.

"You betcha." Sophie laughed.

Josh ran to find the toys Sophie had set up in the back room. Cathy set Nikki down in there too so she could enjoy watching

Josh play. Zack, being only one month old, was sound asleep in his car seat. The kids' contentment gave Cathy and Sophie some uninterrupted time to talk. "Sophie, you never told me how you dealt with Kevin's death. Do you mind me asking?"

"No, I don't mind. It was hard. The last thing Kevin said to me before he died was, 'Sophie, I'm going home to be with Jesus. Someday I want you to join me there. Please open your heart and ask Him into your life.' I tried to have an open mind. I actually kept going to church, until . . . " Sophie got very quiet.

"Are you all right?"

"Yeah, it's just hard to talk about."

"I know, I'm sorry. You don't have to go on."

"I want to. I got a call from the doctor several weeks after Kevin died telling me that the autopsy revealed he was born with a heart defect. The doctor was surprised that Kevin lasted as long as he did. He said that most likely Kevin and his family weren't even aware of his situation. Kevin didn't even know. I got so angry. I blamed God and I still do. He made Kevin with a bad heart. It was His fault that Kevin died."

"Oh, Sophie, I'm so sorry. That must have been hard. I can't say I know exactly what you're going through; all I can do is speak from my own experience. When Nikki was born with her disorder, I didn't want to accept it. I prayed and asked God to heal my girl. I didn't want her to be different. I didn't think I could handle all the possible medical problems, but God has given me the strength to deal with it. I can honestly say now that I wouldn't want Nikki to be any other way. If she had been born without a disorder, she wouldn't be the Nikki I know. She'd be someone else. You saw at Nikki's birthday party how many people her life has impacted. What I'm trying to say is that Kevin was who God made him. From what you've told me, you wouldn't have wanted him to be any other way. He was God's creation, bad heart and all. Would you trade the time that you had with him? Would his parents say it would have been better if he had not been born? What about his friends? The list I'm sure goes on and on. Sophie, instead of blaming God, thank Him for making Kevin and for the time that you spent together." Sophie was very quiet as she listened to everything Cathy was saying, and there were tears in her eyes.

"Cathy, it's just so hard. I still miss him so much. You've given me a lot to think about. I'm not sure how I feel about it all."

"Just one more thing, and then we can move on to something a little lighter. Don't forget Kevin's last words, and consider giving Jesus a chance."

They enjoyed the rest of the afternoon talking about less serious subjects. When Cathy had to pick up pizza to treat the men who were helping them move, she asked Sophie to come with her. Sophie wanted to see the new house and the neighborhood. She felt as if she were saying goodbye to a neighbor and hello to a friend.

* * *

"It's been a big day for you, hasn't it, Miss Nicole? Do you like your new home?"

"Seefas, I just love being with my family, wherever we are. But Mommy and Daddy seem to be very excited about our new home, so I am too."

"You have a good heart. Are you still liking your baby brother?"

"He is sweet. He's starting to stay awake longer, and he smiled at me today when Mommy put him under the play gym with me. I think Zacky and I will be close. I had fun at Sophie's today. I was glad that she came to see our new house. She still doesn't pay much attention to me though."

"I heard her and your mommy talking. I think I'm starting to understand why it's so hard for her to get close to you. She's comparing you to what happened to her husband, and she's scared to feel the pain of losing someone again."

"We just need to continue to pray for Sophie." Nikki yawned.

"We will. You should probably get some sleep now."

CHAPTER NINETEEN

"Cathy, I love your new house. How do you like it?"

"Thanks, Lisa. It's great. It's a little adjustment when it comes to cleaning, but I love the space." Although they'd been living in the new house for a couple of months, it was the first time Lisa had come to work with Nikki since the move.

"Nikki's getting cuter all the time. Her hair's getting longer, and I love her curls. She's practically mastered her head control, and she has her rolling down. I'm impressed, Nikki. Keep up the good work. Now we're going to start working on sitting up. It's going to take a while but I think you'll eventually get it." Nikki responded to Lisa by cooing at her and giggling a little. "How is she doing physically? Is she still seizure-free?"

"She has been extremely healthy. She hasn't had another seizure since we brought her home from the hospital after our big scare. Her heart hasn't given her any problems either. The cardiologist wants to see her again in another couple of years, just to check up on her."

"Sounds like she's doing well." Nikki was tired from therapy and fell asleep. Lisa and Cathy continued talking. "Since I became a Christian, things have been a whirlwind. My husband agreed to go to church with me, and about a month later he became a Christian. Our kids, who are teenagers, thought we had gone crazy and wanted nothing to do with going to church. We have been praying for them. Recently, my oldest girl, who's seventeen, said, 'Mom, we've been discussing it, and we thought we'd give church a try. We see the changes in you and Dad and, well, we like what we see." Cathy was surprised because she hadn't even known Lisa had kids. Until now, Lisa had been private about her personal life.

"That's great, Lisa. How many kids do you have?"

"Four. Two girls, one's seventeen and the other's fourteen, and then I have twin sixteen-year-old boys."

"So, is this the weekend your kids are going with you?"

"Yes. All six of us are going to church together. I can hardly believe it. If you had told me several months ago that we would be doing this as a family, I would have laughed at you. It's amazing to see how God's changing my family. I'm praying that my kids will love church and, more importantly, fall in love with Jesus."

After Lisa left, it was bath time. Cathy put Josh in the bathtub, then filled a little container with water and laid Nikki and Zack down on towels in the living room in front of the fireplace. Nikki loved her bath and would giggle the minute Cathy started getting her undressed. Zack, on the other hand, started to cry. Nikki turned and put her hand on Zack's arm. Zack settled down. Cathy was astonished; it seemed Nikki meant to comfort Zack. After that, Zack didn't cry, and they both enjoyed their baths. After Cathy got her kids dressed, they all went down for naps, including Cathy. Val was coming over later to babysit so Cathy and Gene could go on a date.

* * *

Val got out a game she'd brought over that she thought they would all enjoy, even Zack and Nikki. It involved charades, with Val and Josh doing all the acting and Zack and Nikki giggling while they watched. Then Josh wanted to play hide and seek; he would tell Val where to put Zack and Nikki, tell her where he was going to hide, and then have her find them. They played several other games, and then Val set up little sleeping areas for everyone to have a slumber party around the Christmas tree. She turned off the lights and put on some Christmas music. Nikki and Zack liked watching the lights on the tree and seemed to enjoy the music. Val and Josh sang some Christmas songs, and Nikki and Zack cooed right along. When all the kids eventually drifted off to sleep, Val enjoyed just watching them. These kids had become very important to her.

When Cathy and Gene got home, they were surprised to see all the kids sound asleep around the tree. "Looks like everyone had fun while we were gone. Were they good for you?"

"Cathy, they were perfect. We had so much fun. Your kids are priceless. I haven't felt a part of a family in a long time. I hope you don't mind that I've sort of adopted yours."

"I'm honored that you feel that way. We love having you around. I've been meaning to ask you, how do you like going to church with Jill?"

"It's incredible. Everyone there is so nice, and Jill and I have started getting together with a group of them on a regular basis. We have also joined a small-group Bible study; I love the leader, and she's been a great mentor."

* * *

Seefas was watching over Nikki sleeping so peacefully. He had enjoyed Nikki's interactions with Val and her brothers. Val was good for Nikki. Outside of her family, not many people treated Nikki like she was a real person who understood what was going on. Nikki started to stir, as she never slept all the way through the night.

"Seefas?" Nikki said in a very sleepy voice.

"I'm here, Miss Nicole."

"I was having a dream about Val. I had so much fun with her tonight. I feel like she's a friend, even though she is much older than me. I'd like to have a couple more friends. Do you think that would ever happen?"

"It could happen."

"Can we pray that Jesus will give me a friend?"

* * *

Cathy was getting their house ready for the Christmas party. This Christmas was a lot different from last year's, when they'd been in the hospital with Nikki. The usual birthday guests were coming for the party, and the Ellertons thought of it as an extra-special celebration because Nikki was so healthy. She was now two and a half and weighed about fifteen pounds.

"Hey, Sweetheart, how's the housework coming along? Everything looks great to me."

"Why, thank you, Gene Ellerton. Now I can get started on the food. Care to join me?"

"I can do that. The kids are all down for their naps." They spent the next hour cooking together, then got the kids up and ready for the party.

"Mom, Papa and Granda are the first to arrive. Can I let them in?" Soon, the rest of the guests arrived, and everyone enjoyed visiting over dinner. Afterward, the kids headed upstairs where the Ellertons had things set up in the bonus room to entertain them. When Cathy noticed that Sophie and Jim were spending quite a bit of time together, she couldn't help but smile. Everyone seemed to be having a good time.

"Hey, everybody, could you gather around please? We have a surprise for Jim and Emily." When the kids had come down from upstairs and all the adults had gathered, Gene walked out with a cake that said, 'Happy Birthday, Jesus, Jim and Emily.' Jim and Emily both had tears in their eyes.

"Before we sing, 'Happy Birthday,' I want to explain this cake to those of you who don't know." Cathy told the story of the cake in the hospital. "This year's cake also has Jim's and Emily's names on it because it was almost one year ago that they became Christians, so it is their spiritual birthdays—a very special time a year for them." Cathy noticed that Sophie seemed uncomfortable, yet she also saw something different in her eyes. Then she noticed little Nikki; her face was glowing, she had one of the biggest smiles Cathy had ever seen. Cathy knew Nikki understood everything going on around her, even though she couldn't communicate.

When everyone had sung "Happy Birthday," Jim had something to say. "I just want to say that I owe a lot to the Ellertons. If it wasn't for their generosity and love for others during their own time of need, I wouldn't be a Christian. Looking around and knowing so many of your own stories, we know that little Nikki is the reason so many of us have a relationship with Jesus. I want to say thank you, Nicole Ellerton, for giving us so much of yourself. You are a very special little lady." Everyone started to applaud, including Seefas, and Nikki closed her eyes with a smile on her face as if she were thanking Jesus.

* * *

"Thank you, Lord. Thank you for making me the way I am, so you could work through me. I love you. Seefas, isn't it great to see the excitement on everyone's faces because of Jesus?"

* * *

"So, Sophie, what do you think of all this?" Jim had come up from behind Sophie.

"Well, I was a little surprised. Cathy didn't mention she was doing this. Were you uncomfortable with it?"

"Not at all. I was thrilled because Emily and I are very fortunate to have found Jesus. Christmas used to be the hardest time in my life. You see, my wife died right before Christmas four years ago, and I blamed Jesus for her death. She was a believer and always tried to tell me about Jesus, but I wanted nothing to do with Him. After she died, I knew He had taken her from me. I always tried to make Christmas special for Emily to make up for her mom not being here, but I never felt like it was enough. This is the first Christmas that I have been excited and not trying to make up for something I couldn't. Jesus has filled that gap, and I know one day I will see my wife again."

Sophie was at a loss for words, shocked by how similar their stories were. Cathy had mentioned it, but Sophie never really paid attention. She wondered if she'd ever be able to feel the peace that Jim did. "Maybe one day, I'll give Jesus a chance."

* * *

"Well, Miss Nicole, what did you think of the party tonight?"

"Seefas, it was incredible. It was so much fun seeing all those people come together who love Jesus. My mommy and daddy really made Jim feel good. There was one person, however, who still hasn't given Jesus her life."

"We need to continue to pray for Sophie. I think there might have been a breakthrough tonight. I heard Jim talking to her, and she seemed to be receptive to his words."

"Jesus is so good."

CHAPTER TWENTY

"Cathy, Nikki's doing great. Our next long-term goal will be to get her to sit up unattended." Lisa was always impressed with the progress Nikki was making; it was very slow, yet it was steady. She never seemed to stay at one place, always moving forward.

"We have really been fortunate. It's been nice having you come to our house for therapy."

"Cathy, Nikki's almost three, isn't she?"

"Yes. Why?"

"Didn't my boss explain to you at the beginning of all this that Nikki will have to go to preschool when she turns three to get her therapy? I will no longer be working with her, at least professionally. As a friend, I will always keep tabs on her."

"Lisa, no way. She's only fifteen pounds, how can I send her away to school? She's my little girl."

"Cathy, you won't be sending her away to school. You can take her and then pick her up. You can stay with her in class as much as you want. I know the teacher she'll have and all the therapists. They're great people."

"I'm sure they are. But, I have a hard time picturing Nikki going to school. I mean, this was the first year I've put Josh in a preschool, and he's four. Three just seems too soon."

"I know it will be an adjustment, but it will work out for the best. Just wait and see."

"Do I have any other choice?"

"Your only other choice would be to pay a therapist and that can get pricey. At school, she'll get physical therapy, occupational therapy, speech therapy, and anything else she'll need. I really think that school is your best choice. Talk it over with Gene and see what his take is on it. You still have a while, so pray about it, and please consider it. You know if you have any problems or concerns, I'll always be there."

"Thanks, Lisa, I'll consider it. Hey, I haven't asked you how it went with your kids going to church with you. Did they like it?"

"Well, yes and no. My three oldest adjusted immediately. They went on a retreat with the youth group and came back excited about Jesus. However, I couldn't talk my fourteen-year-old girl, Jessica, into going on the retreat. She's skeptical and wants nothing to do with Christianity. We're all praying for her; one of my boys said, 'Mom, with all of us praying, Jessica doesn't stand a chance.' Hopefully, he's right."

"I have an idea. I know it's still a couple months away, but why don't you bring your family to the kids' birthday parties this year? It would give Jessica a chance to meet other kids who love Jesus and know that all Christians aren't psycho! I'm not saying you're psycho." Cathy and Lisa both laughed.

"I know. Jessica seems to think we are. She just can't understand the transformation that's taken place in all of us. Her older sister has been trying really hard to turn her around, with no success."

"You know, one thing that I've learned lately is that God is the only one who can change someone's heart. We'll join you in praying for her, and seriously, do think about bringing everyone to the birthday party. If nothing else, it will be fun."

"Thanks, Cathy. Just let me know when, and we'll be there." They talked a while longer and then Lisa had to go to her next appointment. After Lisa left, Cathy decided to load the kids up and take them to the park on this beautiful spring day. She gave Annie a quick call to see if she and the kids wanted to meet them there, and Annie said they'd love to.

At the park, Cathy and Annie set out blankets for the little ones to play on, then Annie's older girls took Josh and Annie's son, Braden, to go have fun on the play structure. Nikki had fun watching all the activity, and Zack, now about seven months old, did too. As they were sitting there, all the little kids that walked by would stop and stare at Nikki. They would ask questions about things like her age and if she would ever walk, and make comments on how cute she was.

One of Annie's daughters, Brooke, had been noticing all this going on. She came over and whispered in Annie's ear, in a loud voice, "Mom, is Nikki popular?" Annie and Cathy both laughed.

"It appears so, Honey." Annie had satisfied Brooke's curiosity and she ran off to play again. "I bet you get this all the time, people coming up to ask you about Nikki."

"Yes, and kids especially seem drawn to her. They're fascinated with her. It's like they know she's different, and they can't figure out what it is, but they love her. Most adults who approach us usually think that Nikki and Zack are twins. They say things like, 'It must be nice to have a boy and a girl for twins.' Sometimes I correct them, but most of the time I just smile, and they go on with their business."

While they were talking, a woman approached them. "Excuse me, I hope I'm not bothering you, but my little girl wanted to come over here and see your daughter. My little girl's three and a half and doesn't talk yet, but she has been pointing over here at your little girl and kept getting up to come over. So, finally I gave in. I hope you don't mind."

"Not at all. I'm Cathy, this is my friend, Annie, my son Zack, and my little girl is Nikki."

"I'm Gina, and my little girl's Lindsey." While they were talking, Lindsey sat down next to Nikki and started stroking her arm with a smile on her face. "I'm sorry," Gina apologized.

"Don't be, Gina. I don't mind at all, and I'm sure Nikki doesn't mind either. Your daughter's never said anything?"

"Not a word. They've had her tested and can't figure it out. They just say, one day she'll start talking. She's seeing a speech therapist right now. I've gotten pretty good at translating what she wants."

"I know exactly what you're talking about. Nikki doesn't talk either; she's actually almost three, but we think we've gotten her needs figured out pretty well." Cathy went on to explain Nikki's story to Gina, then Jordenn, Annie's oldest, came over and said that they were all getting tired and were ready to go. At that, Gina got up to go, took Lindsey's hand, and thanked Cathy for allowing them to come over to see Nikki.

"Come on, Lindsey, we've got to go now." As they walked away, Lindsey turned around and said, "Nikki." Gina gasped, and Cathy and Annie laughed. All Gina could say as she turned to go was, "Thanks." All three ladies' eyes filled with tears, and Cathy and Annie simultaneously said, "Thank you, Jesus."

* * *

When Nikki was tucked in her crib, ready to go to sleep, she said, "Seefas, it was another exciting day today."

"It sure was, Miss Nicole. What did you think of little Lindsey?"

"It was amazing. While she was sitting next to me, I seemed to be able to understand what she was saying, without her saying anything. Then when she said my name, I was so excited and thanked Jesus right along with Mommy and Annie. Do you think she can talk now?"

"I don't know. But what we do know is that Jesus used you to touch another life."

"Do you think I'll ever see her again?"

* * *

"Granda, when is Papa getting here? What are we going to do when he gets here?" Josh had heard Granda talking to his mommy and wanted to know all about the fun things she'd mentioned.

"He'll be here soon. Why don't you go find something that we can all play together?" Josh thought for a minute. Because his brother was barely one, and his sister couldn't talk, he knew that he had to get something they could do also.

"I know the perfect thing, Granda, I'll be right back." Josh ran upstairs, coming back with a handful of Winnie the Pooh toys; musical ones for his sister, squeaky ones for his brother, and a Pooh game for him and Granda to play. They'd been playing for a while with everyone having a good time when they heard a knock at the door.

"That's a Papa knock." Josh yelled, and Nikki and Zack looked excited too. When Josh opened the door, Papa had a strange looking doll on his arm that talked to him.

"What's that, Papa?"

"Well, Josh, this is my friend, Joe. Can you say hi to my grandkids, Joe?"

"Hello, grandkids." Josh stood there with an open mouth, Zack hid his face, and Nikki giggled. Papa was a ventriloquist; he'd just gotten a new dummy, and he thought that the kids would have fun talking with his new friend.

"He talks. How does he do that, Papa?" Josh was very curious to know how Papa's doll was talking.

"Joe, can you tell Josh how you talk?"

"Sure can. You see your Papa helps me talk." They went back and forth for quite a while. Granda commented later on how attentive Nikki seemed while this was going on. Joe even got Nikki to laugh out loud several times.

* * *

The kids had enjoyed the day with their grandparents and it was now time for bed. Gene decided to read some passages from the Bible on Heaven for their devotions. Josh and Nikki seemed very interested in what their daddy was saying, while Zacky played. Josh asked a lot of questions, and then they spent some time praying.

* * *

"Seefas, Heaven sounds wonderful. Do you miss being there?"

"Oh, Miss Nicole, Heaven is amazing. All the beauty you see here on earth is just a glimpse of what Heaven is. I long for all of us to be there together one day, where we can worship our Lord forever. But I love being with you. God has entrusted you to my care, and it is an honor that I wouldn't trade for the world."

"I can't wait to go there. My daddy said that in Heaven I'll be able to run around, and he and Mommy will be able to understand what I'm saying."

* * *

"Cathy, Zacky's going to be walking before you know it. I can't believe how fast time has gone by."

"I can't either. I'm so glad that we've continued to be friends, Sophie, even though we aren't neighbors anymore." Cathy and Sophie had become even closer since the Ellertons' move. Cathy was grateful for that. It had been a while since they'd talked about Jesus, and Cathy felt she should broach the subject. She wanted Sophie to learn to love Jesus. Sophie still had emptiness inside, and Cathy knew the only one who could fill that void was Jesus. Jim had told her that he'd had a great conversation about Jesus with Sophie at the Christmas party and felt that she might be starting to break down her walls. "You and Jim are starting to become pretty good friends. I'm glad."

"He is a very nice guy. I learn a lot from him. The way that he's dealt with his wife's death amazes me. I do think, however, that he's giving Jesus way too much recognition for it."

"What do you mean by that?"

"I think maybe Jesus is a crutch he's using because he doesn't want to give himself too much of the credit for moving on with his life."

"Oh, Sophie, Jim was at the end of his rope before he came to know Jesus. He felt like he was going to fall off the deep end. We get to the point in our lives when we have to accept that we can't do it on our own, so we need to relinquish control of our own lives and give it to Jesus. That's what Jim finally did, and only then was he able to move on."

"That's way too scary for me. I'm not ready to hand my life over to someone else, especially Jesus. Look what happened to Kevin when he did that. Jesus took him away from me. I'm happy for Jim; whatever works for him is great. But it's not for me." After Sophie had talked with Jim at the Ellertons' Christmas party, she thought maybe she would be able to give Jesus a chance, but the more she thought about it, the scarier it had become. It was tempting at times to give in to Jesus, but for some reason, it was one of the hardest decisions she'd ever have to make, she wasn't ready to do that. Although everyone made it seem so easy, Sophie felt like she must be missing out on the secret because it seemed anything but easy to her.

"Sophie, I'm not giving up on you. I'm going to continue to pray that one day, you will let Jesus into your life. I promise your life will never be the same again, and you will wonder what took you so long." Cathy decided to drop it at that, as she knew that Sophie wasn't ready and only God knew what the right timing was going to be.

"Mom, Sophie, you got to come see Nikki!" Josh came bolting down the stairs very excited.

"What is it, Buster? Is she all right?" Cathy was worried because it was hard to tell what Josh was so excited about. Thoughts of Josh finding Nikki having a seizure went through her head.

"She's great, she's being silly." Because Josh was laughing, Cathy's curiosity was piqued, and she started up the stairs after Josh. However, Sophie wasn't following.

"Sophie, you have to come too. Hurry!" Sophie couldn't let Josh down, so she hesitantly went upstairs after Cathy and Josh.

Josh, Nikki, and Zack were all in the bonus room, and Josh had his animal books laid out on the floor. All the books were turned to pages about sheep and little Zacky was crawling on the floor making the sound of sheep. Nikki was laughing so hard that she was crying. Cathy had never heard her laugh that way before. She was clearly having fun.

"Mom, you have to hear this, it is so funny. I was reading in the Bible (which meant Josh was looking at the pictures and making up words) and I was naming all the animals that

God has made. After each animal, I would start making the sound that it makes, and Zack would copy me. When we got to the sheep and started making the sound that they make, Nikki started laughing. At first, I thought she was laughing for some other reason, but Zack liked the sheep's sound the best and would keep making it, and every time Nikki would laugh. It's so cute, Mommy, Nikki loves the sounds that sheep make. It made me and Zacky laugh and Nikki started laughing even harder."

Cathy was so touched by this, as it was further evidence that Nikki truly understood what was going on around her. Cathy looked over at Sophie, and she was astonished to find that Sophie had a smile on her face. Sophie genuinely loved Josh and Zack, and Cathy prayed that one day she would add Nikki to that list.

"Sophie, next time you come over, you can spend some time playing with me, Zack and Nikki. Maybe we can do sheep sounds again with Nikki." Josh always tried to get Sophie to include Nikki, and he'd told his mommy that he wouldn't give up until he succeeded.

"We'll see, Josh. But I do need to go now. It's been a lot of fun, and we'll do it again real soon." After Sophie left, Cathy spent time playing the animal game with her children.

* * *

"So, Nikki, I'm very curious about what was so funny today?" Seefas had enjoyed watching Nikki interacting with her brothers and her mom.

"Josh and Zack were doing all kinds of animal sounds, and, even though they didn't know, I was doing them also. When it came to the sheep, no matter how hard I tried, every time a very funny squeal would come out. It would make me laugh, and then my brothers started laughing, which made me laugh even harder. It was so much fun."

"I'm glad that you enjoyed yourself. It was fun for me to watch you playing with your brothers."

"Did you see Sophie, Seefas? She smiled at me. I don't think she's ever done that before. I think one day she's going to learn to love me."

"How could she not? You will eventually win her heart."

CHAPTER TWENTY-ONE

Josh was so excited he could hardly contain himself. "Mom, does Braden really get to spend the night after my birthday party?"

"Yes, Sweetheart, he does. We thought it might be fun for you to have your first overnight guest as a present." Cathy could hardly believe that another year had gone by so fast. Nikki was turning three, and Josh was five. They were both going to be in school this year; Nikki was going to preschool, and Josh was going to be in kindergarten. Every birthday gave Cathy a chance to reflect on the past year. Lisa was bringing along her family this time. There were also the usual guests. It was sure to be another great party.

"Mom, I have my room all set up for Braden to spend the night. When is everyone getting here?"

"I think I hear the first car pulling up right now."

"All right!" Josh ran to see who was there. It wasn't long before all the guests arrived and the party was in full swing. It was fun to see how all the people in their lives were now connected. Val and Jill had pretty much become inseparable. Jim and Sophie had become friends, and Jim joined Cathy and Gene in praying that Sophie would one day come to know Jesus. Lisa's kids were around the same age as Ryan's youngest kids, and they seemed to be hitting it off.

Nikki was the first to open gifts, along with her two brothers of course. Cathy noticed that Jessica, Lisa's youngest daughter, seemed very interested in watching Nikki open her presents.

She was smiling for the first time that day, which made Cathy feel good.

"Is it my turn now, Mom?"

"Yes, Josh, you can start opening." The rest of the party went well, and everyone had a good time. Soon, it was time for everyone to go home, but Josh didn't mind because he got to have a friend spend the night.

* * *

"I think it's time we start thinking about getting these kids off to bed. What do you think, Sweetheart?"

"Oh, Mom, do we have to?"

"Daddy's right, Josh, it's time. But we are setting up a bed for Braden in your room, if you boys want to, we can set up the small TV in your room and you can watch a movie until you fall asleep."

"Thanks, Mom!" Josh ran up and gave Cathy a kiss. "Let's go get ready for bed, Braden." Then the boys were off with great enthusiasm.

* * *

The summer had gone by way too fast. Cathy woke up with great anxiety, not only because it was hard to have her oldest child starting kindergarten, but Nikki was also going to start school on this day. When Lisa told her a few months ago that Nikki would have to go to school, Cathy struggled with the concept. It hadn't exactly gotten easier, but Cathy was resigned to the idea. Nikki's teacher, Margie, had called to introduce herself and she seemed like a very nice woman. This eased Cathy's mind a bit along with the fact that Margie told her that she could stay with Nikki as often as she wanted. The day arrived, and Cathy prayed that she would get an overwhelming peace walking into Nikki's classroom.

"Mom, are you ready to go? I am excited to start kindergarten. I can't believe I get to go to school where we go to church. That is so cool."

"Do you have your backpack and jacket?"

"Yes, I do. I'm all set." Cathy got Nikki's stuff together and then loaded Nikki and Zack into the van. First, Cathy dropped Zack off at her parent's house because she was planning on staying that first day with Nikki at school. She felt sad taking Josh to his first day of kindergarten. She couldn't believe her boy was growing up so fast. After taking lots of pictures and getting hugs, it was time to head to Nikki's school.

"So, Nikki girl, are you ready to take on this new adventure?" Nikki gurgled back at her mom, who was still amazed by how much she seemed to understand. Pulling into Nikki's school, Cathy became a little teary-eyed. Her little girl was growing up too.

"We're here, Sweetie. Time to meet your teacher and all your new friends." As Cathy was pushing Nikki in her stroller up the ramp to her new classroom, she nearly ran straight into one of the other moms.

"Cathy? Is this where Nikki's going to be going to school?"

Cathy could hardly believe that she was looking at Gina. She hadn't seen Gina and her daughter Lindsey since the day they'd met at the park. Nikki started giggling. "Is Lindsey going here?"

"Yes, she is. She is going to be so thrilled to see Nikki. You know, ever since we met you that day, Lindsey continues to say Nikki's name over and over. She hasn't said anything else yet, but I have a feeling with Nikki being here, all that is about to change." As Cathy and Gina said their goodbyes, Cathy felt encouraged because she knew God had a purpose for Nikki being at this school.

Once they got into the classroom, Lindsey saw Nikki immediately and ran straight to her saying her name. The teacher and all the therapists stopped what they were doing, and a silence fell over the class. While Nikki and Lindsey shared a very special moment, Cathy walked over to meet the teacher.

"Cathy Ellerton? I'm Margie, Nikki's teacher."

"Hi, Margie. Nice to meet you."

"I'm sure there is a story behind what just took place between Nikki and Lindsey. I am anxious to hear it. We were just discussing Lindsey and how to help her with her speech problem when you two walked in." Cathy shared with Margie what had taken place at the park and went on to share that she had been apprehensive about Nikki going to school—until now. Cathy told Margie that she felt God had a big part in placing those two together. When Cathy said this, she noticed that Margie seemed a little uncomfortable; Cathy decided to pray for Nikki's teacher.

"I'm anxious to meet your girl, so why don't we go over and you can introduce me." They walked over to where Nikki and Lindsey were.

"Sweetheart, this is your teacher, Margie." Nikki smiled and seemed comfortable with Margie already. Margie was a young, energetic teacher, with a knack for placing others at ease immediately.

"Nikki, I'm excited to have you in my class. I've heard just wonderful things about you from your past therapist. I couldn't wait to meet you for myself." Margie later told Cathy she was surprised how little Nikki was. She said that she was told she was small, but had no idea how small. Although Nikki was long, she still only weighed sixteen pounds. She was a petite little girl who looked like a doll.

"Time to get class started, so everyone grab your mats, and come sit down for circle time." The kids who were able to get their own mats followed Margie's instructions, as the therapists helped the others. They had a chair set up for Nikki in the circle, and the physical therapist sat beside her and helped her participate in all the songs and stories they were doing. Nikki really enjoyed the music time. The day went fast for Cathy, and she was excited to have been there. All her anxieties went away, and she was actually looking forward to the school year. Nikki had seemed to really enjoy herself, but Cathy could tell that she was tired after working hard during her therapy.

"Well, Sis, what do you say we go pick up Josh from school and see how his day went?" Nikki cooed in response, and off they went. Josh was energized about his day at school and he wanted to hear all about Nikki's day. After picking up Zack from Papa and Granda's, they all went home to take naps.

* * *

"Today was an exciting day for you. Did you enjoy yourself?"

"Oh, Seefas. I loved it. Can you believe that Lindsey's in my class? I thought I would never see her again. Remember when you said it was in Jesus's hands if I ever saw her again?"

"Yes, Miss Nicole, I do."

"I guess Jesus knew all along that we would be in the same class, and meeting her that day at the park wasn't just a coincidence."

"I think you are absolutely right there. He knows everything before it happens. I think that Jesus has a special plan for you in Lindsey's life."

"Do you think that Lindsey loves Jesus?"

"I'm not sure, but I have a feeling she will if you have anything to say about it."

"You're right about that. Do you think my mom will try to get to know Lindsey's mom? I would love it if Lindsey could come over to my house sometime."

"I think we should leave that in Jesus's hands as well. What do you think?"

"I think that's a wonderful idea. Thank you, Seefas."

"For what?"

"Being the best angel any girl could ever hope for." At that, Nikki put her tiny arms around Seefas' broad shoulders and squeezed real tight.

CHAPTER TWENTY-TWO

"Hi, Sophie. I'm so glad that you could come over today. Josh and Zack have been asking for you." Zack was now just over a year old and was saying a few words.

"I'm glad that I could come. Where are those boys of yours?"

"They are up in the bonus room playing with Nikki. They are pretending to be brave heroes and Nikki's the princess."

"How can Nikki be the princess?"

"Well, they made a little fort, which they call their castle, and Nikki's lying in it. She is having so much fun, she loves having her brothers play with her. Of course, Zacky just copies everything his brother's doing; he doesn't quite get the game. But nonetheless, they are all three having a great time. Why don't we let them know you're here?" Sophie was still having a hard time picturing Nikki being the princess, but she followed Cathy upstairs. Once they got up there, they stood in the doorway for a few minutes to watch the kids play.

"Oh, Princess Nikki, Sir Zack and I have been searching all over and we cannot find the dragon." Josh was talking to Nikki, and in turn Nikki started giggling, which made Zack giggle.

"Princess Nikki, what do you want us to do? Should we keep searching for the dragon, so we can protect the castle?" It was all so cute. Josh was so serious, Zack was running circles around Nikki, and Nikki kept on laughing.

"I will find the dragon for you, and he will harm us no more." Josh turned around to leave and saw his mom and Sophie standing in the doorway.

"Sophie! Do you want to play with us?" Josh was very excited to see her, and Zacky ran up and hugged her legs. Nikki gave a few gurgles of her own.

"I don't know, Josh. I'm not very good at this sort of game." Cathy knew Sophie was hesitating because Nikki was also playing. Sophie still avoided Nikki whenever possible.

"I'll teach you. Come on." It was evident that Josh wasn't going to take no for an answer, so Sophie finally gave in.

"I'll catch up on some work while you all play up here." As Cathy was leaving, she heard Josh say, "You can be Nikki's mom, the queen." Cathy smiled as she headed downstairs, thinking that she wished she could be as bold with Sophie. She said a little prayer that maybe this would make Sophie more accepting of Nikki. When she got down stairs the phone was ringing. It was Lisa.

"Cathy, I wanted to share with you what happened last night. Ever since Josh's and Nikki's birthday party, Jessica has been talking nonstop about Nikki. Well, last night at dinner, she asked Greg and me if she could start volunteering to work in the nursery at church with Nikki. We were thrilled, of course; anything to get Jessica excited about church."

"That's great. I know they could use the help in the nursery. Has she given any more thought about the youth group?"

"No, not yet. I want her to get involved, so she can make some Christian friends. I figure this is a step in the right direction."

"Absolutely. Thanks for sharing that with me, and we'll continue to pray for Jessica."

"Thanks, Cathy. Hey, how do you like Nikki's school?"

"I have to admit, you were right. Her teacher's great, and Nikki seems to be really enjoying it. Oh, and you know that little girl, Lindsey, that I told you about. The one we met at the park?"

"Yeah, I remember. The one who hadn't talked and then said Nikki's name?"

"The very one. She's in Nikki's class. Nikki's teacher said that she says Nikki's name all the time and wants to be next to her constantly, but she still hadn't spoken any other words. Then the other day, she said a complete sentence out of the blue. They were putting Nikki's chair by two other little kids and Lindsey said, 'Nikki sit by me.' Everyone couldn't believe it."

"You're kidding me. That's great. Sounds like Nikki has a reason for being in that class."

"You're right, Lisa. I should know by now that God has a purpose for everything. I wasn't very excited when you told me that Nikki had to go to school this year, but I see now that it was the right decision. I'm excited to see what else the year holds for her."

"I'm sure the year's going to bring about great things for Nikki. I'll be anxious to hear about them."

"I better go. I hear Sophie and the boys coming down the stairs. I wonder how it went up there. I'll talk to you later, Lisa."

"Bye, Cathy."

"Hi, you guys, how did it go?"

"It was a lot of fun, Mom. Nikki's still upstairs though, could you go get her?" Cathy wasn't that surprised that Sophie didn't volunteer to bring Nikki down with them. Cathy, however, was glad that the boys got Sophie to play with the three of them together, and Cathy was anxious to hear details.

When Cathy and Nikki got down the stairs, the boys were talking about their playtime.

"Sophie, didn't Nikki make a great princess?"

"Yeah, I guess, Josh." Cathy laughed when she heard them talking.

"So, Josh, did you ever find the dragon and put an end to his terror?"

"Yeah!" Zacky had to put his two senses in.

"Yes, Mom. Zack and I found the dragon with the help of Sophie."

"I thought Sophie was the queen."

"Yes, she was, but she wanted to help us search. She said that she was the kind of queen that didn't like to stay home."

Cathy laughed. "So, Sophie, you don't like to stay home much, eh?"

"Well, you know. We queens never get to have any fun."

"Mom, when we told Nikki that we got the dragon, she squealed. We laughed so hard, even Sophie." Cathy looked over at Sophie, and Sophie looked away. Cathy wondered if Sophie was softening a little toward Nikki.

"Thanks for a fun day, boys, but I have to go home now."

"All right, Sophie. Thanks for playing with us and Nikki."

"Um, you're welcome. Bye, Cathy. I'll give you a call later this week."

* * *

"Wow! You had a fun day today. Didn't you Nikki?"

"It was great, Seefas. That's the first time that Sophie has played with me."

"She's eventually going to see how awesome you are."

"Do you really think so?"

"Yes, I do."

"I guess we shouldn't stop praying about it, huh?"

"You're right. Jesus is listening to your prayers, and all things will work together according to His plan."

"I know Jesus hears me, and I know that He loves Sophie. She will come around one day. Thank you for reminding me that Jesus is in control. You're a pretty cool angel, Seefas."

"You think so, do you? Well, you're a very cool girl."

* * *

"Mommy, Mommy, Val and Jill are at the door. Can I let them in?" Cathy could just barely hear Josh yelling from downstairs. She thought he said something about Val and Jill but thought she must have been mistaken because she wasn't expecting them.

"What did you say, Josh?" Cathy asked as she walked down the stairs holding both Nikki and Zack. She had gotten pretty good at doing that since Nikki now had head control. Zack was fourteen months old and able to walk, but he still preferred his mommy to carry him.

"I said, can I open the door for Val and Jill?" At first Cathy was delighted that she had heard correctly, but then she became nervous that something was wrong. Val never just showed up without calling. It wasn't that Cathy minded; it was just very unusual.

"Sure, Buster. Go ahead and let them in." Josh ran to the door very excited.

"Hi, Val. Hi, Jill. Are you here to play with me?"

"Josh, how's it going? We'd love to play with you. But first, we would like to talk to your mom, if that's okay with you." Val was so good with kids and they adored her.

"Hi guys, to what do we owe this unexpected surprise?"

"Hey, Cathy," Jill said. "We just wanted to share with you some exciting news."

"Yeah, we felt like it was very fitting to share with you since we both feel like you had a big part in making it happen."

"Okay girls, you got my attention. Tell me already, what is so exciting?"

"Jill and I were asked to become small group leaders in our twenties' group at church. Can you believe it?"

"That is fantastic. You two will do a great job." Cathy felt so proud of them and how far they had come in their Christian walk, for they were both new believers. It was so exciting for her to see their love for the Lord continuing to grow stronger. "So, tell me details. How did this come about?"

"Well, as you know, Jill and I have become more and more involved in our church. When we joined our small group study, we were in awe. We couldn't believe the love that our leader had for the Lord. She was so wise in the study of the Bible. We gleaned so much from her."

"Yeah, it made Val and I want to learn more ourselves. We made a deal with each other: every night before bed we would read the Bible, and, in the morning, we would share with each other what we learned."

"Our leader started noticing the difference in us, and this morning we got calls from her." It was evident by the sound in Val's voice that whatever her small group leader said had had a tremendous impact on her.

"What did she say?" Cathy was getting anxious to hear the rest of the story. Val continued.

"She told each one of us individually that the excitement that we had for God's Word was so contagious that she felt confident that we are ready to take on our own group. We are going to be coleading a group with four girls in it." Val and Jill both looked ready to burst at the seams with pure exhilaration.

"I am so proud of both of you, and I have to say, I'm not very surprised. It has been fun watching the two of you grow in the Lord. You both will make terrific small-group leaders; the girls in your group won't be able to help picking up on your excitement."

"We both feel like you and your family, especially Nikki, had a lot to do with this." Nikki had been sitting there quietly taking this all in with a permanent grin stuck on her face. Then when Val mentioned her, Nikki let out a loud squeal of delight and everyone laughed.

Val continued. "Seriously, it's thanks to you, Nikki, that we even have a relationship with the Lord. We both talk about you constantly at our group." Nikki again became animated. Val and Jill thanked Cathy and decided to take the three kids down to a nearby park. It was around lunchtime, and Cathy packed everyone a picnic lunch. When they got there the first thing Josh wanted to do was go down and feed the ducks. They decided the best place to set up their lunch would be at a picnic table near the pond. While Cathy got lunch set up, Jill took the boys to feed the ducks, and Val took Nikki on a walk around the park.

Val treasured the one-on-one time with Nikki. She enjoyed hearing the sounds that Nikki would make over the things that brought her pleasure. Val was amazed how the little things seemed to catch Nikki's eye, like a flower in full bloom, a bird singing in the tree high above them, a girl being pushed on the swing by her daddy, children laughing, the list seemed endless. Nikki always taught Val how to stop and enjoy the things around her.

As they were walking, a group of young girls approached them. They were fascinated with Nikki and commented on how cute she was. Val had gotten used to this happening; when she would go places with Cathy, kids just seemed to flock to Nikki. Val talked to them for a few minutes and Nikki was soaking it all in. One of the girls asked Val how old Nikki was. Val was telling her that Nikki was three and was explaining a little bit about Nikki's disorder when one of the girls rudely interrupted.

"She's one of *those* kids."

Val wasn't sure how to respond to her. "I'm not sure what you mean by that."

"She's one of those kids who shouldn't even be here. My dad told me that the world would be a better place if moms would just abort babies like her. He says they're the reason our health insurance is so high." Val couldn't even speak; all she could think about was protecting Nikki from the awful things this girl was saying. How could anyone be so cruel? Val looked down at Nikki and saw tears in her eyes, but she also saw something else that she couldn't quite figure out. Then a voice behind her broke the silence.

"Hey, Val. What's going on over here?" Val turned around and was surprised to see Jim Drake standing there with Emily and some of her friends. It turned out that some of these girls were Emily's friends too.

"Hi, Jim." Val was so shaken that she could barely speak.

The girl began, "Mr. Drake, I was just explaining to this lady what my dad says about . . ."

Jim was quick to interrupt her. "I heard what you said, Amanda, and I want to tell you something about this little girl. You see I know her very well. Her name is Nikki Ellerton, and she changed my life." All the girls were silent except Amanda.

"How could she have done that?" Amanda asked in a very mocking tone. While they were talking, Cathy, Jill, and the boys had come up from behind Jim. Cathy couldn't figure out what was going on, so she decided to let Jim handle it.

"This little girl can't talk, she can't walk, she can't even sit up all by herself, but I'll tell you what she can do. She can laugh, she can make you smile, she can melt your heart, and she makes you feel like you are the most important person in the world. Because of this girl and her family, Emily and I came to know the Lord. If Nikki's mom would've chosen to abort her, Emily and I would be living very lonely, empty, despairing lives. Nikki has had more of an impact on people's lives than most of us ever will."

When Jim was done speaking, he looked around and was shocked to see a crowd of people gathered around him. Jim caught Cathy's eye, and she smiled at him. Then he looked at Nikki, and she was looking right at him smiling with tears in her eyes. Amanda walked away a little put out, but the rest of the girls gathered around Nikki smiling and talking to her.

Val walked over to where Jim and Cathy were talking. "Thanks, Jim. I didn't know what to say when Amanda started talking bad about Nikki. I just wanted to take Nikki and run."

"I'm glad I was there. I know Amanda's dad, and I was surprised to hear his view on certain things. I think I have a challenge on my hands."

"Thank you, Jim, for sticking up for my girl. It tears me apart to hear such hurtful things being said about my baby. I wish I could always protect her from other people's hurtful remarks, but I know I can't always be there. I wish I could talk with Nikki about it and understand how she feels when this happens."

"That reminds me, Cathy. When Amanda said those things, I looked down at Nikki and saw tears in her eyes. But there was something else there, something stronger than her tears. I can't quite explain it, but it made me feel better."

* * *

Later that night when all was quiet around the Ellerton home, there were two people who stayed up talking.

"This was a hard day for you emotionally, wasn't it, Miss Nicole?"

"Oh, Seefas. I had so many emotions running through me. I knew that something bad was about to happen because I could tell in the way you were acting. You looked like you were ready to fight a battle."

"Sometimes I forget that you can see things other people cannot. When the Lord gave me this assignment, He warned me that there would be times that you would need my strength. This, Miss Nicole, was one of them."

"You gave me courage, and I also felt the presence of the Lord, but I wasn't sure what was coming. Then when Amanda said those awful things about me, I was hurt. I don't think that I have ever felt that kind of pain before. I didn't like it. Then something weird happened: I felt Jesus talking to me."

"What did He tell you?"

"He reminded me of the price that He paid on the cross. He told me that He went through similar things, with people saying very bad things about Him. He told me that when people say things like that to me, they are saying it about Him too. He said that He was crying right alongside me, that I am special and He loves me very much."

As Nikki was talking Seefas started to tear up. He knew that the Lord did feel the pain of His children and remembered what it was like for Jesus while He was down here on earth.

"When Jesus spoke to you, how did that make you feel?"

"Strengthened! I saw Amanda in a different light. I saw the pain in her eyes, I saw a girl who was unhappy, and then I felt love for her. I guess you could say, I saw her through Jesus's eyes." Nikki said this with such passion that Seefas couldn't help but stop to thank Jesus for what this little girl was teaching him. Never had he seen a child grasp what it was like to put others first, even at the expense of her own feelings. He felt such love for Nikki; he treasured the relationship that they were building. But, more than that, he loved watching Nikki's relationship with Jesus grow stronger every day.

"Well, Miss Nicole, I think that you should probably get a good night's sleep. Today was a very hard day. Hopefully you won't have to go through too many like this one." At this, Nikki gave a very big yawn. Seefas couldn't help but smile. He remembered that even though Nikki was wise for her age, she was still very much a little girl.

"I am very sleepy, Seefas. Could you sing me to sleep? I love hearing you sing songs to Jesus."

CHAPTER TWENTY-THREE

After the incident at the park, Cathy was apprehensive about taking Nikki to school. She didn't want to risk Nikki being hurt again. Cathy knew that she needed to trust Jesus and place Nikki in His hands.

Cathy was planning on spending the day with Nikki. As they drove up to the school, Nikki seemed to get excited; it was as if she knew exactly where they were.

"Are you ready for another school day, Nikki?" Nikki squealed in delight at her mom. Cathy laughed. "I'll take that as a yes."

Cathy was excited to see the progress that Lindsey was making; she was starting to say a few more words. Nikki's teacher, Margie, made several comments that the impact Nikki had on other kids was a big help in the classroom. She would also remark that Nikki glowed and had a real warmth to her. When Cathy would respond by saying things like, "It's her love for Jesus," Margie would get a funny look on her face and get quiet. Cathy would just smile and say a silent prayer that Nikki would be able to impact one more life for Jesus.

As Cathy and Nikki were leaving school later that day, they ran into Gina, Lindsey's mom. Cathy filled her in on the day and told her that she noticed that Lindsey was saying a few more words. Gina responded like she always did, "Thanks to Nikki." They talked a little longer and Cathy invited Gina and Lindsey to have a play date soon.

* * *

That night after they got the kids tucked in, Gene and Cathy lay in bed talking.

"So, Sweetheart, how was your day?"

"Pretty good. Ryan came to work very excited this morning."

"Why? What happened?"

"I guess over the weekend he had the privilege of leading his neighbor to Christ. I was so happy for him. He said he felt like that was the best thing he's ever done. He asked me if I felt that way after leading him to Christ. I told him, 'Absolutely.' I told him that it only gets better." They talked for a while longer and they could hear their daughter laughing in the other room. Nikki and Seefas were having a conversation of their own.

"Was it fun having your mom with you today at school?"

"Yes, Seefas. I love when my mommy gets to come with me. She seems to enjoy being there."

"Your teacher seems to see Jesus in you as well. I wouldn't be surprised if she learns to love Him before the year's over."

"I will pray that she will. I also still need to pray for Sophie. I want so badly for her to fall in love with Jesus. "

"Jesus hears your prayers. I see subtle changes in Sophie; I think she's eventually going to come around."

"I know Jesus hears my prayers. Remember when I prayed that my mom would invite Lindsey and her mom to come over sometime?"

"Yes. I do remember that."

"Well, today Mom asked them, and Lindsey's mom said yes. I can't wait for Lindsey to come over to play. Jesus is so good to me. I love him so much." Seefas just smiled and gave Nikki one of his famous bear hugs.

* * *

The Ellerton household was full of excitement. Gene had taken the day off so they could all go to the zoo together, and they were going to pick up Sophie on the way. Jim and Emily were going to meet them there. Josh had arranged the whole thing. The time seemed to drag on, especially for Josh, but the moment finally came for them to leave.

On the drive, Josh kept telling Sophie how much Nikki loved the zoo, and he told her that she needed to watch Nikki's face as she observed the animals. "You will have a lot more fun that way," Josh told Sophie.

Sophie tried her best to be excited about that, but she was worried. She knew that Josh would be watching to make sure that she paid attention to his sister. She had told herself repeatedly that the only reason Kevin wasn't with her anymore was that he was born with a heart defect, eventually deluding herself into thinking that people born without defects live forever. Although she knew logically it wasn't true, she'd used these thoughts to build a wall around herself, refusing to get close to anyone born with any sort of problems. She felt that if she opened herself up a little to Nikki, she would start caring about her, and that scared her. It was going to be an interesting day; on top of it all, Jim was going to be there. She wasn't sure what to think of him. She felt comfortable around him until he started talking about Jesus, and this confused her.

"Hey, Sophie. Are you all right?" Cathy interrupted Sophie's thoughts.

"Uh, yeah. Why?"

"Because we're at the zoo and everyone's out of the van except for you," Cathy said lightheartedly and started to laugh. Sophie laughed along with her and shrugged it off so that Cathy wouldn't ask any more questions.

"There's Jim and Emily. Hurry let's run." Josh said as he started to take off.

Gene ran ahead with him while Cathy pushed Nikki and Zack in their double stroller. Although Nikki was three and Zack was one, they were about the same length and both weighed about sixteen pounds, which still caused many people to mistake them as twins.

"Hey, gang. Glad you guys made it. Thank you, Josh, for inviting us along on your outing to the zoo."

"You're welcome. Thank you for coming, Jim," Josh said, sounding as grown-up as he could.

Then Jim leaned down to give Zack five and gave Nikki a kiss on the cheek. Nikki let out her squeal of delight. "I bet you're excited to see all the animals eh, Nikki?" Nikki laughed. "I'll take that as a yes," Jim replied.

"Josh has this whole day planned out. He even helped his mom make the sandwiches for the picnic," Gene said, looking proud. "Well, what do you say we get this show on the road?"

"Yay!" Josh and Zacky said in unison. The whole group of them started on their way. Josh ran ahead holding Emily's hand. Gene and Cathy tried to keep up while pushing the little ones, and Jim and Sophie brought up the rear.

"Sophie, have you thought anymore about giving your heart to Jesus?"

"I've thought a lot on the subject of me dying and Jesus saying, 'I never knew you.' To tell you the truth Jim, that does scare me to death. The problem is, I have a hard time believing that if I'm just a good person, He won't accept me anyway. I mean, there are some really bad people out there who don't deserve to go to Heaven, but I'm not one of them."

"Sophie, the thing is, it says in the Bible that we do not get to Heaven by doing good works. We could not do enough to earn a spot in Heaven. Our sins separate us from God the Father. Nothing we can do could bridge that gap. That's why Jesus had to come and die for our sins. As a faultless lamb, He took our sins upon Himself, died in our place, and rose again three days later. Because of that, when we receive Jesus and the gift that He gave us, we confess our sins and we are forgiven. That is the only way, Sophie, that we can enter into Heaven to spend eternity with our Lord." Jim was very passionate when he talked about this subject, something that didn't go unnoticed with Sophie.

She was about to respond when Josh yelled, "Sophie come over here and watch Nikki. The monkeys are her favorite." They were standing by the monkey cage and there were two little monkeys right up against the cage in front of Nikki. It was as if Nikki and the monkeys were playing together. Nikki would squeal and the monkeys would respond by making noises of their own and doing a little dance. It was very entertaining and cute. Sophie couldn't help but laugh out loud. This surprised everyone, most of all Sophie.

The rest of the day went a lot like that. Josh kept making sure that Sophie was watching what Nikki was doing. He was convinced that Sophie would miss out on all the fun if she didn't pay attention to Nikki. Cathy was thrilled. For the first time, it seemed like Sophie was enjoying being around Nikki. Cathy paused to thank Jesus, praying that this would be just the start in what could truly be a beautiful relationship between Nikki and Sophie. Cathy couldn't help overhearing bits and pieces of Jim and Sophie's earlier conversation; she'd noticed that Sophie hadn't seemed as defensive as she usually was. Cathy felt sure that Nikki could be the one that would finally win Sophie's heart for Jesus. There were a lot of people praying for Sophie. Cathy was confident that in the end, Sophie would receive Jesus in her heart. It just seemed to be taking an awfully long time.

After a fun picnic lunch and touring the second half of the zoo, they decided to call it a day. On the way back from the zoo, all three kids fell asleep. Sophie was sitting in the back of the van between Josh and Zack and seemed to be deep in thought. Gene had turned on the radio for the ride home. It was tuned to their favorite Christian radio station, and as Cathy listened to the words of the songs, she wondered if Sophie was noticing them. It was amazing how some songs just seemed to share Jesus's love so deeply. Music could be a very powerful tool, and Cathy prayed that it would start to stir Sophie's heart. When they reached Sophie's house, she thanked them for a truly wonderful day. "I can't remember when I had so much fun. When your little boy back there wakes up, tell him he did well. You two have amazing kids. See you later."

As they drove away, Cathy said, "Gene, did you notice that Sophie said 'kids' and not 'boys?' Do you think that she just might have included Nikki into that equation?"

"Who knows, Cathy? There just might be some hope there after all." Cathy and Gene both smiled as they sang songs to Jesus right along with the radio.

* * *

"You had a pretty exciting day at the zoo, didn't you Miss Nicole?"

"I loved it. God had such creativity when He created all the animals. Every one of them is unique and silly looking." Nikki started to laugh. "I guess that's how He made us people. We each have special qualities, and we can be a little silly too."

"You are absolutely correct." Seefas took great pleasure in watching this content child who never took anything for granted. "Sophie seems to be warming up to you. She actually seemed to enjoy being around you."

"I noticed that too. I think she even smiled at me, maybe just once, but that counts, doesn't it?" Nikki was very animated; she had been praying that one day Sophie would love her like she loved her brothers. She had also been praying that Sophie would come to love Jesus, and that was the most important thing to Nikki. "Seefas, do you think that Sophie's starting to come around to love Jesus?"

"I'm not sure, but it does seem that her hard heart is starting to soften. I think Jesus is working on her, and I think He will win out in the end."

* * *

"Lisa, I'm so glad that you were able to come over for a visit and work a little with Nikki."

"My pleasure. I miss working with her; she is my favorite, after all." Occasionally on her days off, Lisa would come and work with Nikki for about half an hour. Today she was surprised at how well Nikki had mastered her rolling; she could roll both ways without a problem. Nikki was also doing great with head control. At school they had started to work on Nikki sitting unattended, but she had quite a way to go before she conquered that. "You are doing awesomely, Nikki. I am very proud of you." Nikki responded to Lisa with her sweet squeals. Lisa and Cathy started laughing, which caused Nikki to join in. Zack waddled over from the toy box and wanted to play the fun game too, making Cathy and Lisa laugh even harder. Eventually a toy he wanted to share with his sister distracted Zack, which gave Lisa and Cathy a chance to talk.

"How's Jessica doing? Is she still enjoying working in the nursery?" Cathy had been praying for Lisa's youngest, the last of Lisa's family to make a decision to follow Jesus.

"It's actually going great. She met a friend who was also helping out in the nursery; she turned out to be one of the pastor's daughters. They really hit it off. Her name is Amy and she has been over to our house a couple of times. Amy invited her over to spend the night this Friday night and Jessica's going. I'm praying that this will make Jessica want to start going to youth group and give Jesus a chance in her life."

"Wow, Lisa that's great. I bet it won't be long until all that happens. Now she knows that it's not just her 'psycho' family who loves this Jesus, but cool people do too." They both laughed. "Seriously, I think that will go a long way with her."

"I think you're right. We just need to keep praying."

"I'm right there with you, Lisa."

CHAPTER TWENTY-FOUR

"All right, my three little ones. We need to get a move on or we'll be late for school." Nikki and Josh were having Halloween parties at their school and needed to go in costumes. Cathy was planning to stay with Nikki again that day at her school.

At Nikki's school, it was fun to see all the little kids dressed in costumes. Nikki was dressed as a little pumpkin; she wore an orange outfit with a green collar shaped like leaves, a little orange hat with a leaf on top, and her brown curls coming down from underneath. Margie, Nikki's teacher, greeted them at the door. "Nikki, you look awesome. Your costume is perfect. We have some real fun things planned for today, so I'm glad that your mom could be here to join us."

"I wouldn't miss this. The room looks great." Margie had the room all decorated like a pumpkin patch. Nikki fit right in with the décor. "What can I help you with, Margie?"

"I'm not sure yet; I'll let you know."

It was wonderful that Nikki was able to have friends. In fact, after school, her friend Lindsey was coming over to play. Lindsey's mom, Gina, was coming too.

After circle time, Margie pulled out a load of paint. The kids put their paint shirts on, and they all had fun making a mess. Margie and her assistants did face painting for the kids who wanted it. They painted Nikki's face orange, which made her pumpkin costume perfect. Nikki kept giggling while they were painting, and Cathy told them that Nikki was very ticklish.

While the kids were involved in their physical therapy for the day, Margie pulled Cathy aside. "I still can't get over the impact that your daughter has on the other children. They are just drawn to her. I've been thinking a lot about what you said about Jesus being the one that makes Nikki glow and draw others to her. Do you really think that's true?"

"Absolutely. I believe that Nikki loves Jesus with her whole heart and that He loves her beyond measure. You know, you could have that kind of relationship with Him too. He desires that from all of us." Cathy and Gene had been praying for Margie to come to know Jesus.

"Oh, I don't know. I don't think He would want someone like me. I understand how He could love you and Nikki, but there's a lot of stuff in my past that you don't know, Cathy." Cathy could tell that there was some deep pain behind Margie's eyes.

"Margie, Jesus came to die for us sinners. There is nothing we could do to make him not love us. It is His desire that everyone come to Him. You're right, I don't know what happened in your past, but there is someone who does."

This really confused Margie. "Who? How do you know?" Cathy noticed Margie didn't seem angry; it was more like she was scared.

"Oh, Margie. I'm sorry. Nobody told me; I was talking about Jesus. He knows all about you and He still loves you. In the Bible it tells many stories about how Jesus reached out to those everybody else felt were unworthy of love." Tears were welling up in Margie's eyes, so Cathy just kept praying as she was talking; she didn't know what to say to Margie. She didn't want to turn her further away from the Lord. Just then one of Margie's assistants rang the bell that signaled it was circle time.

"Time to get back to work," Margie said as she walked over to where the kids were gathering.

* * *

Lindsey and Nikki were in Nikki's room. Cathy had felt that they would have the most fun up there. Nikki was sitting in her special chair that a friend of theirs had made for her. Nikki had only had it for a short time, and it seemed to fit her to a tee. Cathy was so excited when they had brought it over for Nikki. It was perfect. Now Nikki was comfortable and ready to play, while Lindsey arranged all of Nikki's dolls around the chair. It was very sweet to watch. Lindsey would place one doll in Nikki's lap and she would have another, and they would play in their own way. Nikki not saying words, but expressing herself with coos and giggles, joined in the fun. Lindsey, having only a few words that she ever said, repeated Nikki's name over and over, and they would both laugh. Cathy and Gina enjoyed watching them for a while, then decided to go down and talk in the living room.

"Thank you so much for having us over. Lindsey adores Nikki."

"I think the feeling's mutual. I could tell Nikki was very excited to have Lindsey over today. It makes me feel good to know that Nikki has such a special friend her own age. I think it's very good for her and me."

"What do you mean by that?"

Cathy paused and thought for a moment. "I'm not sure. I guess sometimes I feel bad that Nikki's missing out on what's considered normal."

"Cathy, I don't think you need to worry about that. From where I'm standing, Nikki is very blessed in the friendship category. The ones who have the honor of being her friend are the ones that are truly blessed." Gina said this with such passion that it really touched Cathy.

"Thank you, Gina, for that reminder. I need reminding once in a while how very special my daughter is. I believe what you said with all my heart. Nikki's life is full of love and contentment. I'm the one that sometimes falls into that lie that Nikki's missing out on life. You know the only thing she's really missing out on is the worldly things. Her life is rich when it comes to relationships, especially her relationship with our Lord Jesus. I don't think Nikki would change a thing. God made her a very special little girl and we are blessed." Gina got very quiet at this point. Cathy could tell something was wrong. "Are you all right, Gina? Did I say something to upset you?"

Gina was quiet for a little longer, then slowly started to speak. "Do you think that God made Lindsey a very special little girl too?"

"Oh, Gina. Yes. I know He did. Lindsey has had such an incredible impact on Nikki. It has been great for her. I'm sure that she has impacted your life greatly too. I didn't mean to sound like Nikki is the only special child."

"You didn't. I'm sorry Cathy. You're right, I'm sure that Lindsey has touched my life in many ways. It's just that I haven't taken the time to let those things sink in. You see, when Lindsey was a baby, and my husband and I realized that she wasn't talking the way other kids were, we freaked. We didn't want our little girl to be different in any way. Frank, my husband, and I started to fight constantly; mostly Frank being upset that Lindsey wouldn't talk and me trying to defend her. It got so bad that finally Frank couldn't handle it anymore and walked out on us. It's just been Lindsey and me for about a year and a half now. Cathy, I'm ashamed to say that ever since that day, I have looked at Lindsey as a burden. I have failed to find the joy in having her as my daughter." Cathy placed a hand on Gina to let her know she was listening if she wanted to go on. "That day in the park, when we first met you, it was the first time that I saw my daughter light up and smile. I felt that Nikki was an angel. This year I have focused so much on the wonderful qualities of your daughter, I failed to see the wonderful qualities of my own daughter."

"Gina, I'm so sorry. I hope that I haven't made you feel that way. Every child is irreplaceable and special to our Heavenly Father. We just need to find their uniqueness and enjoy it. It took me a while to see Nikki's, and, once I did, I was blown away by what I had been missing." Cathy went on to explain to Gina how she had felt in the first year of Nikki's life. Gina was shocked, but it seemed to help her. "Gina, pray that Jesus shows you Lindsey's gifts, and I think you will be blown away too."

"Thank you, Cathy. I'm glad we talked. It has helped me more than you know." Just then, Gina heard Lindsey yelling for her. This startled both Gina and Cathy because Lindsey wasn't very vocal. They both ran upstairs, and what they saw made them laugh. Lindsey had dressed up in some clothes that she had found in Nikki's closet. Nikki had so many clothes of all sizes because people were constantly giving them hand-me-downs. Lindsey had also dressed Nikki up. They looked so cute. Nothing matched, of course, and there were clothes and toys everywhere. Both girls had huge smiles on their faces, and Lindsey started talking nonstop. She started telling her mom and Cathy about all that they were doing and would stop to laugh several times in the process, and Nikki would laugh right along with her. Gina burst out crying, and with tears of joy she bent down on her knee and pulled Lindsey to her and held her real tight. This was the first time in their lives that Gina hugged her daughter this way, and Lindsey started to cry too as she said, "I love you, Mama."

* * *

"Seefas, did you see what happened today? Lindsey talked a whole bunch. She didn't just say one-word sentences: she went on and on. Her mom was so surprised, she started to cry. Oh, then Lindsey cried. It was so cool. Oh, Seefas, did you see it? Did you?"

"I can tell you are a tad excited." Seefas laughed. "It was wonderful. I loved watching the bonding that took place between mother and daughter. It brought tears to my eyes too."

"Lindsey is such a great girl. We really have a lot of fun together. It's been exciting to see her learn to talk and express herself."

"What do you mean by express herself?" Seefas had an idea, but he was curious to what was going on inside of Nikki's head.

"Well, Lindsey seems to be able to show emotion with me. I can tell when she is happy, sad, or mad about something. But she was different around her mom. It was like she was a robot with no emotion when her mom came around. It always made me sad, so I started to pray for their relationship. That's why today was so exciting to see the bond that took place between them. I think this is going to be the start of a beautiful thing." Nikki was an astute little girl who cared deeply for other people. Seefas loved Nikki very much.

* * *

Cathy had just gotten the kids all set up in the bonus room to play. They loved playing there; they felt like it was their own little clubhouse. The boys had all their cars out, and Josh had set up the track. They put Nikki by the start and gave her a flag to hold, telling her that she was responsible for telling them when to go. Nikki had some control when she held things, but not a lot. When the flag just happened to fall, the boys would yell "Go!" and Nikki would laugh. The boys loved to include Nikki in everything they did. Cathy loved the bond that her children had.

She was straightening up downstairs a bit because Lisa was coming over for a visit. She had just finished tidying up when Lisa arrived.

"Hey, Lisa, I'm so glad that you were able to come by."

"Me, too. Where are your precious children? It's very quiet down here." They both started to laugh.

"They are upstairs playing. Nikki is the flag starter for their car race."

"The boys are so good with her. It's very sweet." Lisa always admired how the boys were with their sister.

"So, how are things at your place? How's Jessica doing? Whatever happened to that sleepover she was going to have at her friend's house?"

"It was amazing. When she got home from Amy's house, she was lit up. I could tell immediately that something wonderful had happened to her. First thing out of her mouth was, 'How could I have been so blind? Mom, you were right about everything.' She went on to explain how being at Amy's caused her to see everything in a whole new light. Amy's dad sat down with her, and she prayed to ask Jesus into her heart. She said she wanted to start going to youth group and wanted to continue to work in the nursery. Can you believe it? I was overjoyed."

"That is awesome, Lisa. I'll have to tell Nikki. I know she has been praying for Jessica."

"I know that Nikki is a prayer warrior. You can just see it in her eyes."

While they were talking there was a knock at the door. It was Val.

"Val, so good to see you."

"I'm sorry for interrupting; I saw Lisa's car outside."

"Not at all. Lisa was just sharing with me that Jessica finally made a decision to accept Jesus into her life."

"That's wonderful. You must be thrilled, Lisa."

"I am, Val, and it's always good to see you."

"Cathy, where are your kids hiding out?"

"They're upstairs playing."

"Your kids sure do love playing together. Hey, I've been meaning to ask you how Sophie's doing. I haven't seen her for a while."

"I think she may be starting to warm up to Nikki. It's hard to tell with Sophie. When we went to the zoo with her, she really seemed to notice Nikki in a new light. When we dropped her off at home, she told us we had great 'children;' she usually makes a point to say 'boys.' I just keep praying for her."

* * *

"Did you enjoy your day with your brothers?" Seefas loved the interaction between Nikki and her brothers. They were so good to her; it always warmed Seefas' heart.

"Oh, yes. I loved it. They are so fun. They include me in everything. Do you think Jesus knew they were the perfect choice for me?"

"Absolutely. He put the three of you together. He knew that each of you needed one another." The simple things in life brought Nikki such pleasure.

CHAPTER TWENTY-FIVE

"Sophie, I'm so glad that you were able to come by today. I've missed seeing you. Is everything going all right?" When they'd taken the kids to the zoo during their last visit, Sophie had seemed to warm a little to Nikki, and Cathy was anxious to see where that relationship might go.

"Things are fine; I've just been putting in extra time at work. How have things been going with you guys? I miss seeing the kids." Cathy's mouth dropped open; she couldn't believe that Sophie had said *kids* instead of *boys*. She didn't want to read too much into it, but even if it was a slip of the tongue from Sophie, it was a start in the right direction. Cathy longed for Sophie to let Nikki into her life.

"We've been doing well. Gene took the kids out for lunch; he likes to do that sometimes on the weekends. He feels that he doesn't get much time with them during the week. They should be back in a little while."

"Great. I'm excited to see them." Cathy liked the change she was seeing in Sophie. Cathy and Sophie talked awhile longer when they got a surprise visitor. Jim had stopped by to share with Cathy what was going on with Amanda's dad.

"Hey, Sophie. Nice to see you, I haven't seen you since the zoo. How are you?"

"I'm fine, Jim. Thanks." Sophie always seemed shy with Jim at first and then she would quickly warm up. They had become good friends.

"Well, I have been sharing a lot with Amanda's dad, Phil. That day at the park, I was so shocked to hear some of his views. Phil's a tough guy, but I had never gotten that impression from him before. I knew that I needed to talk to him about it, and I decided the best way to approach him was to share my story about Nikki. He told me that he was familiar with Nikki from what Amanda had told him. He was angry with me and felt that I had embarrassed Amanda in front of her friends and that I put him down as well. It was hard at first to get through to him. It was apparent that Amanda had not really listened to what I'd said at the park, so the story she shared with her dad was lopsided."

"Were you able to share your story with Phil? Did he listen to what you had to say?" Cathy asked.

"Yes. I was finally able to share with Phil about how Nikki changed my life. At first he was skeptical; he'd made up his mind long ago about kids with special needs. It was hard to break that façade."

"Did you get through to him?" Cathy was anxious to know.

"Cathy, let Jim finish." Sophie, able to relate to Phil's point of view in some ways, was anxious to hear the rest of the story too.

Jim laughed. "All right. I'll go on. Phil's first response was, 'Jim, you're crazy. There's no way that any person could be like that, especially a handicapped person. Every person has an agenda. No one makes you feel like you are the most important person in the world.' Phil also wondered how she could convey that without being able to talk. Finally, after a couple hours of explaining to him about Nikki and explaining how Jesus made her to be a special little girl, I was able to go into the story of Jesus and what He did for us by dying on the cross."

"So, what was his response to all your rambling?" The import of Sophie's question was not lost on Phil; she had a hunger to know more, not about Phil, but about Jesus.

"Well, let me tell you. Phil is a big man with a tough exterior, and, for the first time, I saw him break down and cry. His whole countenance changed. He got down on his hands and knees right then and asked Jesus into his heart. He would really like to meet Nikki one day, and he's very concerned about Amanda. He feels like his views have made the wrong impact on his daughter. He asked me to pray for her." Cathy started to cry, and Sophie looked in deep thought. Jim was wondering what was going through her mind.

"Jim," Cathy said, "Gene and I have been praying for him. I think Nikki has been too. I can't wait to tell her."

As if on cue, they heard the garage door open. Gene and the kids were home.

There was a lot of excitement as they came into the house. It was apparent they'd all had a good time; even Nikki was shrieking in excitement. Josh, first to notice their visitors, went running in to give hugs, followed quickly by Zack.

"Hello, everyone." Gene walked over and gave Cathy a kiss, then turned his focus to their company. "Jim, Sophie, good to see you both. How have you guys been doing?"

Sophie was quick to speak up. "I was visiting with Cathy and then Jim showed up to share with us about his friend, Phil." Cathy smiled at Sophie's response. It was like Sophie wanted to make sure Gene didn't think that the two of them had come together. It struck Cathy as kind of funny that Sophie didn't seem to mind the idea; it was more like she was embarrassed and had to blurt something out.

"Oh, who's Phil?" Gene directed his question toward Jim.

"Phil is Amanda's dad. You know the girl that Val and Nikki ran into in the park?"

"Yes, I remember Amanda. Cathy and I have been praying for her and her dad. I just didn't know his name. So, how's it been going with him?"

As Jim told his story again, it was apparent that Gene wasn't the only one interested in hearing it; Jim also had Nikki's full attention. When he finished, Nikki gave a loud shriek and had a big smile on her face. This caught Sophie's attention right away, and Cathy noticed that a smile seemed to slowly appear on Sophie's face.

"I told you that I thought Nikki had been praying. I think that she just confirmed that for all of us." Everyone laughed at Cathy's observation. She was proud of her daughter. Josh and Zack hadn't been paying attention to the conversation until they heard everyone laughing; now they didn't want to be left out.

"Mom," Josh blurted, "guess who we saw when we were at the restaurant?"

"I don't know. Papa and Granda? Uncle Nate and Aunt Lynn? Eddie and Annie?" Cathy kept guessing and Josh kept shaking his head no. "All right, Buster. I give up."

"We saw Nikki's teacher. She came over and said hello to us."

"You did? Was Nikki excited to see her?"

"Yeah." Zack had to get into the conversation somehow. "She nice." Zack was only one and a half, so his vocabulary was still not very large.

"We didn't talk with her very long, Gene added, "but Nikki did seem excited to see her. That seemed to make her teacher's day." They talked a little longer about Nikki's teacher, and then

Jim said that he had to be going; he needed to pick up Emily at a friend's house.

"Thanks for stopping by and sharing with us about Phil. We'll continue to pray for Amanda." At that, Jim said his good-byes and left.

* * *

"You touch a lot of people's lives," Seefas said, in a way only a very proud protector could.

"And a lot of people touch mine. I feel so blessed to have so many wonderful people around me who love me so much. "Jim's news today was very exciting. I'm thrilled that Amanda's dad came to know our Lord. We need to keep praying for Amanda though." Nikki loved hearing that someone else found Jesus. She knew that was the best decision they would ever make.

"We will keep praying. We should also keep praying for your teacher. Why don't we pray right now?"

* * *

School was coming to an end. It was Nikki's last week before summer break. Cathy had mixed feelings about it. She was excited to have the kids home and not have to be on a set schedule, but she had just found out that Margie wouldn't be Nikki's teacher next year. Margie was being transferred to a different district; she didn't want to go but another teacher with seniority was being transferred here. Cathy felt like she hadn't shared enough with Margie about Jesus. She had figured she wouldn't be overbearing and that she still had next year to share Jesus with Margie. Cathy felt like she'd let Margie down. She prayed that the Lord would open up an opportunity for her to talk with Margie before the last day of school. Today was the day Cathy had previously arranged to stay at school with Nikki for the day. Perhaps an opportunity might present itself.

* * *

After dinner that night, Cathy needed to run to the Fred Meyer pharmacy to pick up Nikki's medicine.

At the pharmacy, Cathy stood in a long line at the counter. She hated standing in line; it seemed like such a waste of time. She was getting antsy because the line seemed to be especially dragging. She felt someone tap her on the shoulder. Cathy turned around to see Margie. Cathy was surprised. "Margie, hi. How long have you been standing there?"

"Well, I've been standing here for a few minutes. I wasn't sure if it was you in front of me, so I kept hoping you would turn around so I could see if it was you."

Cathy said a silent prayer that God would give her the opportunity to talk more with Margie about Jesus. The two women chatted until it was Cathy's turn. When they were both done, they went next door to get a cinnamon roll. As they bought their rolls and found seats, Cathy mentally searched for a way to bring up the subject of Jesus.

Margie interrupted her thoughts. "We haven't had a chance to really talk since that Halloween party months ago. Did you really mean it when you said that Jesus knows everything I've done and that He still loves me?" Cathy couldn't believe that Margie broached the subject. She said a silent prayer of thanks before diving into the conversation.

"Margie, with all my heart, I believe it. He loves you, and He's waiting for you to reach out to receive Him."

"Cathy, I did something horrible, and I've never been able to forgive myself. If I can't, how could He?"

"Because Jesus has the perfect love for us imperfect people. He died on the cross for our sins. He saw you, Margie, when He died. He took your sins upon Himself. On our own, we fall short. Nothing we do is good enough to spend eternity with Him. But when we receive the gift that Jesus gave us by dying for our sins, we can ask for forgiveness, and the blood of Jesus washes our sins away."

Margie had tears in her eyes. "Do you really mean that?"

"Yes, I do." Cathy kept praying that this would be the night that Margie received Jesus into her heart.

"Cathy, do you want to know why I decided to work in special education?"

"Yes. I would love to hear your story." Cathy had always wondered what gave people the passion for working with kids with special needs. Having a disabled child herself, she knew the joy they bring; but when you don't have that knowledge first hand, what puts that desire in your heart?

"When I was a teenager, I got pregnant. My boyfriend, Jack, was very supportive. He believed that he was as much to blame for our situation and said he would support me all the way. I was scared to death. I didn't know how to be a mom, and I was so young. I slowly got used to the idea and even got a little excited; that is, until one day." Margie started to tear up. Obviously this discussion was very hard for her.

"What happened to make your excitement go away?"

"Oh, Cathy. This is the awful part; the part I would do over in a heartbeat." Margie paused for what seemed like a long time, and Cathy wasn't sure if she should say anything. Finally, Margie continued. "At one of my doctor appointments, the doctor told me and my mom that my baby had . . . problems. He said my baby would most likely be born with a severe genetic disorder. He told me I was young and shouldn't have to worry about something this big. He told me all about abortion and said it wasn't a big deal, a lot of people did it. I wasn't sure I wanted to do that, but my mom really encouraged me to. I called my boyfriend that night and told him what the doctor said. Jack said it didn't matter what any doctor says, he didn't believe in killing babies. I got so mad at him. I told him, I wouldn't be killing a baby because technically it wasn't even a baby yet. I told him that he would probably just split after the baby came anyway, and I would have to do it alone. To make a long painful story short, I went ahead and had that abortion." Margie started to cry. Cathy scooted her chair closer to Margie and put her arm around her.

"Margie, are you all right? You don't need to go on if it's too hard."

"I want to. This is the first time I've talked about it since that terrible day, and it's somehow freeing. People are wrong. My baby was a baby. It's ludicrous that people think they're not babies until the day they're born. I killed my baby, and I have had to live with that guilt every single day. Why didn't anyone tell me that when I walked out of that abortion clinic, I was walking into a nightmare that would never end?" Margie put her head in her hands and cried even harder. Cathy put her hand on Margie's, not sure what to say. Margie started calming down and looked into Cathy's eyes. "Now that you know what I've done, do you still think Jesus would forgive me for killing my baby?"

"Oh, Margie. Yes, He will. Jesus loves you and is waiting for you to reach out and ask Him for help. He wants to give you His gift of life."

"Jesus loves me? Even after what I've done, He loves me? How can that be?"

"Margie, God created us to have a relationship with Him, but He gave us a free will. His desire is that all would turn to Him and love Him. Unfortunately, not everyone makes that choice. He knows that we are sinners, and yet He loves us anyway. He knows what you did, and He has been waiting for you to turn to Him and receive His forgiveness. He wants to take this burden from you. The way Jesus can do this is for you to accept that He died for you and confess your sins to Him. You need to invite Him into your life to be your Savior. Only then are you able to receive His forgiveness and receive His gift of eternal life. Margie, are you ready to turn your life to Him and receive His gift?"

"I want that more than I've ever wanted anything in my entire life. Cathy, could you tell me how to do that?" Cathy said a silent prayer of thanks.

"Of course, I can. Margie, do you believe that Jesus died for your sins and rose again from the dead?

"Yes. It's something I never paid much attention to before. In fact, I always thought it was a made up story. But slowly over this past year of meeting you and Nikki, it started becoming more than just a story. It has become very real to me. I believe now with all my heart that Jesus loves me, and I am ready to receive Him into my life." Margie and Cathy bowed their heads, and Cathy walked Margie through the prayer of making Jesus the Lord of her life.

* * *

When Cathy got home, she told Gene and the kids what happened with Margie. That night their prayer time before bed was spent praising Jesus for the change in Margie and thanking Him for once again working through their little girl to draw another soul to Him.

When Nikki was tucked into her crib and the lights were turned off, she was able to talk with her angel. "Seefas, I'm so happy for teacher Margie. I had no idea that there was so much hurt going on inside of her. I know Jesus is going to help her get better and not have such sadness in her heart. Seefas, did they throw another party in Heaven tonight over Margie?"

Seefas laughed. He loved the sparkle that appeared in Nikki's eyes when she was excited. "Yes, they did. There was great rejoicing over another one of God's children turning from the darkness to the light."

Seefas loved hearing Nikki pray; she had such sincerity and desire to see others come to know Jesus. This was the time that Seefas cherished the most, being able to pray with his sweet Nikki.

CHAPTER TWENTY-SIX

"Mom, what time are we leaving to go to the birthday party?" Josh was calling to his mom from upstairs. Cathy couldn't believe how quickly her kids were growing up. Josh was turning six, Nikki four, and little Zacky would be two in just a couple of months. Cathy looked over the guest list, amazed that every year it grew longer. This year, Val was bringing Anne, a girl from her Bible study group, and Lindsey and her mom were joining them as well. Gene and Cathy had decided to hold the party at an aquatic park that provided pizza and cake, and everyone could enjoy the water activities. Josh especially was very anxious to get there.

"We'll be leaving as soon as everyone's ready to go. It won't be much longer, Buster," Cathy answered Josh, heading up the stairs to gather everyone's swimsuits. This was one of Cathy's favorite times of the year. Not only were they celebrating the kids' birthdays, but they were also celebrating the way that God was working through their family. The day she'd learned her daughter had a chromosomal disorder, Cathy never dreamt that it would turn out to be such a blessing.

"All right everyone, time to pile into the van and get going." Gene's remark and the shouts of joy from the boys brought Cathy out of her thoughts. Cathy picked up Nikki and headed for the van.

They were the first to get to the aquatic park, so they were able to get the party room set up. Soon the party was in full swing, with some people swimming, others hanging out talking.

Cathy loved sitting back and observing all that was going on around her. Most of the kids were in the water swimming; Val, Jill, and Anne were looking after the littlest ones—Nikki, Zack, and Lindsey. The pool had a little kid section with its own slide and a fountain that sprayed water straight up in the air. The kids were really enjoying themselves. Anne was holding Nikki and going down the slide with her. Nikki loved it, giggling each time.

"Mommy, come over here and watch me," Josh was in the wave pool, where he was playing with his friend Braden and many of his cousins.

Josh came running out of the water and gave his mom a big hug. "Can you take us down the slides? Some of the other kids are doing it, and it looks like a lot of fun."

"Sure thing, Buster. Why don't you get everyone together and we'll go." They headed over to wait in line for the slides, and Cathy was surprised to see Jim and Sophie waiting in line together.

"Hey, guys. Braving the slides, eh?" Cathy couldn't remember ever seeing Sophie so relaxed. She looked like she was having a fantastic time.

"This is awesome. I think this is about our tenth time down. I don't think I've had this much fun since I was a kid." Sophie was beaming.

"She's like a kid in a candy store." Jim seemed very amused by Sophie's attitude.

"I want to go down the same one as you, Sophie." Josh chimed in with enthusiasm. It was evident that Josh was noticing a different side to Sophie too. After a couple times down, Cathy left Josh and the other kids in Jim's and Sophie's capable hands. She wanted to get things ready for pizza and presents. All the guests were spread around the aquatic center; even Cathy's parents had decided to check out the hot tub. Gene, Ryan, and a couple of the other guys were trying to outdo each other on the diving board. As Cathy headed toward the party room, some of the other moms said they would help her set up.

"Great party, Cathy. Lindsey's having so much fun. Thanks for inviting us."

"I'm glad that you and Lindsey could make it, Gina. How have things been going between the two of you?"

"Ever since that day at your house, things have been magnificent. Not only is Lindsey talking nonstop, our relationship is better than it's ever been. Remember you told me to take the time to find my daughter's gifts?" Cathy nodded. "Well, I did that and found out that my daughter is incredible, and I wouldn't want her to be any other way." Cathy loved the excitement that she saw in Gina. It reminded her of the way she was when she finally accepted Nikki for who she was. Cathy was happy for Gina and Lindsey.

Everything was ready. All the kids entered the party room talking a hundred miles a minute. Val, Jill, and Anne came in carrying the little ones.

"Are you enjoying yourself, Anne? I'm really glad that you were able to join us."

"Thank you for inviting me, Cathy. It has been a joy being here. I love spending time with Nikki. She is an absolute delight."

"Well, I appreciate you, Val, and Jill watching over the little ones. It has been a big help."

"Anytime, Cathy. They are all wonderful. I have always enjoyed little children."

"I can tell." Cathy really liked Anne; she had enjoyed getting to know her. "Well, I'd better give everyone instructions on the food so they can get started." Cathy told everyone to help themselves to the pizza, salad, and pop. She reminded them all to save room for cake and ice cream.

"Great party, Sweetheart. Everyone seems to be having a great time."

"Including you. I saw those tricky dives off the diving board, Gene Ellerton. I didn't know you could do that kind of thing."

"Well, yeah. I still have a few tricks up my sleeve that you have yet to learn."

"Is that so? I can't wait to see what else there is." Cathy loved her husband's playful attitude. She really appreciated all the support that he gave to her. "Oh, by the way, did you see who was hanging out with Sophie on the slides today?"

"No. But I'm sure you're going to tell me," Gene said, with a smile on his face.

"Jim was. They looked like they were having a lot of fun together."

"Cathy, they're friends. Quit trying to play matchmaker." Gene was worried that Cathy was pushing too hard for something that neither Jim nor Sophie were ready for.

"I didn't do anything, honest. I had nothing to do with it. I just thought it was interesting, that's all." Josh came running up at that point and interrupted their conversation.

"Can we open presents now, Mom?"

"It's a perfect time for opening gifts. Why don't you let everyone know?" Josh immediately started yelling for everyone to gather around. Cathy wasn't sure who would help Nikki open her presents this year. Nikki had been blessed with so many new friends.

Cathy decided to ask Lindsey, who, of course, was thrilled.

Like always, Josh let his sister open her presents first. Lindsey and Nikki giggled the whole time. Cathy was shocked when she picked up the next present and read that it was from Sophie. It was the first time she had ever brought Nikki a present. Cathy looked at Sophie, who avoided eye contact. Cathy smiled and said a silent prayer of thanks. Could Sophie really be warming up to Nikki? Cathy sincerely hoped so. When it was Josh's turn, he barely waited for his mom to read the gift cards; he was so excited to see the present and get back to swimming.

On the way home, everyone was quiet. They were worn out from playing hard at the party. Seefas took this opportunity to talk with Nikki. "Nikki, it looked like you were having a lot of fun at your party."

"I loved it, Seefas!" Nikki said in an excited, yet tired voice.

"What was your favorite part?"

"I loved spending time with all my friends. But I think my most favorite part was Sophie's gift. She usually only buys for Josh." Nikki had never complained about this. She didn't mind not getting a present from Sophie, but she felt sad because she wanted Sophie to like her.

"I know, Nikki. I think it's great." Seefas never understood why Sophie treated Nikki the way she did. He knew that it had made Nikki sad. He had been praying with Nikki that one day Sophie would come around. Maybe this was the first step in that happening.

"Seefas, do you think Sophie's starting to like me?" Nikki asked in a very soft voice, for she was almost asleep.

* * *

Cathy couldn't believe they were going on their trip; it seemed like they were just celebrating the kids birthdays. Josh and Zack were full of excitement as they looked out the window of the airplane. It was Zack's first plane ride, and it had been a few years since Josh had been on one. Nikki was full of squeals as they flew over the clouds.

The Ellertons were on their way to Kansas for a Saterlee family reunion. Cathy's dad was from an enormous family, and the majority of them lived in Augusta, Kansas. Cathy's uncle was even the mayor of Augusta, and the reunion was taking place at the Saterlee City Park. All of Cathy's brothers and sisters and their families were going to be there and, of course, her parents. Cathy was nervous and excited; she hadn't been back to Kansas since she was thirteen. The Ellertons were going to be staying in the daylight basement of Cathy's cousin, Denise.

Although the flight was uneventful, things got exciting about five minutes after arriving at Denise's house. It was late at night and Nikki was sound asleep in her car seat. Instead of waking Nikki, Cathy decided to bring her down the stairs in her carrier. Cathy thought that she had reached the bottom, but to her dismay there was one more step. Cathy fell and dropped Nikki's car seat. Nikki stayed fast asleep; Cathy, on the other hand, was in excruciating pain. Gene and Denise's husband, Don, encouraged her to stand up and put some weight on her foot, telling her it would soon feel better. When Cathy tried, however, she felt like she was going to pass out from the pain. Worried about their mom, Josh and Zack started to cry. While Cathy rested on a bed trying her best to conceal how much pain she was in, Gene quickly got the kids ready for bed so he could take Cathy to the emergency room.

X-rays determined that Cathy had broken her foot. "Great way to start our vacation. I'm sorry, Honey."

Cathy looked so distraught and cute that Gene had to hide the fact that he was about to start laughing. "It's not your fault.

Just think, at least we'll never forget this trip. Everything's going to be fine, just wait and see."

First thing the next morning, the boys came racing into the room where Gene and Cathy were staying, wanting to make sure their mom was all right. When they saw her cast they both started talking a mile a minute.

"Does it hurt, Mom?" Josh had been very concerned; he didn't want his mom to be in pain.

"Want me to kiss it and make it better, Mommy?" Zacky had the sweetest look on his face. Cathy just wanted to wrap both her boys up in her arms and give them lots of kisses.

"It hurts a little. The doctor gave me medicine to help with that, so the pain is not too bad. You two are going to have to be Daddy's big helpers since I can't get around too quickly." Cathy loved her kids; they were always so concerned about other people and had big hearts.

Nikki started to squeal from her made up bed on the floor, and Gene picked her up and brought her to Cathy. "I think your little girl wants to make sure you're okay too."

Cathy took Nikki in her arms and gave her lots of kisses. Nikki giggled in delight. "Yes, you will have to be a good helper as well."

* * *

"Mom, look! That sign says 'Saterlee.'" Josh was very excited and kept rambling on. "And look at all those people at the park. Who are they? Why are they here? Don't they know that we are supposed to have a family reunion here today?"

"Well, Buster, all those people are here for the reunion. Papa comes from a very large family, so you will get to meet a lot of new people today."

"You mean that all those people are in my family?"

"Yes, all of them. They're all related to us somehow."

"Wow. Cool. Let's hurry." Josh was jumping out of the car, thinking that his family was taking way too long.

"Zacky's family too?" Zack was climbing out of the van backwards looking up at his mom.

"Yes, sweet boy, your family too."

Gene put Nikki in her stroller and retrieved Cathy's crutches. "You all right, Sweetheart? Are you going to need help?"

"I think I can manage. Thanks, Gene. It's a little embarrassing seeing all my relatives for the first time in almost twenty years, and I show up looking like this."

"You look adorable. Besides you'll get to sit there looking cute with our daughter and be able to watch everything going on around you. That way everyone will have to approach you. Now I wish I had a cast on."

Cathy laughed. She knew that Gene was feeling a tad out of his comfort zone with meeting so many people for the first time. "You can sit with me and be available to my every whim."

Gene laughed. "We'll see. Although, I'd guess someone will have to keep an eye on our adventuresome boys."

Soon the reunion was in full swing, and Gene was kept plenty busy keeping up with the boys. They wanted to do everything. Cathy couldn't maneuver very well, so she and Nikki found a shady spot to hang out. They were not bored, however; everyone made their way over to talk with them. It was fun seeing all her cousins and meeting all their new additions.

One of those was a cute little girl with blonde hair and big blue eyes named Leslie. Cathy thought that she must be around seven. She wasn't sure to whom Leslie belonged, but she was quite friendly.

"I think Nikki is pretty. Does she like to play?"

"Yes, she enjoys that very much. She needs to stay in her stroller right now though. Would you like to show Nikki around the park?" At that both Leslie and Nikki got excited. Cathy laughed.

"I think that she wants me to do that. Can she talk?"

"No, not in the way we understand. But, I think that she does understand everything we say to her. You can talk to her like you would anyone else. I'm sure you two will have fun."

"Thank you. You are a very nice lady." Leslie was very polite.

"And you are a very nice girl. So who in this big crowd do you belong to?"

"My mom is Cheryl, she used to be a Saterlee. She's the daughter of Scott and Joanne Saterlee. Do you know them?"

Cathy laughed. "I sure do. Your grandpa is my cousin." At that Leslie and Nikki were off to explore the park. Cathy was one of the youngest cousins in the Saterlee family. In fact, the ones closest to her age were her cousins' kids. So while Scott was her cousin, his daughter Cheryl was only a couple of years younger than Cathy.

"Hey, I saw our daughter being pushed around the park by a little girl. When she went by me, I heard Nikki laughing. What's that all about?" Gene thought that it was great that his daughter was having a good time.

"That's my cousin's granddaughter. She kept coming over to see Nikki, so I finally suggested they go for a stroll. What are our boys up to?"

"They are with Jenny and the girls and a few new cousins they have met." Jenny's the wife of Cathy's brother Craig. "Do you need anything? I was going to go shoot some hoops with some of the guys."

"I think I'm good, but a little thirsty. Do you think you could get me a soda first?" Cathy gave him her biggest, most charming smile.

"You don't have to win me over with that smile of yours. I would be glad to get you a soda." Gene always thought it was funny when Cathy called pop "soda." Gene came back with a root beer for her and leaned down and kissed her forehead. "There you go, my wounded wife."

"Thank you, dear husband. Now go and show 'em what you're made of."

Gene was off and before long Cathy's cousin Cheryl came over. "Thank you for letting Leslie take your daughter everywhere. That's very brave of you. Leslie's having a wonderful time. I think she has introduced Nikki to everyone here."

Cathy smiled. "I'm sure that Nikki has loved every minute of it."

"I'd say so. Every time she meets someone new she lets out a loud squeal of delight. It makes everyone laugh. She's a real sweetheart. Do you remember, Frank, Aunt Josie's son?"

"Yes. He doesn't seem very happy. What happened to him?"

"He's been in a lot of trouble lately with the law. Silly, stupid things really. Lots of traffic tickets that he refuses to pay. Once when a cop pulled him over, he freaked out and took off. He keeps getting arrested, and then he gets out on bail. Aunt Josie's not sure what's going on. No one can seem to get through to him. I haven't seen him smile in months, until today that is."

Cathy hadn't heard about what was going on with Frank. Her only memories of him were from her childhood and Frank was about five years older than her. "So what happened today?"

"Well Leslie was determined to introduce Nikki to anybody and everybody. So she walked up to Frank. I could tell that he wasn't sure what to think of Nikki when he first saw her. But Leslie, in her determined little voice, introduced the two of them. Nikki started laughing. I hadn't seen her do that with the others. But she was laughing so hard—a cute little belly laugh. Leslie started laughing, and soon Frank couldn't help himself, and he started laughing too. I had been walking around with them, just to make sure Leslie didn't run Nikki into someone or something. Then after the three of them stopped laughing, Frank asked if he could escort the ladies around. He's been with them ever since."

"Leave it to children to break through a tough exterior." Cathy loved when she heard stories like this. Nikki just seemed to know what people needed.

"You have a special little girl, Cathy. She captured hearts today." Cheryl left and Cathy got to visit with more people. The reunion came to an end too quickly for all of them.

* * *

Nikki, who still didn't sleep all the way through the night, would periodically just wake up to have a little talk with Jesus and Seefas, then drift back to sleep. That night, when the house became quiet and Nikki woke up, Seefas asked, "So, did you have fun today with your cousin Leslie?"

"I had a blast. She's great. We went all over the park. My favorite part was meeting Cousin Frank."

"I was wondering about that. What made you laugh so hard when you met him?" Seefas was still trying to figure out what tickled Nikki.

"When Leslie introduced me to him, he had the funniest look on his face. It was like he was saying who's Frank? He seemed so distracted that it just made me laugh. He was too serious for me; I knew I had to get a smile on his face. And what better way—laughter's contagious, you know?" Nikki said this so sincerely Seefas couldn't help but laugh.

"You're right. It is contagious."

"Then Frank hung out with us the rest of the day, and I saw him smile lots. He's really a nice guy; he just needs to learn to smile more. I think he would be happier if he did." Nikki was speaking in a very sleepy voice. "I think I better go back to sleep now. Goodnight, Jesus. Goodnight, Seefas."

"Goodnight sweet Nicole. Sweet dreams." Seefas loved this little girl, and he loved her heart most of all.

CHAPTER TWENTY-SEVEN

"What's taking so long for Nikki's bed to be finished?" Josh was excited to see what Nikki's bed was going to look like. Gene and Cathy had decided that she shouldn't have to sleep in a crib any longer, so Cathy bought a bed that would work for Nikki. They needed to make sure she couldn't fall out of it and that it would work forever, if need be. Cathy found a pink bed with a cottage house as a headboard. The roof of the house was purple, and it was perfect. Nikki wouldn't be able to roll out because of a three-inch border around the bed.

"Dad, Nikki's getting excited to try her new bed. Can you please hurry?" Josh entertained his brother and sister while Gene and Cathy worked on the bed and came in every few minutes to check on the progress.

"We're almost done, Buster. You can tell your sister it won't be much longer." Josh took off down the hall yelling the update.

"I really do think Nikki will love her bed. I can't wait to have her try it." Cathy was trying to be patient and help Gene as much as she could, but she was almost as excited as Josh.

"Well, why don't you go get her? I think we're ready for the big moment." Gene had to admit he was just as anxious to see Nikki's response to her new bed. Cathy went to the bonus room to gather up the troops. She came back carrying Nikki with Josh and Zack running ahead of her.

"Zacky, look at her bed. It's so cool. There's actually a house on her bed." Josh and Zack were about to jump on the bed when Gene told them they had to let their sister try it out first.

"Sissy, hurry up. I want a turn. I want a turn." Zack could hardly wait to jump on his sister's bed. Cathy set Nikki down on the bed, and immediately Nikki started giggling and screeching. She rolled around a couple of times and giggled more. Soon the whole family was laughing.

"Well, Sweetheart, I have to admit this was a very good move on our part. Our daughter loves her bed. It was worth getting it, just seeing her expression." Gene loved seeing his daughter get tickled about things.

The kids spent the rest of the afternoon playing on Nikki's bed.

* * *

Val arrived to have dinner with the Ellertons; she said she wanted to see Nikki's new bed and volunteered to go up and get the kids. After a few minutes, Cathy heard laughter coming down the stairs.

Cathy wasn't surprised to hear the laughter because her kids loved spending time with Val. It took Cathy back to the day they all met at Olive Garden. Who would have thought that Val would become such a big part of the family?

After dinner, they played games and laughed a lot. Zack was two now and at a very entertaining stage. He always knew how to get his sister laughing. Josh didn't want to be outdone by his brother, so he would come up with his own entertaining antics.

After the kids were sacked out upstairs, Gene went into his home office to get a head start on his work for the upcoming week. That left Cathy and Val alone to catch up. Cathy asked her how things were going with her mom and brother.

"I've actually been seeing them more often. I decided that I needed to make an effort because I knew neither one of them would. So now the three of us get together once a month at my apartment."

"That's great. Has your mom found a job that she's able to hold down?" Val's mom became an alcoholic after Val's dad died several years earlier, and keeping a job was difficult for her. Val's brother also struggled with alcohol.

"Actually, my mom and brother shocked me last night. They came over and announced that they had joined an AA group together and have been going for several months now. They hadn't wanted to tell me until they knew they would be able to follow through. They have both been sober ever since. So about two weeks ago my mom got a new job, and we're all hopeful that she will be able to keep this one. It's going to change her life tremendously. I'm hoping that they have clear minds again, and I can share with them about Jesus. Before when I tried, they wouldn't even remember what I said the next time I saw them."

"That's very exciting about your brother and your mom getting help. I wish more people would be willing to accept the help that's out there. We will keep praying for all of you. I think God will continue to work in your family." Cathy was happy for Val, knowing how heavily her family's drinking problem weighed on her heart.

"Thanks, Cathy. You know, I would love for them to meet Nikki and all of you sometime. I talk about you guys a lot. I think they would be open to it. What do you think?"

"I think that's a wonderful idea. We'll have you all over for dinner one night."

"Maybe next month, instead of my mom and brother coming to my house, we could come here. I'll talk to them about it."

"Sounds like a plan. How's everything going with your Bible-study group?" Cathy was proud of Val and Jill on how far they had come in their walk with the Lord. When they had told her they were going to be leaders of a small group, Cathy knew they would do an awesome job at leading others in their faith.

"I love it. Everyone is committed to doing their lesson and every week someone has dug a step further and comes with thought-provoking questions. It's fun to dig deeper into the Word."

"The Bible is so full of treasures that it takes a lifetime to discover them all. Anne's come far in her walk, hasn't she? It's been fun getting to know her. I'm glad she was able to come to the kids' last birthday party."

"She has become a great friend. She, Jill, and I are quite the threesome now. Oh, and she invited me to go with her family to stay on a houseboat for a week. I'm really looking forward to it. I haven't had a chance to meet them yet. I think it will be a lot of fun."

"Val, I'm so glad that you have great Christian friends now. I know that they have been a source of strength for you. I'll be looking forward to hearing about your adventure. I've always wanted to go on a houseboat; you'll have to tell me what you think." Val and Cathy talked awhile longer, but it was getting late, so they said their good-byes and Val headed home.

* * *

Seefas was watching over Nikki, who was sound asleep in her new bed. Nikki seemed to really love it and looked so peaceful lying there. "Lord, this little girl is a treasure that the world is slow to recognize. Thank you for the people that she's been able to touch. I think about people like Amanda, who still sees Nikki and others like her as insignificant. Somehow, break through that façade and help them to discover the blessing of knowing these children. Thank you for using Nikki to teach me new and exciting things. Always in your service."

* * *

Cathy was worried about starting out the new school year. She couldn't believe how fast time had flown. Josh was going into first grade, which meant he would be at school all day, and Nikki was starting her second year of preschool with a new teacher.

She took Josh to school first and walked him in to get him all settled. "Mom, I'm fine. School's a lot of fun. I can't believe that I get to have hot lunch. All my friends are here; I'm fine." Cathy appreciated that Josh loved school; it really made it easier when she had to spend so much of her time at Nikki's school. This year, however, she got to be a teacher's assistant in Josh's class once a week and was looking forward to that.

"Well, Buster. I'll be excited to hear about your day when I pick you up. Have a fantastic time, Sweetie." At that, Nikki and Cathy set off for Nikki's school.

When they arrived, Nikki was very animated, giggling and squealing. "Wow, sweet girl, you are excited to start school, aren't you?" Cathy got more giggles in response. As they got out of the car, the helpers from last year greeted them, plus a few new faces.

"Cathy, Nikki looks great. I think she's grown over the summer." It was Joanne, one of the helpers from the year before. Several standing there said she seemed excited to be there and that they couldn't believe how tiny and sweet she was. Nikki just giggled in response and had them all laughing. She had already won hearts.

Joanne introduced Cathy to some of the new people, and they all filed into the classroom. Cathy asked if she could stay that first day, and no one had any objections. After a few minutes Cathy still wasn't quite sure who the teacher was; she whispered to Joanne, who laughed and introduced her to Gary. Cathy was surprised. She wasn't expecting a young, laid-back male teacher. Most workers at the school were women.

Gary grabbed a guitar and said that it was circle time. All the helpers worked to get the kids gathered. One of them rolled Nikki's stroller to the circle. Cathy was excited because music was one of Nikki's favorite things. Gary started singing fun songs that had motions to them, and the kids were having a magnificent time.

After circle time when the kids went to their different therapies, Cathy spent a little time catching Gary up on Nikki. "Have you ever considered getting a wheelchair for Nikki?" Gary asked.

"We've discussed it, but since she's still so little I didn't know if it would be beneficial for her to get one." Cathy had struggled with the idea; she didn't want people labeling and feeling sorry for Nikki. But she and Gene had talked about it and were open.

"She would benefit greatly from one. You can get chairs that go in so many positions now. She would probably be more comfortable in one than the stroller. If you want, I can give you a number for people who do this sort of thing."

"Sure. I'll take the information and discuss it with my husband." The school day went by quickly. Nikki's class was only a couple of hours each day. They went to Grant and May's to pick up Zack and then home for naps. Soon it was time to pick up Josh. "How was your first day of all-day school?" Josh was beaming, so Cathy figured she already knew the answer to that question.

"It was awesome, Mom. Do you know you get three recesses in first grade?" Leave it to a boy to mention recess first.

"That's great. Did you meet any of the new kids today?" Josh had been nervous about the new kids coming in. But once he knew people he was great and outgoing.

"Actually, Mom, there's a new boy, Kyle. We hit it off right away. We looked for snakes the whole recess. He said that he wants to have me over to his house to go snake hunting." Cathy was proud that he was able to reach out of his comfort zone and befriend someone on the first day.

* * *

That night at dinner, Josh talked nonstop about his first day of school. Next, Zack had a turn telling Gene about his exciting adventures with Papa, then it was Cathy's turn to fill him in on Nikki's day. "I was really nervous about her new teacher, but he's great. I like him already. He won me over with his guitar playing and singing. You know that's right up Nikki's alley. He also gave me some information about possibly getting a wheelchair for Nikki. What do you think?"

"I think that it's a great idea. The question is what do you think? When we've talked about it before, you've been hesitant."

"I wasn't sure at first, but I've been thinking about it all day, and I think it's a good idea. If Nikki will be more comfortable and it will help her gain more upper body control, who am I to stand in her way. We will deal with the looks and the questions from people feeling sorry for us. It's part of our lives, and we know that she brings us nothing but joy."

Gene was thankful to hear Cathy's words; he always knew that he had to let her come to places like this without him pushing. He learned a long time ago that God is the only one who can change hearts. "Well, all right. Why don't you call the wheelchair vendor tomorrow, and we'll get the ball moving on this?"

Cathy looked at her daughter, who seemed to be following right along in their conversation. "So what do you think about all this?" Nikki cooed and giggled in response.

"I think she's trying to tell us that we're making the right decision." Gene smiled at his little girl.

* * *

That night when everything was quiet in the house, Seefas and Nikki were catching up on the day. Nikki was rolling around on her bed, looking all around. "I love my bed; it's like a whole new view compared to the crib. It's so comfortable; I love the colors and my little house. Did you see that Josh filled my house with all my Precious Moments dolls?"

"It looks great. Your brothers did a great job decorating your bed for you." Seefas wanted to ask Nikki about her day at school, but the timing hadn't been right. "Today was a big day for you, starting a new school year, with a new teacher. What did you think about all that?"

"I loved my teacher. Can you believe he plays the guitar and sings all those silly songs? I loved it. I can't wait to go back tomorrow and sing more songs." Nikki had always enjoyed music; she and Seefas would often sing together at night.

"What do you think about the idea of getting a wheelchair?"

"I'm excited about it. Some kids at school have them, and I wondered what it would be like to have one of my own. I wonder if Mom will be able to get an appointment set up soon."

"I hope so. We'll have to wait and see. You're getting to be such a big girl. I love seeing you get excited about the little things in life. You should close your eyes now and try to sleep."

Nikki threw her arms around Seefas's broad shoulders. "I love you, Seefas. Goodnight."

"Goodnight, sweet girl. I love you too."

CHAPTER TWENTY-EIGHT

"Are you sure this evening is a good idea? Cathy, I don't want us to come across as matchmakers and seem pushy." Cathy had invited Jim, Emily, and Sophie to come over that night for dinner and to play some games.

"Gene, we're having some friends over that's all."

Gene knew his wife better than that. "Cathy, you have been trying to push those two together since we met Jim and Emily. I'm not sure Jim wants his relationship to go any further with Sophie; that is, unless Sophie takes the step in inviting Jesus to be part of her life."

"I know. They just really seem to hit it off, and Jim could play a big part in Sophie finally coming to that place. I just don't think it hurts for their friendship to become stronger, and who knows what could happen down the road." Cathy really meant that. She understood Gene's point about Sophie needing a relationship with Jesus before she could build a romantic relationship with Jim. But she truly felt that Jim was having an impact on Sophie and didn't see anything wrong with providing the atmosphere for their friendship to grow.

* * *

Everyone was enjoying their dinner when Cathy realized she hadn't asked Jim lately if Phil had been able to get through to his daughter Amanda. Phil felt that it was his fault that Amanda was so negative about kids like Nikki because, before Jim led him to the Lord, Phil had been the exact same way. "Have you talked to Phil lately about how things are going with Amanda?"

"Yes, it's not going too great. Amanda has become bitter at her dad and says he's been brainwashed. In fact, Emily's having a very hard time at school because Amanda blames her for her dad's change."

"I'm sorry to hear that. What's going on at school, Emily?"

"At first it wasn't too bad. Amanda would come up to me and ask what my dad did to her dad; she would say it in a kind of joking way. Then she started getting mad at me and would call me names. Now, she is threatening to beat me up. Dad has to come pick me up every day from school so that I don't have to worry about Amanda."

"Emily, I'm so sorry you have to endure that." As Cathy said this, Nikki put out a hand and touched Emily.

Emily almost started to cry. "You understand don't you, Nikki? Amanda was also mean to you. I'm sorry for the words she said to you."

Nikki responded with her little coos. It was very touching to watch. Nikki obviously understood Emily's words. Cathy noticed that even Sophie seemed touched by the interaction going on between the two girls.

"From what Phil is telling me, I think Amanda is just very confused and not sure what to do with the feelings she's experiencing. He feels bad that she's taking this all out on Emily. Phil's working on trying to control the situation. I think we all need to continue to pray for them."

Jim wasn't sure how to help. He hated that his little girl was going through this, and he was trying to shield her from getting hurt. Fortunately, both he and Emily understood the situation and were trying to figure out the best course of action.

"We have been praying for all of you in this situation, and we won't stop." Cathy decided to change the mood a bit. "Anyone up for some desert?"

"Are you sure you don't want any help?" Sophie asked. She felt a little strange leaving Gene and Cathy to do all the work.

"We've got it covered. Do you guys mind taking the kids in with you? I'm sure they will entertain you until we're done." Cathy was wondering if Sophie would take Nikki or wait for Jim to make that move.

"Sure. We can do that." Sophie stood up and paused to see if Jim would take Nikki, but Jim was preoccupied with something the boys were showing him. Sophie just stood there, took a deep breath, and moved toward Nikki. Cathy was watching discreetly from the kitchen.

"Well, Nikki. Would you like me to take you to the living room?" Sophie said this so quietly that Cathy almost started to laugh.

Nikki started giggling and cooing, and Sophie couldn't help but smile. "I'll take that as a yes." She picked up Nikki in her car seat and transported her to the living room. Cathy almost started to cry. This was the first time since Sophie found out about Nikki's disorder that she picked Nikki up.

In the living room, everyone, Sophie included, was laughing while watching Nikki. Josh had gotten them making animal sounds, one of the kids' favorite games, and Nikki was making the cutest noises and big belly laughs.

Josh saw his parents and ran over to them. "I think Nikki is making the sheep sound. Remember, it's her favorite one? But listen, it really sounds like a sheep. Do it again, Nikki." At that Nikki made that cute sound again. If you listened closely, it did sound like a sheep.

"My sweet girl, are you telling us what a sheep says?" Cathy leaned down and gave her daughter a kiss. In response, Nikki belted out a very loud squeal and everyone laughed some more.

Her proud daddy said, "I'm pretty sure that was a yes." The rest of the night went much the same way. While playing board games, everyone seemed to have the giggles. It didn't matter what it was, it would strike one person funny, and the laughter was contagious.

* * *

"Seefas I don't remember ever having so much fun. I hope we have more nights like this one."

"I could tell you were enjoying yourself, and I think you got yourself wound up. I can't believe you're still awake," Seefas said with a twinkle in his eye. "What was your favorite part?"

"Hands down, it was when Sophie carried me to the living room. I think that is the first time she has ever carried me at all, even in my car seat. Maybe next time she will hold me without my seat."

"That would be great. I think her wall around you is starting to come down. How could it not? You are so easy to love." Seefas had a hard time understanding why it was taking Sophie so long to accept Nikki. With most people, Nikki was a little magnet they are drawn to. But Sophie had kept her distance for so long, Seefas had wondered if she would ever come around.

"Seefas, will you pray with me tonight? I feel like there is so much to be thankful for but so many needs too. We should continue to pray that Sophie will one day come to know Jesus as her personal Savior, and we need to pray for Amanda and Emily. This whole thing is hard on Emily, but I know that she really cares about Amanda and wants to help her. Could we pray and maybe sing a little before I go to sleep?"

Seefas and Nikki bowed their heads before the Lord and lifted up their prayers and songs to Him. Seefas treasured this time with Nikki more than anything else. After Nikki fell asleep, Seefas kept watch over her and continued to pray. He didn't know what exactly, but he felt like hard times were ahead.

* * *

"Cathy, it's Mom. Dad fell getting out of the hot tub, and I can't help him up. I think he has broken something. Can you come over and help?" Cathy wasn't quite registering the words. Her mom seemed way too calm to match the words she was saying.

"Um, Gene just called a few minutes ago. He should be driving by your place about now. I'll call him and have him stop by to help. Mom, I think you should probably call 911."

"Okay, thanks, Sweetheart; I will do that."

Cathy got off the phone and called Gene right away. He said that he was only one minute from there and would be glad to stop.

* * *

When Gene got to the Saterlees', he found May sitting on her bed talking to Grant through the screen of a sliding glass door. Gene said hello to May and headed out to where Grant was on the ground. Grant seemed very out of it, and Gene knew that he probably shouldn't try to move him on his own. "The ambulance should be here any time; just hang in there."

Grant looked up at Gene and gave him a brave smile. "I'm a Marine; I've been through worse." Grant was a retired major from the Marine Corps and was tough. He'd been told a few times in his life that he probably wouldn't make it, but he was a fighter and always proved his doctors wrong.

May came through the door with the medics right behind her. They took over from there and got Grant loaded on a stretcher. The medics said they'd be taking him to Mount Hood Medical Center, and May and Gene could meet him there.

Gene knew that Cathy would want to be with her dad, so Gene drove May to his house. Gene went in to give Cathy an update, and she was in the car within minutes.

"How are you holding up, Mom?"

"I know your dad's a fighter. I just felt so helpless today, like I should have done more to help Dad."

"Mom, Gene said that *he* wouldn't have been able to lift Dad; there is no way that you could have done that. It's not your fault. The best thing that we can do right now is go and be with him. He'll be all right. God's got His hand on him."

At the hospital, they had given him something for the pain, so he was sleeping.

"Are you his family? I'm Doctor Graham." May and Cathy turned around to see a tall, young-looking doctor. Later May commented that he must have been at least six foot seven.

"Yes, I'm his wife, and this is our daughter, Cathy. Do you know if he broke anything?"

"Unfortunately, your husband has broken his hip, and it will require surgery. He will need to stay here overnight. My recommendation is that you contact Doctor Givens. He is an excellent surgeon and does his surgeries over at Portland Providence. If you would like, I could put a call in to him right now and see if he would be available to come over and talk with you."

"That would be great. Thanks, Doctor Graham." May was a tad overwhelmed with all the information. Everything seemed like a blur, from this morning to this moment. She and Grant had gone into the hot tub together. When she got out, he said he was staying in a few minutes longer, and now they were here.

"Have you eaten anything today? Do you need me to get you anything?" Cathy knew her mom didn't do well if she went too long without eating.

"I ate right before your dad fell. That's what I did when I got out of the hot tub. What about you? I'm fine staying here if you want to go home for a while."

"I think I might do that. I'll grab something to eat, and I know the kids will want to come visit Dad. If it's all right, we will be by later this afternoon. Are you sure I can't get you anything before I go?"

"I'm fine. You go. I'll see you in a little while." Cathy leaned over to kiss her mom.

"I love you, tell Dad when he wakes up that I love him and I'm praying."

* * *

When they got to the hospital the boys were very anxious to see their Papa and make sure he was okay. Cathy was touched that her kids had very caring hearts. "I'm anxious to see him too, but you need to remember this is a hospital. You can't be running down the halls and being loud."

"We know, Mom." Josh said this in such a grown-up way that it made Cathy and Gene both smile. "We just want to make sure that Papa is okay."

Nikki squealed in response, and Cathy smiled. "I know you want to make sure Papa's okay too." When they got to the room, a man was talking with Grant and May. Cathy and Gene hesitated to go in, but Grant saw them and motioned them in.

"How are my wonderful grandkids doing? Come give your ole Papa a hug." The man in the room was Doctor Givens, the surgeon. Gene took the kids down to the waiting room until the doctor was done talking with them.

"I was just telling the doctor of my medical history and the fact that I've had prostate cancer for seventeen years and have outlived a lot of my doctors." Grant was a stubborn man and a fighter. Whenever a doctor told him he didn't have long to live, Grant wouldn't tell the family because he didn't believe it.

"The cancer worries me regarding surgery. We're going to run tests and make sure it's safe to do." The doctor seemed knowledgeable, but Cathy wasn't impressed with his bedside manner.

"I understand Doctor Givens, but I'm sure I'll be fine to do surgery. Whatever tests you need to run, let's do it so we can get this over with." Cathy loved her dad's determination. She knew if anyone could survive this, it was him.

After the doctor left, Grant wanted his grandkids back in the room with him. He introduced them to everyone who passed by the room. One nurse came in, and Grant said that she had been very helpful to him and Granda, so he wanted to make sure she met the kids, especially Nikki.

"And this is my special granddaughter, Nik-nak patty-whack." At that Nikki gave a loud squeal and everyone laughed. Nikki loved when Papa called her that. It was his special name for her.

* * *

That night when everyone was in bed Nikki and Seefas had their special time together. "Seefas, I'm worried about Papa. Do you think he's going to be okay?"

"I don't know, but Jesus does. Should we pray and ask him to watch over Papa?"

"Oh, yes, yes. Let's do that. I know He is with my Papa right now and loves him even more than I do." Seefas and Nikki bowed their heads and went before the throne room of Heaven, interceding for Nikki's Papa.

CHAPTER TWENTY-NINE

"Hey, Cathy. The boys and I are running to the store to pick up a few things, and Val just pulled up." The boys loved going to the store with their dad. They always hoped that he would buy something for them, which he usually did.

Gene let Val in as they were heading out the door. "Hey, Val. Great to see you, we'll be back shortly. Cathy's in the living room with Nikki."

"Thanks, Gene. Hey, boys. See you when you get back." Both the boys gave Val giant hugs.

"Hi," Cathy greeted Val as she walked into the living room. "You know, you really didn't need to come early and help. I'm happy to have you and your family here tonight. I'm excited to meet your mom and brother."

"I know. Truthfully I just wanted to give you an update on my life before the gang was all here."

Cathy could tell that Val was dying to tell her something. "All right. What's going on? Spill the beans."

Val walked over and picked up Nikki, who smiled at her. "Hey, sunshine girl. Good to see you too. Well, remember when I told you I was going to go on vacation with Anne and her family?"

"Yes. I have been wondering how that all went. I can tell by the smile on your face that it was spectacular."

"I guess you could say that." Val was grinning from ear to ear.

Cathy laughed. "All right already. Tell me."

"Okay. Anne comes from a big family, like yours. There are six kids, and she is the youngest, at least, one *of* the youngest. She has a twin brother and Anne is a full five minutes younger than him. Their older brothers and sister are all married. So there are four boys and two girls. Anyway, as I said Anne has a twin brother named Adam, and he is very cute."

Cathy started to laugh, which made Nikki laugh. Val held Nikki up and gave her a kiss. "I knew there had to be a boy involved—not sure if anything else puts a smile on a girl's face quite the same way."

"Funny. Well, we hit it off. We have a lot of the same likes, and he is so easy to talk to. Anne, Adam, and I spent the whole time together with a string of nieces and nephews following closely behind. By the end of the trip they were calling me Aunt Val."

"So have you seen him since?" Cathy was so happy for Val. She loved her like a sister and wanted her to be happy.

"Tons. We also talk on the phone almost every night. I guess you could say that Adam is now my boyfriend." Val blushed.

"What does Anne think about all this?"

"She's thrilled. She keeps saying she should have thought of the two of us way before the trip. She says we're perfect together."

"We're home." Josh was yelling as he and Zack ran into the living room. "Did we miss all the fun? Why is everyone smiling? Even Nikki looks happy." This made Cathy and Val laugh, and Val blushed even more.

"Do you remember that Val's mom and brother are coming over?"

"Oh, yeah. Can't wait to meet them. When are they coming?" Josh loved having visitors, and Zack was bouncing around excitedly.

"Not too much longer." The boys ran off to play.

Gene said that he would finish up last minute details for dinner. "How's it going with your mom and brother? Has your mom been able to keep her job? Are they still sober?"

"Cathy, it's been an amazing month. They have both stayed sober, and mom's job is great. My mom and I talk on the phone almost every night. I've been able to share the whole adventure with Adam with her. I feel like I have my mom back. My brother is also doing fantastic. He got a new job that he absolutely loves. The difference in the two of them is nothing short of a miracle. They have also been open to hearing about Jesus. They're not there yet, but they're close. They are very excited to meet Nikki and all of you." The doorbell rang. "Mom, I think they're here."

Both the boys ran to the door.

"Come in. I'm Josh."

"I'm Zack. Nikki's my sister, but she can't tell you her name." Cathy smiled at her boys.

"I'm Cathy and this is my husband, Gene, and I guess you've met the rest of my family. We are so glad you could come."

Val knew her mom and brother were shy, so she took over the introductions. "This is my mom, Tanya, and my brother, Paul." Val gave her mom a hug. "I'm so glad that you guys wanted to meet the Ellertons. They have changed my life."

"Thank you for all you have done for my daughter. I know that her life is better for meeting you all. I have especially been excited to meet Nikki." At that Tanya walked over to Nikki sitting in her car seat. "Hi, Nikki. My name is Tanya. You are a special little girl."

Nikki looked up into Tanya's eyes and smiled. She even threw in one of her special squeals and everyone laughed.

"I think we are ready to eat," Gene said as he led everyone into the dining room.

"Are you a cook?" Tanya asked with a puzzled look on her face.

"I like to do it when I have the time."

"Wow. I haven't met too many men who like to cook. Cathy, you're a lucky lady."

"I think so. He's really good at it too."

"So, Val, does your Adam like to cook?" Tanya looked at her daughter and Val blushed.

"I'm not sure. I guess maybe I'll ask him next time we're together."

Dinner went great. Cathy liked Val's mom, but her brother hadn't done much talking, so it was hard to get to know him.

"Hey, Gene, I'll clean up dinner," Cathy said. "You go rest. Thanks for making dinner."

"My pleasure. Hey, Paul, you like football? Want to go in the office and see if the Seahawks are winning?"

"Sounds good to me."

"Seahawks!" Josh and Zack yelled together.

"We watch too?" Zacky looked up at his dad with a smile on his face.

"You bet. We'll let the ladies do some bonding." The guys disappeared into the other room.

"Cathy, I'll help you clean up the dishes."

"Thanks, Val. Tanya, if you wouldn't mind, could you take Nikki into the living room while we get things cleaned up?" At this, Nikki let out a squeal.

"Sounds like Nikki wouldn't approve if I said no." Tanya picked Nikki up out of her high chair and went into the living room.

"Do you think it was okay to ask your mom to do that?" Cathy hadn't thought it through before asking; not everyone was comfortable around Nikki.

"I don't think she minded at all. In fact, I think she was probably excited to get to spend some one-on-one time with Nikki. I talk about Nikki so much, Mom has felt like she knows her."

"I really like your mom, and she seems like she's really enjoying herself. However, your brother is quiet. Is he always like that?"

"Paul takes a while to get used to new people, but once he warms up you can't get him to stop talking."

Cathy laughed. "I hope we aren't too intimidating." At that very moment they heard hoots and hollers coming from the office where the guys were watching football.

"Sounds like he might already be warming up."

"Sounds like, probably thanks to the Seahawks." Cathy and Val both started to laugh.

"Well, everything looks good in here. Shall we go see how your mom and Nikki are faring?" Val agreed and, as they started toward the living room, they heard Nikki doing one of her sweet belly laughs. They stopped to peek around the corner to watch what was going on before going in.

Tanya had Nikki under her play gym and was tickling her and playing peek-a-boo with her. It was clear that they both were having a great time. Cathy and Val couldn't help themselves and started to laugh.

Tanya turned around when she heard them. "Cathy, your daughter is a precious jewel. No wonder Val was so drawn to her. If you ever need someone to watch her, I would love to. I'm sure a lot of people have offered, but I'd like to put in my request. I would love to spend more time with her. You can't help but feel joy when you're around her. Precious."

The rest of the night went well. By the end of the night Paul was talking pretty much nonstop to Gene in the other room.

They all agreed that they needed to do this again soon. Tanya had mentioned that next time, Adam should join them, and, of course, Val blushed.

* * *

"Nikki I believe you stole another heart tonight. Val's mom loved you." Seefas was proud to be Nikki's guardian angel. He loved seeing her impact so many people.

"I loved her too. I had so much fun with her when mom and Val were in the kitchen. Did you hear her say that she would like to watch me sometimes? I think that would be so much fun." Nikki's eyes were dancing with excitement.

"I sure did. It's interesting that Val's mom had a similar reaction to you as Val did in the beginning. They have a lot in common."

"I noticed that too. Val told Mom today that her mom and brother haven't asked Jesus to come live in their hearts yet. But she said they were close. We need to add them to our list of people to pray for."

"There are a lot of people all over the world who still need to receive him. Missionaries go out all the time to places that haven't been reached. But, you know, Nikki, you have quite the mission field of your own, and it keeps getting bigger. That's a wonderful thing."

Nikki smiled. "That's true; I haven't thought of it that way before. Seefas, can we pray right now for all those people on our list? I know that Jesus is going to do great things in their lives."

* * *

Cathy was thankful for the night before with Val and her family. Now they were in the waiting room while Grant was having his hip surgery, a procedure the doctor was only willing to go ahead with because of Grant's determination. Craig, Jenny, and the girls had driven up from Salem, and Gene, Cathy, and the kids were also there to support May.

"Gene, can you watch the boys? I'm going to take Nikki on a stroll around the hospital. Just sitting here is hard." Cathy was anxious about her dad's surgery. He was a stubborn man; when he wanted something, it was impossible to change his mind. Cathy was worried that his previous cancer might affect her dad's health going through a surgery like this. She knew all they could do was pray and support her parents through this time.

Cathy was so absorbed in her thoughts that she almost ran Nikki's stroller into a gray-haired woman passing by. "Wow. Sorry my mind was somewhere else."

"That's okay. What a cute little girl you have here. What's her name?"

"Her name is Nikki." Cathy was used to people asking about her daughter.

"You seemed lost in thought. Is everything okay?"

"It's just that my dad's having hip surgery right now. I'm just worried about him." Nikki looked up at her mom, smiled, and gave a little coo.

"Did you just see that?" The woman looked very intrigued. "Can your daughter talk?"

"No, she can't, but she has her own way of communicating. She's very content."

"I see that. When you said you were worried about your dad, it was like your daughter said he was going to be all right. I could even almost hear her say that. That's why I asked if she could talk. I couldn't tell if I heard something or not. I think she knows something we don't."

The woman was studying Nikki.

"I think she has a close relationship with Jesus. I believe she sees her angel. There are too many times that she is intently looking at something that I can't see and carrying on like she would if she was looking at me."

"Really?" The woman continued to look at Nikki. Cathy wasn't sure what to say but sensed the woman's interest and waited. After a few minutes the woman started to say something but then stopped.

"What is it?" Cathy was confused by the woman's reaction.

"This is going to sound bizarre to you, especially if you're a Christian. I have been a psychic for twenty plus years, and I have always prided myself in being able to read people. But in that simple gesture of your daughter's, she seemed to have more understanding about life than I've ever had. Does that sound strange? I can't really explain what I felt."

Cathy just started to pray, she didn't fully understand what the woman witnessed with Nikki, and she felt at a loss for words. Then Nikki reached her arm out as if reaching for the woman's hand. The woman reached down, took Nikki's hand, and started to cry. Cathy teared up witnessing this nonverbal communication between Nikki and this random woman they almost ran into.

"Thank you, Nikki. I understand. Somehow, I understand." The woman looked at Cathy. "I have dabbled in the darker things of the world, like witchcraft. I loved the power that it gave me. I really believe that my ability as a psychic was a direct result of that. Right now, your daughter has shown me that it was of the devil; it didn't have any light to it at all. The peace that I see in your little girl, the love that she just extended me, I have never seen in my entire life. She showed me Jesus. She really did. My life will never be the same." She reached down and took hold of Nikki's hand. "You are a very special girl. Thank you." Nikki cooed, and then the woman was gone.

Cathy just stood there in shock, wondering what just happened. She looked at Nikki and saw tears of joy in her eyes. "Jesus knew what He was doing when He made you, my dear daughter. You are a blessing. I love you. Thank you, Jesus." Cathy leaned down and kissed Nikki on the cheek. "What do you say we walk back and see if there's been any word on Papa?" Nikki giggled and they headed back toward the waiting room.

When they got back to the waiting room, Cathy told everyone what had just happened, and they all sat there stunned for a few minutes. Then May spoke up. "Dad will be glad to know his surgery wasn't for nothing."

"Mrs. Saterlee?" May looked up to see Doctor Givens standing there. "Everything went great. We just wheeled him down to the recovery room. When he wakes up you guys can take turns going in to see him."

May smiled. "Thank you, Doctor." Then she turned toward her family. "And thank you, Jesus."

* * *

"Do you know what that was all about at the hospital with that woman?" Seefas witnessed the whole thing but could not figure out what the woman had experienced.

"I'm not sure, I think she saw Jesus. I really didn't do anything. I just reached my hand out to her, and Jesus took over. It was kind of cool to watch. I think Jesus spoke to her heart and changed her right there. It's hard to understand the way Jesus transforms lives sometimes. Seefas, I can't wait to stand before Jesus in Heaven. Do you miss that?"

"Miss Nikki, when I'm not there my heart longs to be, but I know that my job right now is to be here with you. The time is coming when I will need to go and give an account before the Lord for what I've been doing here."

"Really? Will you come back?" Nikki seemed a little worried.

"Yes. Another angel will come for just a short time to care for you while I'm gone, then I will be back."

"Good. I will miss you. But I'm happy that you will get to be home again, even if it is for a short time. Seefas, I don't think there is a better angel than you."

CHAPTER THIRTY

"Hi, Nikki. Did you have a good weekend?" Gary met Nikki and Cathy at the door as they were going into the classroom. "Hey, Cathy, we have a surprise for you guys. They dropped off Nikki's wheelchair this morning. They said if there's any problem with it you can take it into their office, and they'll adjust it for you." After talking about the wheelchair months earlier, Gene and Cathy had gone into a wheelchair manufacturer and ordered one. They took measurements for Nikki, and Cathy was able to pick out the color: hot pink.

Nikki seemed to know exactly what Gary had said, for she squealed with delight. Cathy laughed. "I guess my daughter is excited about that. I'd love to see it and see what Nikki thinks about it."

Gary went into the other room and came back pushing a hot pink wheelchair. Cathy took Nikki out of her stroller and set her in the wheelchair. Nikki giggled and squealed, then she immediately crossed her legs like a little lady. Nikki loved to do this. Cathy looked at Nikki and smiled. The wheelchair made Nikki seem older. She seemed very comfortable in it.

"Do you like it, Nikki?" Nikki looked at her mom and giggled. Everyone laughed. "I guess we won't be needing her stroller any longer. Gary, I'm not going to be able to stay today."

"That's fine. I think Nikki will love school today. We go to music class. I think that is her favorite thing to do here."

Time flew by and before Cathy knew it, she'd gotten everything done, and it was time to go pick up Nikki and Zack. She walked into Nikki's class and loved seeing her sitting up in the wheelchair. Nikki parked in front of a computer with a huge mouse. Cathy looked at Joanne, one of Nikki's helpers. "Is she actually doing something on the computer? She looks so grown up sitting there."

Joanne laughed. "She sure is. The mouse is extremely sensitive, and she barely has to even bump it, and it changes what's on the computer. It's a program with bright lights and music. She seems to really like it."

Cathy walked over to Nikki, leaned down and gave her a kiss. "Hey, big girl, are you having fun on the computer?" Nikki looked up at her mom and giggled.

"Did Joanne tell you about music class today?" Cathy turned around and saw Gary walking up.

"What happened? Did Nikki behave herself?"

"Always," Gary said. "Nikki stayed behind for a few minutes to finish eating her lunch. When they got there with the other kids, the music teacher was looking around and asked, 'Where is my favorite pupil?' They didn't know who he was talking about at first, and he said, 'Where's Nikki? I don't have another student who enjoys my class as much as she does. I need my star pupil in here.' They laughed and said she'd be there in a few minutes. Sure enough, when Nikki got there, she shined. She is a real fan of music."

Cathy was touched and nodded. "She has always loved music."

"It's fun; when I play the guitar and sing for the kids, I love watching Nikki. She's stolen hearts around here."

* * *

"What do you think about your new wheelchair? I love the color; it suits you." Seefas loved to see Nikki reach new milestones.

"I love it. It gives me a whole new perspective than always being down low in the stroller. And did you see, Seefas, I got to play on a computer? I see Josh do that all the time at home. I never thought I would be able to do it."

"I did see that. It seemed like you had tons of fun at school today."

"I did. Music class day is my favorite. My music teacher is funny, and he has a round tummy like Santa Claus and kind of does a big ole belly laugh. I like him." Nikki was giggling.

"I think it's mutual. I heard Gary tell your mom that you are the music teacher's favorite." This made Nikki giggle more and the laughter was contagious. Pretty soon they were both laughing so hard they couldn't stop. After a while, Seefas forgot why they were laughing.

* * *

"Mommy, when Sophie gonna be here?" Zack loved getting his mom's full attention when his brother and sister were at school. He especially liked when visitors came over because he got all their attention too.

Cathy heard a car door close outside. "You know what, kiddo? I think she just got here. Do you want to go to the door and check with me?"

"Yay! Hurry mommy, race you to the door." Cathy cherished her time with Zack. Sometimes it felt like he was growing up faster than the other two had. She wished time would slow down. Cathy remembered her older sister saying, "Just wait until your kids start school, then time will cruise by." Cheryl was right; once Josh had started school, time flew way too fast.

Cathy opened the door for Sophie, and Zack attacked her legs. "Hey, look who it is. It's my most favorite Zack in the whole world!" Sophie picked Zack up and gave him a big hug then spun him around.

"Do it again, Sophie." Sophie spun him one more time while Zack giggled. Then she put him down, and he was off up the stairs yelling something about his favorite toy he wanted to show her.

"Josh and Nikki are at school?" Sophie sort of asked this nonchalantly as she sat down and looked through a couple magazines on the coffee table. Cathy noticed that Sophie threw in Nikki's name and not just Josh's.

"Yes, they are. I need to pick Nikki up in a few minutes."

"She has a new teacher this year, right?" Sophie continued to look through the magazine not wanting to make eye contact with Cathy.

"She does. I was worried about it at first, but I really like him. She has a male teacher who plays the guitar and sings to the kids. He's nice. He also got us in contact with a wheelchair manufacturer, and Nikki has a new wheelchair. It's bright pink. She really likes it." Cathy was so pleased that Sophie was asking about Nikki's school. This was a huge step. Could she be warming up to allow a place for Nikki in her heart?

"I'm glad. By the way I ran across an old school mate the other day. I haven't seen her in a couple of years, and I guess she's throwing a Valentine's party. She invited me to come and told me to bring a date." Sophie seemed a little hesitant to tell Cathy about it.

"Is it something you want to go to?"

"I would love to. I guess tons of people I went to high school with years ago are going to be there. It would be fun."

"I sense a hesitation. What's up?"

Sophie looked at Cathy like the answer was obvious. "The date part. I don't have a date. She specifically told me to bring a date. I guess that makes sense since it's a Valentine's party. Cathy what am I going to do?"

"Well, do you have anyone in mind?" Cathy immediately thought of Jim, but she didn't want to be presumptuous, and she didn't want Gene to accuse her of meddling again.

"The only person I could think of was Jim." Sophie looked embarrassed. "He's really the only guy I know well enough to ask. Do you think he would think it odd or be uncomfortable if I asked him?"

Cathy was thrilled but tried to respond with a cool head. "You guys are friends. I don't think he would feel uncomfortable at all. I think that Jim would be a great person to ask."

"Are you sure? I don't have to go to the party; it was just a thought." Sophie was backpedaling fast.

"Sophie, I think you should go. It would be lots of fun, and I think Jim would be honored that you felt comfortable enough to ask him."

"I'll think about it. Thanks, Cathy, for the feedback."

"Hey, it's already time to go get Nikki. Would you like to go with me and Zack?"

"Sure. Why not?" Sophie picked Zack up and gave him another twirl. "Would you like me to carry you to the car?"

"Zacky would love that!" Zack gave Sophie a hug.

* * *

"What did you think when you saw Sophie with your mom today?" Seefas himself was surprised to see Cathy drive up with Sophie.

"I thought that it was very cool. Sophie has never been to my school before and, knowing how she feels about special-needs kids, I was shocked. She actually came into the class with my mom." Nikki had been praying for so long that Sophie would accept her and love her like she did Josh and Zack. "I think she's starting to let me into her heart."

"It does appear that way. We need to keep praying for her."

"I know the most important thing is her loving Jesus, not me." Nikki started to giggle.

"What's so funny?" Seefas was sort of snickering himself.

"Did you see the look on Sophie's face when she walked into my classroom today?" Nikki was still giggling.

"Come to think of it, I did." Now Seefas started laughing a little harder.

"See looked like she just stepped into the land of Oz, like she just saw the wicked witch. It didn't last very long; her face softened after that, but I happened to catch it. It made me laugh too."

"I think it was seeing you laugh that softened Sophie up."

"Seefas, I'm glad she's coming around. I think she's going to find Jesus soon too. That's my prayer, and I won't stop praying until she does."

CHAPTER THIRTY-ONE

"It was nice of your parents to watch Zack for you while we go shopping." Cathy and Val were out shopping for Josh and Nikki's birthdays, which were just around the corner.

"Dad would keep the kids every day if he could."

"How is your dad doing after his surgery?"

"He can't get around nearly as well as he used to. He used to walk to our house all the time, and now it's a struggle just to get to the car." Cathy had been worried about her dad, even his general health seemed to be deteriorating a little. Having the kids come visit really perked him up.

"Sorry to hear that. I know that your dad is an on-the-go type of guy."

"The funny thing is, even though he can't move very well now, he still is. It drives him crazy to just be hanging out at home, so he's on the go as much as ever. In fact, he still goes to Multnomah Bible College to hang out with the military guys there."

"You're kidding? That's great." Val had always admired Cathy's father, so much so that she even called him Dad.

"So how's everything with you? I want updates on everyone."

"Well, where should I start?" Val said, blushing.

Cathy laughed. "With your love life, of course."

Val turned even redder. "Okay. The more I get to know Adam, the crazier I am about him. It's funny; he's anxious to meet Nikki. He says she sounds like an angel."

"Bring him over. I'm dying to meet him myself."

"Unfortunately, he has to go out of town for a while on business. I told him as soon as he gets back we'll come visit you guys." Val looked disappointed.

"Does he go out of town often?"

"Yes, but he says now he has someone to look forward to getting home to see." Val smiled.

"That is very sweet. Oh, bummer. He's going to miss the kid's birthday party." Cathy was thinking that would have been a great opportunity to meet him.

"I know. He said he'll catch their next one."

"He should come to Zack's. It will be sooner than next year's party."

"Thanks. I'll invite him. Hey, look at these plates; they're perfect for the kids. They have animals all over them."

"Yep. Animals, of course, is the birthday theme. I think Nikki loves them as much as the boys." Cathy laughed thinking about her kids playing the animal game. "How're your mom and brother doing?"

"Fantastic! Mom can't stop talking about you letting her watch Nikki the other night. She said she can't remember having so much fun. She took her everywhere with her. She said everywhere she went people came up and asked about Nikki. Well, I guess you're used to that; I've seen it firsthand."

Cathy laughed. "I'm glad she had fun. I told her she could do it again soon."

"Last week, Mom called and asked me to come over because she really needed to talk with me. I got worried because she said that it was very important."

Cathy looked concerned. "Was she okay?"

"Better than okay. She said she was ready to ask Jesus to come into her life and be her Lord. She was glowing. I've never seen her more excited than I did that night." Val looked very happy and relaxed. For the first time she could truly rest, now that her mom belonged to Jesus.

"Val, that's wonderful. I can't wait to tell Nikki. I think Nikki is a little prayer warrior. I don't know how I know; I just think she is."

Val laughed. "I think you're right. You'll never believe what happened next. My brother called me a couple days later and told me Mom had him over for dinner because she really needed to talk to him. Mom led Paul to the Lord." Val could hardly contain her excitement. "Can you believe that?"

Cathy was starting to get as excited as Val. "How awesome that your mom was the one to lead your brother to the Lord."

Val still had news she was having a hard time keeping it in. "There's more, if you can believe it. I also had the extraordinary opportunity to lead one of my coworkers to the Lord. Her name is Sarah, and I've been praying for her for a long time. Now she wants to come to Jill's and my Bible study."

Cathy was blown away by how far Val had come in her walk with God. "God's working through you, girl," Cathy said as she gave her a hug. "Hey, I think we have everything we need for the party. Do you have time to go with me to pick Nikki up from school?"

Joanne greeted Cathy and Val as they entered the classroom. "Gary was gone today, so Nikki had a substitute. She wasn't thrilled about having to drive all the way to Gresham from Beaverton this morning, so when she got here she was a little on the cranky side. But, lo and behold, she met your daughter, and, long story short, Nikki melted her heart. She said she would drive to Gresham anytime."

Cathy looked down at her daughter and kissed her forehead. "You were at it again, eh Sister?" Cathy, Val, and Joanne all laughed as Nikki let out a squeal.

* * *

"Seefas, Mom and Val told me all about Val's incredible week. I'm so excited that Tanya and Paul both came to Jesus. And then another one of Val's friends. Can you believe all three of them gave their hearts to Jesus this week?"

"That's just the people you know; there are lots more in the world who did the same thing. There was a lot of rejoicing in Heaven this week." Seefas looked Heavenward longingly.

"Oh, Seefas. I can't wait to be able to witness the party that takes place there one day."

"It is definitely something to behold."

"You miss it don't you?"

"I do, but I love being here with you. This is the assignment that Jesus gave me, and it brings me great joy."

"One day we'll be able to walk together in Heaven, won't we?" Nikki was getting very animated. "Will you show me all the beautiful things?"

"You bet, Sunshine!"

Nikki became serious. "Seefas?"

"Yes?"

"Our true home is with Jesus, isn't it?" Nikki said this with a big yawn.

"Oh, yes. This time here is only temporary. You will spend eternity with the Lord. He is preparing a place special for you.

Now, close your eyes, Nikki, and get some sleep." Seefas sang to Nikki until she drifted off to sleep.

* * *

"I can't believe another year has gone by already. It's crazy how time flies. Josh is now seven, and Nikki will be five tomorrow. Zack is going to be three. Honey, please slow down the time for me." Cathy sighed at Gene.

"I know; time is going by fast. But, you know, there are good things about every stage of life. We just need to enjoy each of our kids' stages to the fullest. Starting with enjoying this huge birthday party we are having in about an hour." The Ellertons had decided to throw the party at the park this year because there were so many people on the birthday list.

Josh and Zack came running down the stairs, yelling at the same time, "Is it time to go yet? We want to go now."

Gene laughed at his boys' enthusiasm. "We'll leave in about half an hour. Clean up the toys you were playing with and start getting ready to go."

"All right. Let's go Zack. Maybe Dad will let us leave early."

Cathy laughed and Nikki squealed. "I think even our daughter is excited to go. What do you say, Dad, could we get there early?" Cathy looked at Gene and batted her eyes in a playful gesture.

"Not you too. All right, that's four in favor of early departure. I guess I can't say no to that."

* * *

Soon the party was in full swing, and everyone was having a great time. Cathy looked around and couldn't believe how many people were there this year. She felt sorry for the other people in the park because they were taking over the whole area. Cathy felt blessed to have such wonderful people surrounding them with love. God had used Nikki in such amazing ways, sometimes it was overwhelming.

Cathy walked up to Gene and gave him a hug. "Great party, Mr. Ellerton."

"Why, thank you, Ma'am. I worked long and hard to throw this here party together, and I paid most of the guests to show up. Looks like they're having a good time." Gene laughed and kissed Cathy on the cheek.

Cathy smiled. "Well, you did good. Hey, did you happen to notice who drove here together?"

Gene laughed. "No, but I'm sure you're going to tell me."

Cathy playfully punched Gene in the arm. "You're right. I am. Jim and Sophie."

Gene got that worried look in his eyes again. "Sweetheart, I told you not to play matchmaker."

Cathy got a little defensive. "I didn't. I had no idea that they were driving here together. I wonder how the party was that they went to."

Gene looked confused. "What party?"

"Oh, I thought I told you. Sophie asked Jim to go to a friend's party with her, and I keep forgetting to ask her about it." Cathy noticed the look in Gene's eyes again. "I had nothing to do with it. Sophie asked me if I thought it would be weird for her to ask him, and I said no."

"Hey what are you two talking about?" Cathy turned to see Sophie walking up to them. Gene took that as his cue to mingle with some of the other guests.

"Hey, Sophie. Sorry I haven't gotten a chance to say hello to you yet."

"Not a problem. Wow, there's a lot of people here today."

"I know. Isn't it great?" Cathy wondered what Sophie thought. Although she had started to warm up to Nikki, she had been cynical about how Nikki could impact so many people.

"Yeah, it is." Sophie was looking around almost like she was soaking it all in. Cathy prayed that Sophie was also warming to the idea of having Jesus be a part of her life.

"Sophie, I keep meaning to ask you how the party went. Did you have a good time?"

Sophie's expression lit up, and Cathy couldn't help but smile. "It was really nice. I was nervous to call Jim at first, but when I finally did, he was very gracious. He didn't laugh at me or make me feel stupid. He just said that he was honored that I felt comfortable enough to ask him."

Cathy wasn't surprised. Jim was a nice man. "Tell me about the party."

"It was really nice. My friend went all out. She had the place decorated to the nines. There were tables set up in her house with lit candles on each one, like a restaurant. She had the dinner catered. The atmosphere was romantic. I guess I should have expected that since it was a Valentine's Day party. I was a little embarrassed; I kept apologizing to Jim. He just smiled and told me it was fine. Jim thought that my friend did a great job throwing the party. It was weird; the way everything was set up, it felt like Jim and I were on a date at a nice restaurant. We talked the whole time. I felt like I left that evening knowing Jim pretty well." Cathy let Sophie talk about the possibility blooming between her and Jim. "We also talked a lot about Jesus. I learned more about Him too. I'm still not sure what to think."

Cathy knew she needed to continue to pray for Sophie. She was sure that one day Sophie would come around. "I'm glad that you had fun. But speaking of parties, I think it's time to open gifts."

As if on cue, Josh ran up to his mom. "Mom, can we open presents now?"

"You bet, Buster. Why don't you start rounding people up?" Josh took off running, yelling for everyone to come watch him open the gifts.

Cathy walked over to where Val, Jill, and Anne were watching all the little ones. Val had Nikki on her lap swinging. Nikki was giggling. "Hey, which one of you wants to help Nikki open gifts this year?"

Lindsey walked over and tugged on Cathy's shirt. "Can I do it again?"

Cathy leaned down and gave Lindsey a hug. "Of course you can." Cathy was thrilled with how far Lindsey had come in a year. Lindsey was now in a regular classroom and doing very well. Gina still brought Lindsey over to play with Nikki about once a month.

After opening the gifts, everyone was eating cake, and Cathy made her way over to talk to Jim. She was anxious to know how things were going between Emily and Amanda.

"Hey, Cathy, great party. I look forward to coming to these birthday parties."

"Thanks, Jim. How are things going between Emily and Amanda? Any better?"

"A little. Amanda still seems bitter and doesn't talk to Emily, but she has stopped calling her names and threatening to beat her up. Now she just passes by Emily like she's invisible. It still hurts Emily, but at least it's better than it was."

"Sorry to hear that. We still pray for Amanda every night. How's Phil doing?"

"Same as you—still praying for his little girl."

* * *

"Did you enjoy yourself today, Miss Nikki?" Seefas had loved watching Nikki interact with all the people at the birthday party.

"I had so much fun. My favorite part was getting to be with all the people that mean so much to me. I love them a whole bunch. Being at the park made me think about Amanda. I heard Mommy telling Daddy on the way home that she's still not wanting anything to do with Emily or Jesus. That makes me sad. Seefas, can we spend time praying for Amanda and Sophie? It seems like maybe Sophie's getting closer to accepting Jesus in some ways, then in other ways it seems like she's still far off. They need our prayers."

Nikki was a prayer warrior, and Seefas could see the love of Jesus radiating from her. "I think that that is a very wonderful idea."

CHAPTER THIRTY-TWO

"Mom, are you sure Dad is up to having the kids come over today?"

Grant had been to the doctor the day before and found out that his cancer has spread into his bones. He had not been getting around that well since his hip surgery, and now this. Cathy was devastated. She didn't want to think about going through life without her dad, and it was so important to her that her kids would remember him.

"Sweetheart, you know having the kids here lifts Dad up. Besides, the doctor said that Dad could go on with his life and that they won't be starting chemo for another couple of weeks." May was doing all right with the news. She was, of course, very sad, but Grant was a fighter, and she wasn't giving up yet.

When they had walked into the Saterlees' house, Papa was sitting in his big rocking chair. "Oh, I'm so glad that my grandkids came to visit." He looked at Zack. "Your name is George, right?"

Zack giggled. "Papa!"

"Oh, I mean Sam." Papa loved teasing the little ones this way, and they loved being teased.

Zack giggled some more. "Papa, my name is Zacky." Zack climbed up on his lap and gave Papa a kiss. "You already know my name. You're just kiddin' me."

Papa laughed. "I know, you're right. Hey my sweet daughter, why don't you hand me my beautiful granddaughter, and she can sit here with me and Mr. Zack?"

Zack laughed some more while Cathy handed Nikki to her dad, and Nikki started to giggle. "I tell you Dad, my children love you."

"I love you most, Papa. I almost wish I could stay here instead of going to the birthday party."

"No sir, Josh. I love Papa most!" Zack climbed off Papa's lap and walked up to his brother trying to look bigger than he was.

Josh just laughed. "Come on Mom, we need to go or we'll be late."

"All right. You two be good for Papa and Granda." Cathy leaned over and gave Nikki and Zack kisses.

"Oh, they'll be good, or I'll lean them over my knee and give them a spankin'." Papa tried to look serious.

Zack laughed. "Papa, you always spank your hand, not us." At that Papa tried to grab Zack, and he ran off laughing.

"Now Dad, you behave yourself too." Cathy kissed her dad and walked out the door with Josh.

"Anyone want some cookies? They're fresh out of the oven." Granda walked in holding cookies that smelled yummy.

Both Zack and Papa together said, "I do, I do." Then Nikki squealed. Papa looked at her and laughed. "I think our Nikki might like her bottle. Could you warm that up for me, May, and I'll feed it to her?"

While Nikki drank her bottle, Granda took a nap and Zack put on a puppet show for Papa using all of Papa's puppets.

"Hey, Mister. Your name George?" Zacky tried to talk in a deep voice like Papa and say the kind of things Papa would say.

"No, my name's Fred. What's yours?" Papa loved his interaction with Zack and sitting there holding Nikki while she ate. What could be better than this?

"Um, it's Purple Tiger." Zack laughed. "I like to eat Freds." He laughed some more and started to go toward Papa.

"Oh, Nikki, help me! Purple Tiger is trying to eat me." Nikki looked up at Papa and smiled with her bottle in her mouth.

"Papa, Nikki can't help you, she's drinkin' her bottle." Zack looked so cute with a very matter of fact look on his face.

"Who's Papa? My name's Fred."

"Papa!" Zack went over and looked up at him. "Your name is really Papa. Nikki's done with her bottle. I'll take it to kitchen." Zack grabbed the bottle and looked at his sister. "Good girl, Nikki."

Papa laughed. "You are getting to be a very big boy, Zack."

"Papa, I almost three."

"I know. You're growing up so quickly."

"I be right back." Zack ran the bottle to the kitchen, then walked back into the living room. "How old are you, Papa?"

"Well, I'm twenty-eight." Grant had told all kids who asked him that he was twenty-eight, even his own kids. That was the hardest year for his children to turn because they would say, 'Now, I'm as old as dad.' The funny thing was all the little ones believed him, and though as they got older they didn't anymore, they still didn't know his real age.

Zack got a serious look on his face. "Wow, Papa. You're old." Papa just laughed and laughed. Then Nikki started giggling. She wasn't sure what was so funny, but just seeing Papa laugh made her laugh, and then Zack started to laugh as well.

"Hey, what's so funny in here?" Granda had woken up from her nap.

"I have very special grandkids." Grant loved to tease May by calling them *his* grandkids instead of *their* grandkids.

"Is that right? Well, I think my grandkids are very special too."

Zack and Nikki started to giggle. "We both yours, right Nikki?" Nikki giggled some more.

Eventually Papa fell asleep rocking both Nikki and Zack. When Cathy got there to pick up the little ones they were fast asleep in their Papa's arms. Cathy treasured this in her heart.

* * *

"Seefas, I love my Papa very much. I'm sad that he's sick." Nikki got tears in her eyes. "Mommy is very sad too."

"I know. He is a very wonderful Papa; you guys have a very special connection."

"Is Papa going to Heaven soon?"

"I don't know that. Only Jesus knows when that will be. Right now you just need to enjoy him and love him. Everyone who loves Jesus is going to Heaven one day."

"I know that, Seefas. I will just miss Papa very much when it's his time to go. But he'll be with Jesus and have no more pain, and I know that will be wonderful for him."

"And you know what?" Seefas said with a smile on his face.

Nikki looked at him and couldn't help but smile back. "What?"

"The best thing about being a Christian and loving someone that's a Christian is that when they die, you have the promise that you will see them again one day."

"That is the best thing ever. Our goodbyes are only temporary. But, I don't have to think about saying goodbye to Papa yet."

CHAPTER THIRTY-THREE

Cathy couldn't believe that Nikki was starting kindergarten. Time was going by so quickly. Josh was starting second grade, and Zack was going to start preschool this year. Driving to Nikki's new school, Cathy had mixed emotions; she was thrilled that Nikki was going to be going to school in Gresham, but she wouldn't be able to stay in the classroom like she did in preschool. Cathy knew that she needed to put Nikki into God's hands; He always had a way of making something good out of what Cathy viewed as a hard situation. And the truth was, Cathy had a hard time watching her kids grow up so fast.

As they rounded the corner to Nikki's new school, Nikki let out one of her sweet squeals. Cathy laughed. "I think someone's excited to be starting kindergarten today." Nikki cooed in response. "Well, it will be interesting meeting your new teacher and your new classmates. I'm sure you will win their hearts."

"Zacky excited to go to school and meet new teacher too." Zack's first day at preschool was also today, and Cathy was dropping him off after Nikki was settled.

"And, I know that you will win your teacher's heart too." Zack, at three already, had such a big heart and truly cared about people. He made friends wherever he went.

Cathy parked along the curb, loaded Nikki in her wheelchair, helped Zack out of his car seat, and they walked up the path to Nikki's class. It was on the side of the school and had a door going to the outside, which the kids would go through instead of having to go through the school building. When they entered the class, they were greeted by a delightful, silver-haired woman. She approached Nikki and bent down to her level. "Who is this adorable little girl?"

Cathy liked her already and felt immediately at ease. "This is Nikki."

"I should have known. I was told that she was just an itty bitty girl. Well, Nikki I hear that you win the hearts of all your teachers and helpers. I'm looking forward to working with you." Then she turned her attention to Zack. "And, who are you?"

"I'm Zacky, and I'm three. I get to go to school today too." Zack was very proud of himself and felt like such a big boy getting to go to school like his brother and sister.

"Well, it's very nice to meet you, Zack." Marie laughed and looked at Cathy. "I'm Marie. You must be Nikki's and Zack's mom."

"Yes. I'm Cathy. It's nice to meet you, Marie. I have to admit I was nervous bringing Nikki to a new school, with a new teacher, but you have made us feel very comfortable. Thank you."

"It's my pleasure. I really enjoy working with these young ones, and I know that I will enjoy getting to know you both." She reached down and tousled Zack's hair. "I wanted to let you know, although it is policy not to have parents stay during the school day, if ever you want to pop in for a visit and see what Nikki is working on, you are more than welcome."

Cathy felt a huge sigh of relief. "Oh, thank you so much. You don't know how much that means to me. I think that was my biggest worry in bringing her today." Cathy leaned down and kissed Nikki on the forehead. "Did you hear that, Sis? Mom can come visit you once in a while here at school?" Nikki started giggling.

* * *

When Cathy pulled into Zack's school, he was bouncing up and down in his car seat. Zack was going to a preschool at a church right behind the Ellertons' home. Cathy had told Zack that if it was nice outside, when his school day ended, she would walk to pick him up. Of course, Zack thought that was the best idea ever.

Walking into the school, Zack was running and pulling Cathy along by her hand. "All right, Zack man, I'm coming." When they got into his class, there were already a few kids in there coloring.

"Mom, I think we're late." Zack said this with a frown on his face and looked up at his mom.

Cathy tried not to smile. "I just think the other kids were early. I bet you'll get a chance to color too."

Just then a pretty woman with long blonde hair and bright blue eyes walked up to them. "That's right, you will have lots of opportunity to color. My name is Mrs. Walker. What's yours?"

"I'm Zack. I'm three years old, and I'm so excited to be here." Zack said this in the most grown up voice that he could muster.

Cathy could tell that he had already won his teacher over. "I'm Cathy. Zack has been counting down the days until he got to come to school." After a few more minutes of talking, Cathy kissed Zack and left him in capable hands.

Cathy felt very satisfied with how this school year was starting out; all her kids were at great schools with great teachers.

* * *

Cathy walked up to Nikki and bent down to kiss her on the cheek. "Looks like you had a good day, sweetheart. I'm glad that you enjoyed your first day back to school." Nikki cooed in response.

Marie walked over to where they were standing. "Your daughter stole the show today, Cathy." Marie told Cathy all about their adventure to the fifth-grade classrooms.

Cathy smiled. She loved hearing stories like that about her daughter. "Kids are drawn to Nikki. We get that kind of reaction wherever we go. My boys are always wondering why Nikki's so popular."

Marie laughed. "She is a likable little girl. She's already captured my heart."

As Cathy was walking Nikki out to the car, a little red-headed girl approached them. She walked over and just stood there smiling at Nikki. Cathy wasn't sure if she should say something or not, but the little girl didn't seem in a hurry to go anywhere. "Hi." Cathy thought she should try to start a conversation. "Do you know Nikki?"

The little girl looked down and in a quiet voice said. "I met her today when she came to my classroom. She seems very sweet. My name's Sally." She hesitated a moment, then said, "Can I give her a hug?"

Cathy smiled. "She would like that."

"Are you her Mom?"

"Yes, I am."

"I think you're lucky to have Nikki as a daughter."

"You're right. I am. Nikki brings lots of joy to our family."

Sally leaned down and gave Nikki a hug and Nikki giggled. That made Sally smile. "You're right. I think she did like that.

Well, I better go. I can't wait to get to volunteer in your class, Nikki."

* * *

At bedtime, Seefas asked Nikki about her day. "You seemed to really enjoy your time at school."

"It was so much fun, Seefas. I really like Teacher Marie, and it was fun meeting Sally."

"Marie seems like she's going to be a great teacher. I think she'll make this school year fun for you. And Sally seemed really taken with you. She is very shy; I wonder what her story is."

"I don't know, but did you hear her say she was going to volunteer in my class? I'm sure I'll get a chance to get to know her better."

"I did hear that. She seemed excited about it."

"Seefas, I wonder if she loves Jesus."

* * *

"I love when you get to come play with us, Sophie!" Zack was jumping up and down, tugging on Sophie's shirt.

Sophie laughed and leaned down to pick Zack up. "I love coming over to play with you too. Have you guys figured out what game we're going to play today?"

At that, Josh chimed in. "We want to play hide and seek. It's one of Nikki's favorite games."

Sophie got a weird look on her face and looked at Cathy for an explanation. "When we play hide and seek, the boys like me to hide Nikki someplace and then go hide myself. Nikki isn't a very good hider, however; she gives herself away by giggling. I think that is the boys' favorite part of the game, seeing their sister crack up laughing."

"All right, I'll give it a go. Are you going to play with us Cathy?"

Cathy thought for a minute. Her first reaction was to play, of course, but she wanted to give Sophie a chance to bond more with Nikki, and she knew if she played, she would be the one hiding Nikki. "Um, actually, if you don't mind I could use this time to get some things done that I've been putting off."

Although Sophie was really warming up to Nikki, she was still worried about letting Nikki fully into her heart. However, she knew that she couldn't tell Cathy that she had to play. "That's fine. I'll play with the kids. It will be fun."

All three kids squealed in delight, and Cathy and Sophie both laughed. "Sophie, you will be in charge of hiding Nikki, and when it's your turn to count, Nikki can count with you. Okeydokey, artichokey?" Josh loved that saying.

"Sounds good, Josh. Let's go." Sophie leaned down to pick up Nikki, who giggled and wiggled in excitement. Sophie couldn't help but smile. "I think Nikki is just as excited as you boys to play."

Cathy smiled as she watched the troop go up the stairs. "Thank you, Lord, for how far Sophie has come in accepting Nikki. I pray that their relationship continues to grow closer. I also pray that Sophie opens her heart to you." Just then Cathy heard laughing coming from upstairs.

"Sophie, that was a great hiding place to put Nikki." Josh was laughing uncontrollably. "She looked just like one of our stuffed animals."

"Except our toys don't laugh, Josh," Zacky said, while laughing himself.

Sophie was laughing too. "She did look pretty cute among all those stuffed animals and dolls. Well, Nikki, even though you got found quickly with that laughing of yours, you're the cutest little toy I've ever seen."

Zack stopped and got a serious look on his face. "Um, Sophie," he said while tugging on her shirt, "Nikki's not really a toy."

Sophie laughed and leaned down and gave him a kiss on his forehead. "I know, Sweetie."

Josh gave a little yawn. "Sophie, I think Zack and Nikki are a little tired. Could you help us set up a movie in the bonus room?"

Sophie smiled. "Sure. Why don't you guys pick one out, and I'll get it going for you. Then I'll go visit with your mom for a while." After Sophie had the three kids comfortable with their movie, she headed downstairs.

"Cathy, you have the cutest kids I've ever met. There would definitely be a hole in my heart without them in my life."

Cathy couldn't help smiling and saying a quick thank you to Jesus, noticing that Sophie no longer said "the boys," but "the kids." "They are wonderful. What are my little darlings doing upstairs?"

"Josh said while yawning that Zack and Nikki are tired, so he had me put a movie in for them."

Cathy smiled. "Of course, he wasn't tired. Thanks for doing that. How are you doing, Sophie?"

Sophie looked troubled at that question. "I'm fine. Just trying to figure out what my heart's telling me."

"Oh yeah, in what way?"

"I've been thinking a lot about Jim lately."

Cathy tried to hide her grin. "Is that so? In what regard?"

"All right, Cathy, don't get too excited."

Cathy looked shocked. "What? I'm not. I was just . . ." Cathy couldn't get her sentence out without laughing. "Am I that obvious?"

Sophie rolled her eyes. "Yes. That's okay. I do like Jim a lot; he's a great guy. It's just that . . ."

Cathy gave Sophie a minute to gather her thoughts. "You don't have to talk about it if you don't want to."

"Actually, I do want to talk about it because it's driving me crazy. There are a few problems with what I'm feeling. One, I have no idea what Jim's feeling, and, two, his whole life is centered around God. Where do I fit into all that? It reminds me so much of the way Kevin was."

"Sophie, I think that maybe you should continue in your friendship with Jim and see where it takes you. Let Jim take the initiative, and just enjoy where it's at right now."

"I know you're right, Cathy. I'm worrying about something that's not even happening. Sometimes I let my mind get carried away and start thinking about all kinds of scenarios."

"I think we all do that, Sophie. I'm just glad that you can have a friend in Jim right now. It's good for both of you."

"You're right. I need to just enjoy our friendship and see where it takes us." Sophie walked over and gave Cathy a hug. "Thanks."

Cathy couldn't believe how much Sophie had changed over the last few years. When they first met, Cathy would have fallen over backward if Sophie gave her a hug. Sophie was slowly dropping that hard exterior and letting people get close to her. Cathy hugged Sophie back. "Sophie, I'm so thankful for our friendship."

* * *

"Nikki, you really like playing hide and seek, don't you?" Seefas asked with a big grin on his face.

"It's one of my favorite games, Seefas, and it was so fun today playing with Sophie. I think she might like me now. I just wish that she would love Jesus too." Nikki had a sad look in her eyes. "She's missing so much in life, not allowing Jesus to live in her heart."

"Yes, she is, but she has a little prayer warrior on her side. Just keep praying that God will get her attention somehow."

"I will, Seefas. I so want Sophie to love Jesus like I do." Nikki got a silly grin on her face.

"What are you smiling about, Miss Nikki? You look like you're up to something."

"I was just thinking how fun it would be for you to hide in my room and for me to try to find you. I'll close my eyes, you hide, then I'll try to guess where you are." Nikki started giggling.

"What's so funny?" Seefas loved his little Nikki so much; he thanked Jesus often for giving him the opportunity to be her guardian angel.

"I'm just picturing you trying to hide in my room without me being able to see you." Nikki laughed harder.

"What are you trying to say, that I'm too big?" Seefas said, trying to hide his own laughter.

"You said it, I didn't." Nikki, by this time, was belly-laughing. Seefas joined in with his deep-barrel laugh. Then they played hide and seek until Nikki was sleepy.

Seefas pulled the covers up and tucked them under Nikki's chin. He leaned down and kissed her forehead. "Goodnight, sweet Nikki."

Nikki looked up at her angel towering over her, with sleepy eyes. "Goodnight, my big, strong angel. I love you."

CHAPTER THIRTY-FOUR

"Mom, when is Val coming over with her new boyfriend?" Josh was grinning from ear to ear like he'd just said something funny.

"Yeah, boyfriend." Zack said, exactly how Josh had.

Cathy laughed and tousled her boys' hair. "She should be here any minute. Now you two be on your best behavior, and no teasing Val, you hear?"

"Yes, Mom," the boys said in unison while running upstairs to play until Val arrived. They had barely reached the top of the stairs when they heard the doorbell ring. Scrambling right back down, they both yelled, "I'll get it."

They were both out of breath when Josh reached the door, calling out, "Hi, Val."

"Val, I was supposed to open the door for you. Josh pushed me out of the way so he could open it."

Val leaned down and picked Zack up and gave him a bear hug. "That's okay, Bud. How about you be the first one to meet Adam?"

Zack turned around and gave Josh a sly smile. "Hear that Josh? I get to be first to meet the boyfriend."

Everyone laughed. Cathy reached out to take Zack from Val. "Well, welcome, Adam. As you can see, everyone's been very excited to meet you."

Gene walked over holding Nikki. "Including this little one." Nikki let out a loud squeal, and everyone laughed again.

"I've been excited to meet all of you. Val talks about you guys nonstop. You are each very special to her." Adam placed his arm around Val's shoulders and the boys both giggled.

"All right, you two." Cathy gave them a warning look. "Why don't we head into the living room? Dinner will be ready in about fifteen minutes."

"I appreciate you having us over, Cathy. I was disappointed that I wasn't able to make it to the birthday party. Val said it was a lot of fun."

"We were sad you couldn't make it too. I told Val that you need to come to Zack's party if you're in town."

"Actually, I just got a promotion at work yesterday. I won't have to do nearly as much traveling. I'm excited about that, especially now that there's someone making me want to be around more often." Adam smiled at Val, and she blushed.

Cathy smiled. "I'm sure Val will love having you around more often."

As this topic was getting a little too mushy for him, Gene quickly changed the subject. "It looks like dinner's ready. Shall we head to the table and continue our conversation there?" After Gene thanked the Lord for the food and wonderful company, he asked, "So, Val. Cathy told me you were thinking about going back to school. Have you decided what area you'll study if you do?"

"I have. I've decided that I want to be a special-education teacher. When I go with Cathy to pick Nikki up from school, something stirs in my heart, and I feel like that's where God is calling me. I just started doing an online program and should be done in a year or two, since I already have my bachelor's degree."

Cathy smiled. "I know you'll be a fantastic teacher with those little guys, Val. Nikki would be thrilled if you were her teacher one day." Nikki giggled. "See, she agrees with me."

* * *

"Mom, now that dinner's over, can Zack and I go upstairs to play until dessert?"

"Sure, Josh. We'll let you know when it's time." At that, the boys bolted upstairs.

"I'll do the dishes," Gene said. "You guys can go make yourselves comfortable in the living room."

Cathy leaned over and kissed her husband's cheek. "Thank you."

Adam couldn't stop watching Nikki. "Your daughter is so animated, and she seems to understand everything we're saying."

"We're not sure what she understands, but we assume everything. We'd rather err on the side of telling her too much than too little. But she's definitely aware of what's going on around her." Cathy leaned over to get Nikki out of her wheelchair and take her to the living room with them. As soon as Cathy picked her up Nikki started laughing uncontrollably. She was laughing so hard she got the hiccups, and everybody was soon laughing along with her.

"Hey, what's so funny?" The boys were yelling as they ran back down the stairs. They didn't want to miss any action.

"Your sister just got the giggles, and it was contagious," Cathy said, still laughing.

The boys started laughing as well. "Nikki's so funny." Zack said, giggling.

"Your kids are very special. Now I see why Val is so drawn to them."

"Thanks, Adam. They are great kids, and we all love Val too. She's like one of the family. That's why we were anxious to meet you."

"I've been telling him how great you all are, and how much you've touched my life and my family's." Val was glad that Adam was getting along so well with the Ellertons.

"Dessert time!" Josh came running in with Zack on his heels.

* * *

"Did you have a fun evening, Miss Nikki?"

"Yes, Seefas. I did. I really like Adam. I think he will marry Val one day."

Seefas smiled at Nikki's insight. "You do, do you? Why do you think that?"

"Because I see the way they look at each other. It's the same way Mom and Dad look at each other."

"So, what was so funny tonight when your mom went to pick you up?"

"You were." Nikki said, laughing.

"I was? Why was I so funny?"

"You got that funny expression on your face that you some-times get. You know, the one like you're trying to figure out a puzzle, but you're just not getting it." Nikki started giggling again. "It's very funny, you know?"

Seefas laughed. "I don't know what you're talking about." He laughed again and started tickling Nikki, which caused Nikki to laugh even harder.

When they'd both stopped laughing, Seefas looked at Nikki. "I guess I *was* trying to figure out a puzzle. You and I have such wonderful conversations that I sometimes forget that your parents can't hear you talk. When your mom was saying that she's not sure how much you understand, it just struck me how deep your understanding really is, and that one day, when you sit down with your mom in Heaven, she'll be blown away."

"Oh, Seefas. I can't wait to sit down with Mom and be able to talk with her, laugh with her, and walk with her. Heaven's going to be wonderful. But I do get to laugh with her here on earth. Every time I laugh, my mom starts to laugh. So we at least get that part together."

"I think that's one of your mom's favorite times."

* * *

"Hi, Mom." Cathy walked into her parents' house and kissed her mom on the cheek. The boys came tumbling in after her, with Gene and Nikki taking up the rear. "Thanks for having us over for dinner. Are Craig, Jenny, and the girls here yet?" The whole family couldn't gather often because the other siblings lived all across the country. But Craig and Cathy made a point of converging at their parents' home about once a month for family time.

"Not yet. They should be here anytime."

"Hey, Dad." Cathy leaned over and kissed her dad, who was sitting in his favorite rocker with Nikki and Zack already in his arms. Cathy was really worried about her dad's health; he was weak from the chemotherapy treatments. "Are you all right holding both of my little ones?"

"You know, this is therapy for me. My grandkids lift my spirits and always make my day happier. They are just fine where they are."

"I love sitting with Papa, Mommy," Zack said as he snuggled up to Papa.

"Papa, when our cousins get here, we are going to put on a puppet show for you. Zack and I decided since you always do them for us, this time we will do one for you." Josh and Zack loved doing things with Craig's girls, who were ten, seven, and five.

"Oh, I look forward to that. I bet it's going to be the best puppet show I've ever seen," Papa said with a twinkle in his eye.

"Yep, it is Papa," Zack said as he climbed off his lap.

Josh looked out the window. "I see them. Uncle Craig and Aunt Jenny and the girls are here." He and Zack bolted out the door.

* * *

After dinner was all cleaned up, Grant was excited to share something with the family. "Can we all gather in the living room please? There's something I want to tell you. Josh, can you go get the rest of the kids? I want you all to hear it." Josh ran to get everyone and within minutes everybody was sitting down waiting to hear Papa's announcement.

At first Cathy was worried when her dad said he had something to tell them. She was afraid it had something to do with his cancer, but seeing how excited he was, her fears subsided.

"Granda and I just sold our house in Florida, and we have decided what we want to do with some of the money."

"What Papa?" all the grandkids said in unison.

"We are going to pay for our whole family to go to Disneyland. We want everyone to go, all six of our kids and their families."

"Yeah. Disneyland." said all the grandkids.

"Wow, Dad. That's very generous. Are you sure?" Craig asked. He was worried about his dad and didn't want to put undue stress on him.

"Absolutely. It will be the best medicine for me. It will be a place where we can all enjoy ourselves." Nikki squealed in Papa's lap. "See, even Nikki's excited."

"Granda and I figured it all out. We will have enough to give everyone traveling money, plus pay for the hotel and park entrance. It's something we really want to do. It will be great to have everyone together; we haven't been since Cassie and Mike's wedding. And little Zack wasn't even born at the time." Grant seemed excited and determined.

"I think it will be great, Dad. Something for all of us to look forward to." Cathy knew that her dad was a determined man, and she felt that this would be good for him.

"When are you thinking, Dad? Have you talked to the others yet?"

"Not yet, Craig, but I was thinking early summer, after school is out and before everyone gets busy with their summer activities. Would that work for all of you?"

"Basketball camp doesn't start up until July, so I think that will work for us." Craig, a basketball coach, always taught camps in the summer.

"Works for us too. Gene will just need to know the dates so he can get the time off."

"I'll call the rest of the kids tomorrow. Dad was like a kid in a candy shop when he thought of the idea," May said. She knew how important it was to Grant to have the family around him, and she didn't know how much longer they were going to have with him. The cancer was getting worse, but she didn't want to worry the children.

"Everybody ready for the puppet show?" Zack came running in excitedly. "We have a special show just for Papa. But, everybody else can watch it too."

The kids brought in chairs and blankets and set up their stage. When they'd all gotten behind it, Josh walked out in front of the stage. "Ladies and Gentlemen, may I present to you, 'Our Trip to Disneyland.'"

* * *

"Oh, Seefas. Did you see Papa during the puppet show? He loved it. I think I saw tears in his eyes."

"I think you're right. He seemed touched by the whole thing. They did a great job."

"My favorite part was when Zack pretended he was Papa going on a roller coaster. That was very funny. Papa said he loved roller coasters," Nikki said laughing. "Do you think he can go on one? He said he's going to try when Josh asked him."

"I think it will probably depend on what the doctor tells him and how he's feeling. Are you excited to go to Disneyland? It will be your first time there."

"I am. Watching the puppet show gave me a good idea what it will be like. All the rides and the Disney characters. It will be so much fun." Nikki was getting excited.

"What do you think your favorite part will be?" Seefas loved seeing Nikki get excited.

"I don't know. I think maybe, everything."

Seefas laughed. "You're probably right."

"It was funny when they pretended they were getting wet on the rides. They pretended to be very hot and said they wanted to go cool down on the rides. Then they got off soaking wet. Uncle Craig said that actually happens on some of the rides. I wonder if I'll get to go on any like that." Nikki had the same twinkle in her eye that Papa had earlier that evening.

"Whatever you end up doing there, I'm sure it will be great."

Nikki became serious. "Seefas, I'm really worried about Papa. He seems weaker every time I see him. I could tell Mom and Uncle Craig were worried about him too."

"Your grandfather's fighting a hard sickness. Cancer takes a lot out of people, but when he's around his family, he brightens up and seems to get stronger."

"I love Papa so much. I want him to be here with me for a very long time." Nikki started to cry.

"Oh, sweet Nikki, enjoy the time you have with him. Nobody knows how long they have here on earth, but God does. He's very special to you and even after he goes to be with Jesus, he'll continue to be special in your heart. Papa loves Jesus, so you know one day you'll be with him again."

Nikki was still crying but a smile managed to make its way out. "That is very good news, Seefas. So when Papa dies, we're only saying goodbye for a short while."

"That's right, sweet Nikki. But right now Papa's still here, and you can continue to enjoy having him around."

Nikki threw her little arms around Seefas' massive neck, a memory that Seefas would treasure forever.

CHAPTER THIRTY-FIVE

"I'm glad that you were able to step away from work for a bit and meet me at Starbucks, Gene." Jim had called Gene because he really needed some advice about his relationship with Sophie. They would meet occasionally at the nearest Starbucks to have a heart-to-heart. Ever since Jim had become a Christian, Gene had been invaluable to him in his spiritual walk.

"On the phone it sounded like you needed to talk."

"I do." Jim took a deep breath. "Here goes. I've developed feelings for Sophie that go beyond friendship, and that scares me. I know that I can't let it go that direction unless Sophie finally turns her life over to the Lord."

Gene was listening intently to Jim and couldn't help but smile a bit on the inside. He was thinking, *So my wife was right. Don't know how she can read these things so well.* He was also praying for the words to help Jim.

Jim was still talking. "I just can't see letting myself get serious about someone whose focus in life is not the same as mine. Christ is the center of my life, and I know He's not of Sophie's. I keep comparing it to, say, if Sophie wanted nothing to do with Emily. Emily is my daughter and the joy of my heart. Jesus is my Savior and the light of my life. What difference is there really?" Jim was rambling on. Gene could tell that this was tearing him apart.

"You're right. There isn't much difference. You would never get involved with someone who wanted nothing to do with your daughter. So I see your point. At the same time, there's nothing wrong with caring about Sophie and praying that one day she will come to invite Jesus to be a part of her life. We are called to be Jesus's light to the world and draw people to him."

"What do I do with all these feelings running around inside of me? I've tried to not let them come, but, well, they came anyway."

"Guard yourself and pray. You never know what's going to happen down the road. One day, Sophie could come around, and the Lord might be preparing you for that day. Until that happens, guard your heart." Gene felt for Jim. He knew that what he was saying was not an easy task.

"I know you're right. I think what I need to do until that day is not be alone with Sophie. I can still talk with her and be her friend, but to be alone with her is probably not a good idea. I hope she doesn't think that I'm giving her the cold shoulder."

"Well, take it one day at a time. There might come a time when you need to be totally honest with her about what's going on inside, and explain why you can't be alone with her."

Jim was quiet for a couple of minutes. "You're right. That day may come." Jim felt better talking it out with Gene. He had known what God was calling him to do, but somehow he was hoping that he had misunderstood God's plan. Saying it out loud to Gene, he knew he had not.

Gene interrupted Jim's thoughts. "Anything new with the Amanda situation?"

"Funny that you ask. I just got off the phone with Phil as I was driving over here. He told me that he is seeing slight changes in Amanda's attitude and is still praying for her."

"That's great. Did he say what changes he was seeing?"

"The other day he was reading his Bible when Amanda walked into the room. Normally, she'd turn her nose up and walk out. This time was different. When she went to leave, she suddenly turned around, walked over, and sat next to him for several minutes, saying nothing. Then she looked up and asked him, 'Do you really believe in all of that?' Phil told her he did and that he had no doubts."

"What did Amanda say?"

"Phil said that it's not what she said next, it's what he saw in her eyes. She told him that she still thought that it was a bunch of lies, but her tone was soft, and she had tears in her eyes. She turned to walk out, but Phil saw a change. He wants us to keep praying."

"We will. I agree with Phil, it seems like maybe her walls are breaking down, and she's not sure what to do with what she's feeling."

Jim nodded in agreement. "I sure wish that Emily could mend the fences with her; I think Em could help her through all of this."

"Friends are needed to help you through tough obstacles." Gene smiled at Jim, implying that he was there for him and his situation with Sophie.

"You're right," Jim laughed. "Thanks for being there, Gene."

* * *

That night at dinner, Gene gave the family an update on Phil and Amanda, since they'd all been praying for them.

Cathy smiled. "God's working, I just know it. I think that Jim's right about Emily being the key to helping Amanda."

Nikki let out a squeal and everyone laughed. Josh then piped in. "I think Nikki thinks that's a grand idea." Gene and Cathy both laughed that he'd used the word *grand*.

Bedtime came all too quickly for the boys. "I'm not a bit sleepy," Zack said as he was yawing.

After they had everyone tucked soundly in bed, Gene told Cathy about the other part of his and Jim's conversation. Cathy couldn't help but smile.

"Cathy, you need to take this seriously. Jim is very determined to not let this go anywhere unless Sophie becomes a Christian."

Cathy pouted. "I am. It's just that you were so sure that I was making all of this up, and now you know the truth."

"Okay, you don't have to gloat. I admit you have a knack for figuring these things out, but we need to help Jim with this and not push him in a direction he's not ready to take." Gene loved his wife's desire to see everyone happy, but he wanted to make sure Cathy understood Jim's heart.

"I understand his hesitation, and I will be good." Cathy leaned over and kissed her husband's cheek. Cathy knew that Jim's decision was wise, but she was sure that soon Sophie would come around. She had already done a one eighty with Nikki, and she knew God was next.

* * *

"Do that again, Seefas. I love the way that you pretend to fight off the bad guys. You are my hero."

Seefas smiled. He was glad Nikki didn't know that, to protect her, he had to fight off the 'bad' guys quite often. "Anything for you."

Nikki yawned. "I think I'm ready to go to sleep. Can we pray before I close my eyes?"

Seefas leaned down and gave Nikki a kiss on the forehead. "Of course, we can do that."

"I want to pray for Phil and Amanda, especially about Amanda allowing Emily back into her life. I think that Jim is right; I think Jesus places friends in our lives to help us in tough times."

* * *

Summer break was about to start. Everyone around the Ellerton house seemed ready for it. The sun was shining and they all had the summer bug. Cathy loved summer time with her kids. She looked forward to a few months of no set schedules and playing together outside and loved the times in their pool. Nikki especially loved the water.

Today Cathy was meeting Val and Jill for lunch at Olive Garden.

Cathy walked into the restaurant and saw them already seated. "Hey, you two. I know something big is going on. Are you going to keep me guessing?" Cathy smiled and she sat down.

Val laughed. "I think we should order first, don't you? That way I can tell you with fewer interruptions."

After ordering, Val leaned back in her chair. "Well, I wanted to tell you about my weekend."

Cathy scanned her memory but came up empty. "I'm sorry, Val. I can't remember if you told me that something special was going on last weekend. I guess I've been busy with three eager kids getting ready for their summer break."

"No, I didn't tell you because I didn't know myself."

Cathy looked over at Jill who was just sitting there quietly with a smile on her face. Cathy loved Jill; she couldn't help but think back to that day when Gene came home and told her about Ryan coming to know the Lord and how soon his whole family followed suit. Jill had been so good for Val. The two had become instant best friends back at Josh and Nikki's birthday party years before.

"Um, Cathy. Are you with us?" Val said with a sly look on her face.

Cathy snapped back into the present. "Sorry, I was just thinking how far you girls have come. I can't wait to hear about your weekend."

"Well, Adam and I had a date planned on Saturday. He picked me up in the morning and we drove to the beach. The day was perfect; we played on the sand and got our feet wet in the ocean. At sunset, we built a fire and roasted hot dogs and ate S'mores. It was beautiful, the sun setting, sitting next to this wonderful man that the Lord had brought into my life. I honestly couldn't imagine anything better than that, until . . ." Val trailed off as if in a dream.

"All right, girl. You're leaving me hanging here," Cathy laughed.

"Oh, yeah. Sorry. Anyway, we're sitting there and Adam leans over and takes something out of his pocket."

Cathy knew what was coming and was excited for Val. "Yes, keep going."

"Adam tells me how blessed he is to have me in his life, and how God knew exactly what He was doing when He brought us together. He said that he never wants to know what it would be like to not have me here and that he wants to spend the rest of his life with me." Val had been hiding her hand under the table. She brought it up to show the most beautiful ring Cathy had ever seen. It was white gold with a princess-cut diamond and what looked like little diamonds dancing all around it.

Cathy stood up to give Val a hug, and there were tears in the eyes of all three girls. "I am so happy for you. You and Adam are perfect together."

"Thanks, Cathy. Sorry I didn't tell you earlier this week, but I wanted the timing to be perfect. I didn't want to tell you over the phone."

"Today was a perfect time. So, have you guys set a date?" Cathy was an old romantic at heart; she loved things like this.

"We want to get married at Christmas time. I love that time of year. That will give us time to go through premarital counseling and to plan the perfect wedding. Of course, I want all three of your kids to be in it. The boys can be the ring bearers, and I want Nikki to be my flower girl."

Cathy was touched. She never even considered Nikki being able to do something like that. "The kids will be thrilled. Thank you, Val."

* * *

Pulling into Nikki's school, Cathy was still thinking about Val's wedding. She couldn't wait to see her three little ones in the wedding party.

As Cathy got out of the car, she was greeted by Marie, who was pushing Nikki out to meet her. "Hey, there's my sweet girl. All ready for summer break?"

Nikki let out a loud squeal, and both Cathy and Marie laughed. Marie smiled. "I think we're all ready for a few months off, but we're going to miss you, Nikki."

"I know she'll miss you too. But we get you again next year, right?" Cathy had come to love Marie as Nikki's teacher. She had been such a great help to Cathy in transitioning out of being with Nikki in the classroom. Even though Cathy could drop in on occasion, it wasn't the same.

"I will be here. Can't wait to spend another year with this little angel." As they were talking, Sally, the little girl with red hair who Cathy had met at the beginning of the year, walked up to them.

"Hi, Sally." Cathy said.

Sally seemed surprised that Cathy remembered her name. "I just wanted to say good-bye to Nikki. Since I'm in fifth grade, I won't be going here next year. I'm going to miss her. Do you think I'll ever see her again?" Sally looked like she was about to cry.

"We can pray that you will one day." Cathy's heart went out to her.

Sally seemed a little surprised by what Cathy said, but then she smiled. "I would like that, thanks. Nikki, I'm going to miss you. I hope to see you again someday." Sally leaned over and gave Nikki a hug and Nikki giggled.

* * *

That night at dinner, everyone seemed excited about Val's news and the idea of being in her wedding.

Once everyone said their prayers and was tucked soundly in bed, Nikki got her time with Seefas.

"Seefas, can you believe it, I'm going to be a flower girl. Mommy says that I get to hold a bunch of flowers and that she'll put some in my hair."

"You will be the prettiest flower girl there ever was."

Nikki smiled. "I knew that Val would end up marrying Adam. I'm so happy for her."

"It is special when two people find each other, especially when they let Jesus be the center of their marriage."

"I know Val and Adam will do that."

"I think you're right."

"Hey, Seefas?" Nikki got such a cute, serious look on her face that it made Seefas smile.

"Yes, Miss Nikki?"

"Mom told Sally that we could pray that we would see each other again. Do you think Jesus will answer that prayer?"

"I think anything's possible with Jesus. I think you'll just have to pray about it, and see what Jesus does."

CHAPTER THIRTY-SIX

The party was in full swing. Cathy stood pushing Nikki in the baby swing, looking around the park at all the friends and family who'd gathered once again for Nikki's and Josh's birthdays. Every year the guest list grew larger, and the Ellertons were touched that so many people played a part in their lives. Josh had turned eight and Nikki six, and in a few months Zack would be four. Cathy felt fortunate to have Gene and her three beautiful kids.

"Excuse me, Mrs. Ellerton." Cathy jumped a little. Deep in thought, she hadn't seen little Lindsey walk up next to her.

"Hi, Lindsey." Cathy couldn't believe that this was the same little girl who, not too long ago, never said a word. Now, thanks partly to Nikki, Lindsey spoke in complete sentences and was in a regular classroom at school.

"Do you think it would be okay if I pushed Nikki for a while? I would love to spend time playing with her."

Gina, Lindsey's mom, had walked up with her. "I will stay here with the girls, that way you can go and make your rounds with the guests."

Cathy smiled at her friend. "Are you sure you don't mind?"

"Not at all; you go. The girls and I will be having fun over here."

Cathy gave Gina a quick hug. "Thanks, friend."

The next people Cathy saw were Jill, Val, and Adam. "Hey, there everyone. Adam, I wanted to say congratulations. I couldn't be happier for you and Val."

"Thanks, Cathy. I feel like a very lucky guy." Adam had a grin on his face that went from ear to ear, and Val turned bright red.

Cathy laughed. "I think Val feels the same way. I'm glad all three of you are here, and I know the kids feel the same way. Where is Anne today? I thought she'd be with you guys."

"She's out of town. She flew back to Ohio to be with her best friend from high school. She sends her love. The rest of us weren't going to miss this fabulous party. We do need to leave a tad early, however. The three of us are meeting up with my brother, and we're going out on his new boat. We've been waiting for a good day, and we haven't had too many of them this month." This June had been unusually rainy. Gene and Cathy had been praying all week for a sunny day, and the Lord had smiled down on them and given them one. "We won't leave until after the kids open their gifts."

"Josh will appreciate that." Cathy laughed. "Wow, Paul bought a boat? That sounds like a lot of fun. Gene and I would love to buy a boat one day." A fleeting thought went through Cathy's mind, wondering if there was a possibility that something would spark between Jill and Val's brother, Paul. Cathy had never thought about that possibility before, but it made sense, especially now that Paul had become a Christian and radically turned his life around.

After a few more minutes of small talk, Cathy excused herself and went looking for Sophie. She wanted to make sure Sophie was okay. Sophie had been having a hard time with Jim pulling away from their relationship while trying to sort out his feelings for her. Sophie also was trying to sort out her feelings for Jim. It was one thing for Sophie to be cautious about falling for Jim because of his relationship with the Lord, but it had thrown her for a loop when he started to pull away.

Cathy spotted Sophie over by the little lake, feeding ducks with Josh, Zack, and a group of the other kids. "Are the ducks getting full?"

"If they're not full yet, they will be by the time the kids get done with them," Sophie laughed.

"Well, it looks like you're having just as much fun as they are." Cathy paused, unsure how to ask Sophie about Jim.

Sophie seemed to notice Cathy's hesitation. "I'm okay, Cathy, you don't need to worry about me."

Cathy giggled nervously. "I know. I just wanted to make sure you were."

"You know, it's not like Jim ignores me. It's just that you can tell that's it not the same."

Cathy wasn't sure how much to tell Sophie. She hadn't really explained to Sophie what Jim was feeling, as she didn't want to betray Jim's trust.

"Cathy, you didn't tell Jim I was struggling with feelings for him, did you?" Sophie looked panicked.

"No, I promise. I didn't tell him anything about that."

"I guess he's a big boy. He probably figured it out on his own." Sophie looked defeated.

"Sophie, I wouldn't worry about it. Jim's just going through some things that he needs to sort out. Things will go back to normal again, I'm sure of it." Cathy changed the subject; she didn't want to say more than that for fear she would give away how Jim was feeling.

Cathy was in the middle of telling Sophie about a dress she bought the other day when she looked shocked and put her hand on Sophie's arm. Sophie turned and saw Jim, Emily, and another young girl. "Cathy what's wrong? Who's that girl with Jim and Emily?"

Cathy started to tear up. "Sophie, nothing's wrong; in fact, I think it just might be an answer to prayer."

Sophie looked really surprised. "Why? Who is that?"

"Did I ever tell you about the girl that Emily was having a hard time with? The girl who thought that Emily and Jim were crazy for loving Jesus and leading her dad to the Lord?"

Sophie was quiet. She did remember that girl, and it sobered her. "Yeah, I remember."

"Well, that's her." Cathy by this time had tears running down her face.

"Really?" Sophie was even touched by seeing Amanda here.

"Let's walk over and say hi." Cathy grabbed Sophie's arm to drag her along. Sophie went hesitantly.

As they were walking over to where Jim and the girls were, Cathy couldn't help but see the irony in the situation. This was the very place where Amanda had attacked Nikki verbally, and now here she was at Nikki's birthday party, with a smile on her face, nonetheless.

When they reached the group, Amanda threw her arms around Cathy and gave her a big hug. "I'm so sorry. I'm sorry for saying those awful things to your daughter a few years back." Then she looked at Emily. "Well, for everything I've done over the last couple of years." Emily reached out her hand and took Amanda's and squeezed it.

"You're forgiven, Amanda. Not only by me, but by Jesus."

Amanda started crying. "It's hard to believe that He would forgive me for all the awful things I've done." Then she looked at Cathy. "Do you really forgive me?"

Cathy pulled Amanda into a big embrace. "Of course I do. We have been praying for you for a long time." Then Amanda and Cathy were both crying, and Sophie was standing there quietly, obviously touched by what was going on.

"Do you think we could find Nikki so I could apologize to her?

Cathy led Amanda to where Nikki was swinging with Lindsey. Gina was pushing Nikki while Lindsey swung next to her.

Cathy stopped the swing and leaned down next to Nikki to talk to her. "Nikki, do you remember Amanda? We've been praying for her for a long time." Nikki cooed in response.

"Do you think she really knows what you're saying?"

"You know, Amanda, we don't know for sure, but we always err on the side that she does."

Amanda walked over and leaned down next to Nikki. "Nikki, I am so sorry for all the mean things that I said about you here at the park a few years back. I've come a long way since then, and I now see how beautiful you are on the inside and out." Amanda leaned over and gave Nikki a big hug, and Nikki started to giggle. Cathy also could have sworn that she saw tears in Nikki's eyes.

"I think she's trying to tell you she forgives you."

The rest of the party went great. But as far as Cathy was concerned, Amanda was the best part of the party. Nikki couldn't have received a better birthday present.

* * *

That night Nikki had a hard time going to sleep, she was so excited about Amanda. "Seefas, that was the best birthday gift ever. Amanda asked me for forgiveness and, better than that, she asked Jesus into her heart."

"I know. God never ceases to amaze me. When things look so bleak and impossible, He comes through."

Nikki got serious again. "Seefas, there still is one person that hasn't asked Jesus into her heart."

"I know, sweet girl. Sophie."

"Seefas, it's been six years. What do you think it's going to take for Sophie to give her life to Jesus?"

"We just need to keep praying."

* * *

"Mom, look. I think I see Disneyland down there. See, Zack, I think it's right there."

"I don't see it, Josh. Mom, Josh is telling me Disneyland is right there, and I don't see it."

Cathy laughed. "The plane will be landing in a few minutes, and then we will rent a car and drive to Disneyland. Then you'll be able to see it up close." The boys had been looking forward to this trip since Papa had mentioned it several months before, and now it was finally here. Grant had planned the trip for the whole family, and everyone was going to be there, all twenty-six of them, including Grant's brother Sam. His wife had died several years ago, and they had no children, so Grant thought that it would be fun for Sam to join them. Grant and May gave each family money for traveling expenses and paid everyone's admission to the park.

About an hour later they were pulling into the hotel where they would all be staying, which was only a block from the park. Josh pointed to where the hotel's pool was located. "Mom, look, I see our cousins. Alyssa, Madi, and Kassidy are all swimming in the pool. Can we go swimming too?"

"Yeah, can we? You know, Mom, Nikki loves swimming." Zack thought that maybe this would convince her to let them go.

"You can run over there and say hi to them. As soon as we get the van unpacked and find our swimsuits we will join them."

"Thanks, Mom."

While Gene finished unloading the van, Cathy called the front desk to see which family members had arrived so far. They were coming from all over the United States: Colorado, Florida, Texas, and Virginia. To her delight, she found that everyone had arrived except for her oldest brother, Chad, and his family, but they were due anytime.

The plan was for everyone to meet for dinner in the hotel dining room and then venture over to the park for the evening festivities.

The afternoon was filled with lots of fun hanging out at the pool, and Zack was right—Nikki did love the water. All the older cousins took turns watching Nikki in the water and pulling her around in her taxi floatie.

* * *

Grant felt weak and hated that he had to be in a wheelchair for the trip, but it was doctor's orders and really the only way that he got the okay to go. Grant had been feeling worse and the cancer was continuing to spread, but he didn't want to worry the family. Just being with all his loved ones was the best medicine he could ask for. As Grant rolled into the dining room with May and his brother Sam, he could see all his kids and their families spread out throughout the dining room. His heart soared. He and May had talked often about how rich their lives were to have such a wonderful family who all loved Jesus.

"Hi, Dad." Cathy walked up to her dad, leaning over to give him a kiss on the cheek. "I think that this was a great idea. Thank you so much for doing this for everyone."

Grant beamed. "Oh, it was my pleasure, darling."

Walking through the park at Disneyland that night, Nikki seemed to be glowing. She had always loved music and bright lights. Cathy leaned over to Gene. "Do you see our daughter's eyes all lit up?"

"I do. The boys are also enjoying it."

"Daddy, do you see Mickey Mouse over there?" Zack was pulling on Gene's shorts.

"I do. All the Disney characters are here. I bet by the end of the week, we'll be able to get our pictures taken with most of them."

"Really?" Zack was glowing.

Gene laughed. "You bet."

* * *

The plan that week was for everyone to meet for breakfast and dinner as a family and then go to the park whenever they would like. The siblings were going to rotate going to the park with Grant, May, and Sam.

The first morning was Cathy and Gene's turn, and the kids were excited to get started. As they were going into the park, Josh and Zack were on either side of their Papa. Zack was jumping up and down. "Papa, where do you want to go first?"

"Well, Zack man, I want to go where you want to go."

"Um, I want to go and see all the Disney characters."

Grant laughed. "All you have to do for that is keep your eyes open as we walk from place to place because they are everywhere."

Zack's eyes got as big as saucers. "Really?" Then he looked to his right and got very excited. "Papa, you're right. There is Goofy."

They made their way over to stand in line for the show Aladdin. While they were in line, Zack got to see all kinds of Disney characters. They would come up and interact with the kids, paying extra attention to Nikki, who would give one of her special squeals.

* * *

The week was going too fast and, all too soon, it was the last day at the park. All the siblings decided to meet at Pirates of the Caribbean and go on that ride together. When it came their time to get on, Gene and Cathy had decided that they would take turns while one of them waited with Nikki.

As Gene was getting on with the boys, the man running the ride asked Cathy if she and Nikki were going on. Cathy was surprised because she didn't think Nikki could go on this ride since there were a couple of drops down a small waterfall.

"Are you sure it's safe for my daughter to go on?"

"Of course. On this ride you don't even need to wear seatbelts." The man smiled at her. "I think she would probably enjoy the ride."

Cathy hesitated. "Well, if you're sure."

"Absolutely."

Cathy got Nikki out of her wheelchair and climbed on board with the rest of the family. "All right, sweet Nikki, ready for this ride?"

Nikki squealed in response. As the ride started, all the kids were wide-eyed. Josh and Zack were a little nervous entering a dark tunnel. Cannons fired all around them, and make-believe pirates were dancing and fighting. Up ahead, Cathy could see their first drop, and she started getting nervous about Nikki. She held Nikki tighter as the drop approached.

"Okay, Sweetie. Here it comes." They came to the drop and started going down. Halfway down, Nikki started laughing one of her belly laughs. Pretty soon everyone on that raft was laughing right along with her.

"That was fun." Josh was excited. "Can we do that again? And Mom, Nikki loved it."

Cathy laughed. "I think you're right. Did you enjoy that Nikki?" Nikki giggled. "Well, up ahead we have one just like it."

Sure enough, at the next drop, Nikki laughed even harder. The whole family decided that it was worth going on this ride again after lunch, just to enjoy Nikki's reaction.

* * *

The next morning in the dining room, before everyone took off to head home, Grant wanted to have a special time of reflecting on the week. Many people shared their highlight of the week, and by far the best one was just being together.

Later that night when the Ellertons had made it back to Gresham, Nikki was tucked snugly in bed. She just lay there for a few minutes reflecting on the week at Disneyland. Seefas watched her for a while, then broke the silence. "A penny for your thoughts, sweet girl."

"I was just thinking about how lucky I am to have such a wonderful family. It was so much fun being together in California. Papa seemed to be better than he has in months. Do you think that maybe Papa's getting better?"

Seefas felt sadness in his heart. He knew how much everyone loved Grant, but he could tell that Grant was getting close to the end of his life here on earth. "I think your Papa can't help but feel good when he has all his family surrounding him."

"I love Papa so much. My favorite part of Disneyland was seeing Papa happy."

Seefas smiled at Nikki's sincerity, then he started to laugh.

"What's so funny?" Nikki was confused.

"I was just thinking about another thing that had to be close to your favorite."

Nikki thought for a minute, then smiled. "Oh, do you mean the Pirates of the Caribbean ride?"

"That very one. You seemed to really enjoy that ride."

"That was a blast. I loved the feeling that I got in my tummy when we went down those waterfalls. I'm so glad that the man said I could go on the ride."

"Me too. It's always fun to experience a new feeling."

"I hope I get to go on that ride again one day."

"That would be great."

"Seefas, I'm worried about my Papa, though. Can we spend some time praying before I go to sleep?"

Seefas treasured these moments with Nikki. "I think that's a great idea."

CHAPTER THIRTY-SEVEN

Cathy had mixed feelings as she drove up to Nikki's school on the first day of a new year. She had just dropped off Josh; he was starting third grade. It was a big deal because not only did he have a locker for the first time, it was also the first year his classroom was inside the church. The classrooms for kindergarten through second grade were in modular buildings outside of the church.

Earlier, Cathy had dropped off a highly excited Zack for the start of his second year of preschool.

But this year for Nikki was an immense step. It was the first year she would be going all day. Cathy felt like Nikki was too little and that it was too soon for her, but Marie assured her that Nikki would do great. Cathy was still uncertain, but she was trusting Marie's advice.

"So, Nikki, a big step for you today. How do you feel about staying at school for a whole day like Josh does?" Nikki looked like she was thinking about the question. Then she let out one of her squeals, and Cathy laughed. "Okay, I guess if you're all right with it, I should be too."

Cathy still felt uneasy as she wheeled Nikki to her classroom, but Nikki was a trooper and went with the flow.

Marie greeted them at the door with that warm, motherly smile of hers. "Nikki, I missed you so much over the summer. I'm glad that you get to be in my class again this year." Marie leaned over and gave Nikki a kiss on top of her head. She turned her attention to Cathy. "Are you feeling any better about Nikki being here all day?"

"I'll be okay. I know that the transition is harder on me than on Nikki. She'll do great and most likely love being here for the full day. As a mom, it's hard to let them grow up sometimes."

"I was the same way with my kids; now they're all grown up and out of the house."

Cathy cringed. "I'm not ready for that day."

Marie laughed. "You have a while, so don't worry about that yet."

Cathy kissed Nikki goodbye and headed back to the car. She left Nikki's classroom with peace, knowing Nikki was in good hands.

The day went by quicker than Cathy expected, and soon she was heading home with her girl. Cathy talked to Nikki about her day. "So, Nikki, Marie tells me that you had a great day. She said that once again she took you to the fifth grade classroom to recruit volunteers and, no surprise to me, you won over the kids. Many will be helping out in your classroom."

Nikki giggled, but Cathy couldn't tell if Nikki understood or if she just liked it when anyone talked with her about anything. "Marie also told me that this year you will start learning how to use a walker at school. Marie said it's called a gait trainer and that it will support your upper body, so you'll be able to focus on using your legs. Sounds like you have some exciting things coming your way this year." Nikki cooed.

* * *

Val's big day finally arrived. All the girls who were part of the wedding had spent the night at her mom's house. Tanya was very gracious to host the overnighter. Cathy was one of the bridesmaids, and Nikki was to be the flower girl, so Val insisted that Nikki spend the night also.

Tanya had a friend, Deeana, who owned a salon and agreed to do all the girls' hair. Deeana had the front room set up like a hair salon and had recruited fellow hairdressers to come and help. Even Nikki was getting her hair done. Cathy felt so pampered, and energy was high in the house that morning. She couldn't help but notice the glow on Val's face. Val had been through a lot in her life, and now all the pieces were falling into place.

After a couple of hours, everyone looked fantastic. Val was having five bridesmaids: Cathy, Anne (Adam's twin sister), Jill (the maid of honor), and a couple of girls from Val's small-group Bible study.

Val walked over to where Nikki and Cathy were being pampered. "Cathy, Nikki looks amazing. I can't believe how long her hair has gotten. It just flows down in soft curls. She's so beautiful."

Cathy smiled; here it was Val's big day, and she took time out to notice how pretty Nikki looked. "Thanks, Val. And you look absolutely stunning."

Val blushed. "Thanks, Cathy. Do you think Adam will think so?"

Cathy laughed. "I think he won't be able to keep his eyes off of you."

Soon it was time to head to the church. Gene was bringing the boys, who were both going to be ring bearers, each carrying a ring. Cathy thought Val was brave to have them do this, especially since Zack was only four.

Cathy stood up front watching the rest of the wedding party walk in. She smiled when she saw Paul, Val's brother, escorting

Jill down the aisle. If Val has anything to do with it, those two would be next, she thought.

Then it was the kids' turn. Zack came down first, then Josh pushing Nikki's wheelchair with one hand and holding the pillow with the ring in the other. Nikki had a basket full of flowers sitting on her lap, and Cathy held her breath hoping Nikki wouldn't accidentally knock them on the floor. Cathy was also trying not to laugh because Zack was walking so slow, being very careful not to drop his pillow. Josh had to keep stopping Nikki's wheelchair from running into him. The three of them eventually made it down the aisle and stood in front of Cathy.

The music changed and everyone stood up as Val, escorted by her uncle, started coming down the aisle. Cathy smiled when she saw Adam's face at his first glimpse of his bride. It was a look of admiration, love, and pride. Cathy made a note to herself to tell Val later that, indeed, Adam thought she looked absolutely stunning.

The service was beautiful. Adam and Val had wanted their wedding service to reflect Jesus, and they succeeded. At the end of the ceremony, everyone headed over to a hotel for an incredible sit-down meal and dancing.

The boys loved dancing, and even Gene picked Nikki up out of her chair and whirled her around the dance floor. Nikki thought this was the best thing ever.

Cathy made her way over to where Tanya was sitting. She noticed Tanya watching Val and Adam dancing. "She looks happy."

Tanya looked up at Cathy, and her eyes were moist. "She does, doesn't she? I was just thinking that she's turned out to be an incredible, beautiful girl, but no thanks to me." When Val was a teenager, her dad had died. Tanya had taken it hard and stopped being a mom.

Cathy felt for Tanya. "Life was hard, but look where you both are right now. I know that Val treasures the relationship that you two have today."

"I'm so blessed to have her forgiveness and to have found Jesus myself." Tanya turned from watching Val and Adam and placed her hand on Cathy's knee. "You know you and your family played a big part in all of this."

"God has a way of bringing people together. You know Val's the one who found us."

"I know she was so drawn to Nikki, and I can see why. She looks like she's having a lot of fun out there with Gene."

Cathy looked over to where Gene and Nikki were dancing, and her heart swelled with pride and joy. She laughed as Gene pretended to dip Nikki.

"I'm so glad that you have let me adopt your family as mine. I still need to have Nikki over to spend the night sometime."

"She would love that. Just say the word, and we'll make it happen."

Tanya laughed. "I will enjoy having her over. She makes me smile."

Cathy looked up as Adam was making his way toward them. He held his hand out to Tanya. "May I have this dance?"

Cathy was making her way toward her boys and noticed Jill and Paul dancing together. "I wonder if Val is noticing her brother and Jill, or if she's caught up in the fairy tale of her night," Cathy thought.

Before Cathy reached her two boys, Val came up behind her. "Hey, are you having a good time?"

Cathy gave Val a hug. "The best. It's so fun seeing you so happy. Today has been amazing."

Val smiled. "It's like a dream. I can't believe that Adam is my husband. Cathy, I've never been happier."

"You two are a remarkable couple. I know that you will be very happy, and God's going to use you two in incredible ways."

"Thanks, Cathy. Hey, have you noticed who my brother's been dancing with all night?"

Cathy laughed. "I have. I was actually just wondering if you had noticed."

Val had a mischievous grin on her face. "Of course I did. I've been keeping my eye on the two of them for some time. Neither have admitted it, but I see a romance in the near future."

Cathy laughed. "You better be careful, or Gene will accuse you of being too much like me." Val looked confused. "Never mind. I'll tell you some other time."

The reception was still going at eleven, but Gene and Cathy thought it best to get the kids home to bed.

* * *

When all was quiet at the Ellerton home, soft whispering was coming from Nikki's and Zack's room.

"Today was so fun, Seefas. I loved being the flower girl, and my favorite part at the party was dancing with my dad."

"You did look like you were enjoying yourself. You were doing a lot of laughing out there."

"I know. Did you see my dad dip me? That was the best. When he'd bring me back up it was like a little gust of wind in my face."

"You have always liked the wind."

"Nothing's better than the wind in your face." Nikki giggled.

* * *

"Thanks so much, Teri, for fitting Nikki in today." Cathy had taken Nikki over to their friend's house for a haircut. Cathy loved Nikki's hair, but it was almost down to her waist and Nikki didn't like sitting still to have it all combed out.

"I can always squeeze Nikki in, you know that." Teri's family had adopted Nikki as one of their own. "So what are you thinking you want done to her hair?"

Cathy paused for a second. "I know that it will be a pretty drastic change, but I'm thinking you should bob it."

Teri hesitated and then smiled. "I think she would look adorable, but that it is a big change. Are you sure?"

"Yep. If I don't like it once it's done, it will always grow back." Cathy sort of had the same philosophy for her hair; she liked trying new things. "In fact, let's give her bangs."

Teri laughed. "You got it." While Teri cut Nikki's hair, Cathy and Teri had a chance to catch up. "So what did you say your kids were doing tonight?"

"Well, Gene and I are going out on a date, and the kids are going to church for a new program they've started called Loved Ones. It's for families with special-needs kids and their siblings. It will be our first time taking the kids there, but they're pretty excited to go."

"What will they do there?" Teri was intrigued.

"I guess they feed the kids dinner, do some fun activities with them, and then they have a time of worship. I hope the kids will enjoy it; they do it once a month. They want parents to take the opportunity to go do something fun during that time."

Cathy looked down at her daughter and gasped.

Teri looked worried. "Cathy, are you all right? Are you already regretting the decision to get her hair cut?"

"No, the opposite. She looks adorable. She looks like a little doll. It actually makes her look older." Nikki was six and a half now, and she almost looked it.

Teri turned her around. "Let me get a good look at you." Teri got down at eye level with Nikki. "You are a beautiful girl. What do you think about your new hairdo?" Nikki giggled in response. Her curls now fell softly around her sweet little face; she really did look like a doll.

That night Gene and Cathy dropped the kids off at church. Josh was a little hesitant until he saw a friend from school, Mariah, whose mom, Shelly, happened to run the Loved Ones program. Feeling more comfortable, Josh ran off to play, Zack at his heels.

Shelly walked over to greet them. "Hi, Gene. Hi, Cathy. Glad you guys were able to bring your kids to share the night with us." Shelly leaned down to talk to Nikki. "And, I'm very excited for you to be here, Nikki." Nikki giggled.

"I think she's excited to be too," Cathy laughed. "Is there anything you need us to do before we leave?"

"Not at all. Your kids are in good hands. We have a lot of volunteers excited to help out with this ministry."

Josh came running over to Cathy and Gene. "Mom, Mom! Guess what?"

Cathy laughed. "What?"

"Jessica is here. She is helping out with the Loved Ones. She was very excited to see us walk in." Jessica, Lisa's youngest daughter, had been skeptical for a long time of her family's new-found religion. Slowly she had made friends with the pastor's daughter and eventually asked Jesus to be her Savior.

"That's great, Buster. You guys will have fun with her."

"I know. Gotta go play now. Love you, Mom. Love you, Dad." Then Josh was gone just as fast as he'd come.

After Cathy and Gene left, Shelly took Nikki into the gym, where the rest of the kids were hanging out. A bunch of the kids ran up to welcome Nikki. One of the girls, Heather, especially loved Nikki. She was an older teenager with special needs, and although she had limited vocabulary, she managed to ask Shelly if she could push Nikki around for the evening. They were together the rest of the night, and Heather made sure that Nikki was included in everything the kids were doing.

They ate dinner, played games, and had a talent show. Heather took Nikki up on stage with her while she sang a song. Nikki sang right along in her own way. Josh, Zack, and Mariah put on a skit about a little dog that got lost. Zack got to be the dog, and Josh and Mariah were the owners, who eventually found the dog.

As the night was coming to an end, they had a time of worship. A couple of guys with guitars led the kids in singing. Nikki loved music; it was her favorite thing to do.

When Cathy and Gene arrived a few minutes early and could hear music coming from the gym, they snuck into the back to see what was going on. They were speechless at what they saw, and Cathy had tears in her eyes. Nikki was toward the back in her wheelchair with her hands raised up to the Lord in worship.

Cathy wiped a tear that slid down her cheek, and Gene put his arm around her. "Gene, do you think she's meaning to raise her hands like that? It really looks like she's worshiping Jesus."

Gene squeezed her shoulders. "I don't think there's any way to really know, but it sure looks that way."

Then Shelly walked over and smiled. "Isn't that the sweetest thing ever? Nikki really loves worshiping."

Cathy was so touched by her daughter's actions, all she could do was nod.

The time of worship came to an end and Josh and Zack didn't want to leave. Cathy thanked Shelly, Jessica, and the rest of the helpers and said that the kids would be back next month.

On the way home, the boys talked nonstop about their time, and Zack was quick to point out that Nikki had a lot of fun too.

"I'm glad you guys enjoyed yourselves. Would you like to go back again?" Cathy already knew the answer or she would not have told Shelly they'd be back.

Together Josh and Zack said, "Yes."

Gene had been skeptical at first, not really understanding what the program was about. Now he thought differently. "That is an incredible program they've started. I think they are going to reach a lot of people through this ministry."

"I think you're right."

* * *

"Seefas, tonight was so much fun. My favorite part was the end when we got to sing and worship the Lord."

Seefas smiled; he had enjoyed singing along and watching Nikki worship. Nikki had such a close relationship with Jesus that Seefas couldn't have been a prouder angel.

"I really liked everything about tonight. I can't wait to do it again. I also really liked Heather. She took me everywhere. I also got to sing with her during the talent show. That was a blast." Nikki giggled.

"You were a star up there. And, by the way, I really like your haircut." Seefas smiled.

"Thank you, Seefas, I really like it too. It makes me feel so grown up."

Seefas laughed. "You are growing up quickly. You are a beautiful little girl on the inside and out."

CHAPTER THIRTY-EIGHT

"Mom, Sophie's here. Can we leave now?" Josh was excited, mainly because he got to skip school, but he was also excited to watch his sister. Today was the Special Olympics. Nikki's teacher, Marie, had been talking about it all year, and the day had finally come. It was put on by a junior high school in Gresham, and the kids who went to that school ran all the events. Gene had taken the day off, and Sophie was riding over there with them. Jim and several of their other friends were also meeting there to watch Nikki compete in the Olympics.

"You bet, Josh. We're ready to head out. Everybody into the car. We don't want to be late." When they pulled up to the school, Cathy was surprised how many kids were there. They found Marie and the rest of Nikki's class and set up lawn chairs and blankets next to theirs.

Cathy pushed Nikki over to greet Marie. "There are so many kids here."

Marie laughed. "Yes, there are. They bring in schools from all over the Portland area. It's really a big event. Soon, they will have everyone walk around the track following the marching band from the sponsoring school. They even have their dance team out there. It's a pretty big deal and the kids all love it. I think the kids helping out enjoy it just as much as our kids do."

"Well, I'm excited to see how the day plays out. My boys are curious how Nikki will be able to participate. They've been looking forward to this all week."

Marie laughed. "They are great boys. Actually they can help out with one of the events Nikki's signed up for. It's the wheelchair race. If Josh likes, he could push Nikki in her wheelchair, and Zack could run along next to them."

"I think they will love that. They will be looking forward to that event."

"Nikki is signed up to do three events. She will be in the wheelchair race, the tennis ball throw, and the softball throw. I will let you know when her event is approaching. Other than that, just hang out and enjoy the day. In about five minutes they will be starting the parade. I will take Nikki around, and you can get her on video if you like."

Cathy laughed. "I think we'll be doing a lot of that." Cathy kissed Nikki's forehead. "Have fun parading around. I'll see you when you get back."

Cathy walked back over to her family and friends. "Wow, what a perfect day for this. The sun is shining and the temperature is perfect." There wasn't a cloud in the sky, and it was supposed to stay right around seventy-five degrees.

"Mom, where are they taking Nikki and the rest of her class?" Zack had noticed all of them heading down to the track.

"Everyone participating in the Olympics is going to parade around the track following the band and dance team."

"Wow!" Zack's eyes got real wide.

Soon the parade was underway. Gene got it all on video. Nikki looked so cute in her pink sun hat and white sunglasses.

Sophie leaned over to Cathy. "Just think—at one time I thought these kids weren't worth being born. What on earth was I thinking?" Cathy hugged Sophie. Cathy remembered the day when she had found out that Nikki was having problems inside the womb, and Sophie had sent her a letter telling her to abort Nikki. Oh, how far Sophie had come since then. The Ellertons and Jim were all praying for her to take the next step, and ask Jesus to come live in her heart.

Cathy had noticed that Jim and Sophie had been polite to each other, but they were keeping their distance. They both had feelings for each other that went beyond friendship, but Jim was not going to take that next step unless Sophie turned to the Lord.

The Olympics were now in full swing, and it was time for Nikki's first event, the tennis ball throw. The whole way down to watch Nikki's event, Josh kept asking how Nikki was going to be able to throw the ball. Cathy had reassured him that he would soon see. When they got to the event, the red-haired girl helping with that event began heading toward them. She seemed familiar to Cathy.

"Hi, Nikki. Do you remember me? I'm Sally. I went to your school last year." Of course, how could Cathy have forgotten? This was the shy little girl who had become so attached to Nikki and was worried that they'd never see each other again.

Nikki giggled. "I think she remembers you. Do you go to this school, Sally?"

"Yes, I do, and I get to help out today. I've been having so much fun, even more now that I see Nikki. I think it's Nikki's turn. Can I take her over?"

"Of course." As Sally pushed Nikki over to have her turn, Josh and Zack both wanted to know who that girl was. Cathy explained to them as Gene got in position to catch Nikki on video.

It was Nikki's turn. "Go, Nikki. Throw the ball real far." Zack cheered his sister on. They placed the tennis ball next to Nikki on her wheelchair and Nikki pushed it off, then Sally caught the ball and threw it very far. "Wow! Great job, Nikki." Zack was jumping up and down. Cathy wasn't sure if that counted, but sure enough Nikki walked away with the first-place ribbon.

Sally also ended up at the softball throw, and Nikki came away from that event with another first-place ribbon. Then it was time for the wheelchair race. Josh and Zack could hardly wait for this one, and even Nikki seemed eager.

Cathy and Gene went over the rules with Josh before he got in position with Nikki, with Zack right next to him.

Gene leaned over to Cathy. "I definitely need to video this one."

Cathy laughed. "I don't think the boys would forgive you if you didn't."

The starter yelled, "Go!"

Josh and Zack ran as fast as they could, and Nikki giggled the whole way. Of course, they won because the other kids were being pushed by teacher's assistants and didn't quite have the same desire to win as the boys did.

As they were leaving, Sally made her way over to them. "Excuse me. I remember you telling me that we could pray that I'd see Nikki again. I think Jesus answered our prayers." They talked a few more minutes, and then Sally gave Nikki a hug and was off to help clean up.

Cathy pondered this in her heart. Jesus had answered the prayer of this sweet girl.

On the way home, everyone was laughing and in a good mood. Sophie even seemed to have enjoyed the day. "My favorite part was watching the three of you race down the track," she said laughing.

"That had to be mine too," Cathy laughed.

Gene was laughing too. "I don't know, Nikki coming home with three first-place ribbons has to be at the top."

Josh and Zack both yelled. "Yeah, and with our help."

* * *

At the end of the day when all the kids were tucked in, Seefas and Nikki had a chance to talk. "Did you have fun today, Nikki?"

Nikki's eyes glowed. "That was so much fun. So many of my friends came to see me, and I got to see Sally again. Right before I left, she told me that she had prayed to Jesus that she'd see me again and that He answered that prayer. She said, 'Maybe Jesus is real.' It made me sad that she doesn't know that beyond a shadow of a doubt. I think we need to add her to our prayer list."

"We will. It was fun seeing you enjoy yourself. What was your favorite event?" Seefas loved watching Nikki do things that put a smile on her face.

"That's a hard one, but I would have to say the wheelchair race. I loved the feel of the wind in my face. That I got to do it with my brothers made it even more special." Nikki was giggling, reliving the moment.

"You sure do like the wind."

"I love it. It always makes me laugh, the feel of it blowing in my face. There's nothing better."

Nikki enjoyed the simple things in life. She was very aware of God's creation. From the feel of the wind to the smell of the flowers, Nikki always noticed.

"Well, I'm glad that you enjoyed the day. I think your family and friends enjoyed it too."

"They seemed to. I love that Sophie's involved in my life now and loves me just as much as she loves my brothers."

* * *

Cathy was meeting Val for lunch, and afterward they were both heading over to Nikki's school to check out her new gait trainer. Although Nikki had received it about a month ago, Cathy's schedule hadn't allowed her to visit the school to see it firsthand. Marie told her that Nikki had made some progress, taking about five steps in it so far. Cathy was thrilled. It was a long way from walking, but it was progress nonetheless. Val was excited to be tagging along. She always enjoyed seeing Nikki with her class, especially since she'd started school to become a special-education teacher.

They were eating at Olive Garden, where they'd first met.

"Thanks for meeting me, Cathy, and letting me tag along to Nikki's school."

"Glad to do it! I always love getting together with you. Is there something specific on your mind?"

Val got a sparkle in her eye. "Actually, yes. Adam and I have been talking for a while now and been praying about it, and the Lord has opened up a door for us."

Val definitely had Cathy's curiosity peaked. "So what is it?"

"We have been talking about wanting to adopt a child with special needs." Val paused and her eyes were moist.

Cathy wasn't that surprised. Val really had a heart for these kids. She was, however, surprised about the timing, with Val still being in school. "I think that's great. What about your schooling?"

"Our plan was to wait until I was done with school, but God opened up an opportunity for us that we couldn't pass up.

I've looked into it, and with all that you can accomplish online now, I can finish up my schooling from home."

Cathy brightened up. "That's great. I know how excited you were about getting your degree. But tell me about this amazing opportunity that has come your way."

Val got excited. "Adam works with a guy whose younger sister got pregnant and she's not married. The plan was for her to keep the baby and raise it on her own, but she had an ultrasound last week that revealed that the baby has Down syndrome. I guess the girl freaked out and wanted to get an abortion right away." Val started to tear up.

Cathy got tears in her eyes too. "People told me I should do that with Nikki."

Val put a hand on Cathy's. "I remember you telling me that."

"So, what happened? What changed the girl's mind?"

Val continued. "Her brother did. Adam led him to the Lord a few months back, and he knew that aborting the baby would be wrong. He asked his sister if she would be willing to give the baby up for adoption. I guess she was skeptical at first, thinking that no one would want to adopt a child with Down. But her brother remembered Adam saying that we were thinking about adopting a special-needs child. Well, long story short, he called and asked Adam if we would consider adopting his sister's baby. It took us maybe a day, and then we said we would love to. We felt like God put this baby in our laps."

Val's story touched Cathy. "It sure sounds that way to me. So when is the baby due, and do you know if she's having a boy or girl?"

Val smiled. "She's due in about four months and she's having a baby boy. We've already decided on a name: Benjamin."

Cathy hugged Val. "I'm so happy for you both. You guys will make amazing parents to baby Benjamin. I can't wait to meet the little guy."

Val smiled. "I can't wait to tell Nikki. I know that sounds funny since we don't know how much she understands, but for some reason I think she'll understand."

Cathy smiled. "I think she will too. I think she'll think that you will make an amazing mom."

Cathy and Val finished eating and headed over to Nikki's school. When they walked into the classroom, Nikki was already in her walker. Marie greeted them at the door, and Cathy introduced Val to Marie.

"Cathy has told me a lot about you. You're the one going to school to be a special-ed teacher, right?"

Val smiled. "That's right, and Cathy tells me that I could learn a lot about that by watching you with the kids."

Marie looked at Cathy and blushed. "Thank you, Cathy. I just love the kids, that's all."

Cathy laughed. "That's a lot."

Marie smiled and changed the subject. "We just got Nikki in her gait trainer. Ready to go see your daughter work some magic?"

Cathy laughed. "You bet I am."

They walked over to where one of the helpers, Julia, was working with Nikki. Nikki had stolen Julia's heart. She was Julia's absolute favorite, and she could get Nikki to do almost anything.

Seeing them, Julia turned to Nikki. "Miss Nikki, look who's here. Are you ready to show your mom what you can do in this thing?" Nikki let out a big squeal and everyone laughed.

Cathy leaned down and kissed Nikki on the forehead. "You look like such a big girl in that walker. I can't wait to see what you can do with it."

Julia pulled out a toy and explained that this was Nikki's favorite and the best incentive to get Nikki to move the walker. She put it in front of Nikki, and Nikki started taking slow but deliberate steps toward it. Cathy held her breath. She couldn't believe that her little girl was taking steps. Nikki took six steps then stopped, obviously tired.

Everyone clapped and Cathy picked Nikki up and swung her around. "Great job, Sweetheart." She kissed Nikki's cheek. "I can tell you worked really hard. I am proud of you."

Julia explained that the most steps Nikki had taken before was five, so this was a record.

Since the school day was almost over, Marie told Cathy that she could go ahead and take Nikki home a little early.

On the way home, Val told Nikki about the little boy she was adopting, and Nikki truly seemed to understand. Val looked at Cathy, her eyes shining. "I think she really knows what I said." At that, Nikki let out a little squeal.

* * *

"Big day for you today!" Seefas was beaming with pride.

"Which part, the walker or hearing about the baby Val's adopting?" Nikki giggled.

"Both. You are really coming along with your steps. I know that it takes a lot out of you, but I'm proud of you."

"Thanks, Seefas."

"Pretty special news about Val and Adam adopting a baby too."

"I know. Val will make an amazing mom. I think it's so cool that she is choosing to adopt a baby who will need extra help."

"I'm not surprised. She loves you so much, and you are an inspiration to her."

"I can't wait to meet baby Benjamin. Do you think that he and I will be friends?" Nikki beamed.

"I think you can count on that."

"Seefas, can other kids like me see their angel too?"

"I'm not sure Nikki. I was pretty surprised when you were able to see me. But I think that there is probably a good chance that they can. Nothing would surprise me now."

"I bet baby Benjamin will be able to see his angel. He'll have so much fun playing with his angel like I do mine." Nikki threw her tiny arms around Seefas. She loved her angel very much.

CHAPTER THIRTY-NINE

"Sophie, do you really need to leave? You haven't been here very long." Cathy knew that Sophie was conflicted and needed time, but she hated seeing her leave like this.

"Cathy, I'm okay. I'm not leaving because of you. I'm the one that brought up the whole Jesus subject again. I'm torn. I believe everything that you're saying, but I'm just not ready."

Cathy took a deep breath and prayed for the words to say. "Sophie, what's holding you back, if you believe?"

"I guess . . ." Sophie stopped, shut her eyes and took a deep breath. "All right, here it is. I'm still angry with Jesus for taking my husband. Okay, so he's a loving God who died for me, right?"

"Yes." Cathy kept praying.

"So on one hand I see this loving God and what he's done in the lives of people I care about, and then I see Him as the God who took my husband. How can He be both?"

"Sophie, I don't know why He chose to call Kevin home. I do know that Kevin is in a wonderful place and completely whole. I also know that Kevin loved you, and his last prayer was that you would come to know Jesus. We may never know until we get to Heaven why He took Kevin at a young age. God has a plan for each one of us, and He won't take us home until that plan is fulfilled. He longs for a relationship with you, and the peace you're looking for won't come until you open your heart to Him."

"That's just it. I long for that, Cathy. I long for that peace. But I need time. I know that I will get there; I just need time. I need to go. I have a lot of errands to run. I'll talk to you later, okay?"

Cathy hugged Sophie. "Sophie, none of us know how long we have here on earth. Don't put it off."

Sophie hugged Cathy back. "Love you, my friend. I'll see you later."

* * *

After Cathy picked up the kids from school, she tried calling Sophie again. She'd been trying to call her all afternoon to make sure she was okay after she'd hurried out this morning. When the call went unanswered, Cathy hung up the phone and checked her watch. Gene was supposed to be home early from work because they were going to a family dinner that evening. She'd barely glanced at the dial when the phone rang.

"Hey, Sweetheart," Gene said. "I guess there was a really bad car accident on the freeway. It happened a couple of hours ago, and they are still working to get it all cleared up, so I'm stuck in traffic. I'll keep you posted on how things are moving."

"Gene, that's terrible. Do you know if anyone was seriously hurt?" Every time Cathy heard an ambulance siren she said a prayer for those involved, so she began praying as she listened to Gene.

"I heard on the news that they had to life-flight one of the drivers, but they're not giving specifics right now."

Cathy continued to pray after she finished talking with Gene. She had already been worried about Sophie; now she was worried about the driver of the car.

An hour went by before she heard from Gene again. "Hey, Sweetheart. By any chance have you talked with Sophie in the past couple of hours?"

Cathy's heart sank. "Why? What's wrong? I've been trying to call her since this morning and haven't been able to reach her." There was silence at the other end of the phone. "Gene, talk to me! Why are you asking?"

In a barely audible whisper, Gene said. "Cathy the car in the accident looks just like Sophie's."

Cathy dropped to the floor and started crying; she was grateful that her kids were upstairs playing in the bonus room. "Are you sure?"

It sounded like Gene was crying when he answered. "It looks just like hers. The news said that the driver was taken to Legacy Emanuel. Why don't you call and see if you can find out anything? I'm through the traffic now, and I'll be home in about ten minutes."

A couple hours later, the Ellerton family was sitting in the waiting room along with Jim, Emily, and several close friends, anxiously waiting for some news. A car had crossed over the median and hit Sophie's car head-on. She had been in surgery for several hours. One of the nurses had been grateful when they'd arrived because the hospital didn't know whom to contact for Sophie. She made a point to keep them updated on how things were going.

The group sat in a circle praying for Sophie. Cathy had told them about the conversation she had with Sophie that morning. An hour later, a doctor walked up to them. "Are you the friends of Miss Sophie Carter?"

Gene spoke for them. "Yes, we are. Is she out of surgery?"

"She's out of surgery, but we had to put her in an induced coma. We won't know more for a few hours."

"When will we be able to see her?" Cathy said through tears.

"We will be moving her to a recovery room shortly, so I'd say in a couple of hours you could go in. Please, only a couple at a time."

The next couple of hours were spent in prayer for their beloved friend. When the nurse came over and said they could take shifts going in, Cathy decided that she should take Nikki in with her. She thought that it would do Sophie good to hear the kids. Although it was against hospital policy, Cathy talked the nurse into making an exception.

Wheeling Nikki into Sophie's room, Cathy felt so helpless seeing Sophie lying there weak and frail. "Hi, Sophie. Nikki and I came in to check on you and let you know that we are here and praying for you." Nikki cooed in response, like she was talking to Sophie too. Cathy went on to explain who was at the hospital and how they had found out about the accident. She told Sophie they all loved her, and someone would be there at all times until she woke up. All the while Cathy was talking to Sophie, Nikki was talking too.

Gene and the boys were the next to go in, then Jim and Emily took a turn. They kept rotating until the nurse said that there could be no more visitors. They decided that Jim and Emily would stay at the hospital, and everyone else would go home to get some sleep. Jim promised to keep everyone posted if there were any new developments.

That night Cathy hardly slept. She kept replaying in her head the last thing she said to Sophie. "Sophie, don't put it off, none of us know how long we have here on earth." Cathy started to cry. "Please, Lord, let her be all right."

Morning finally came. Gene took the day off of work to stay with the kids, and Cathy headed to the hospital. Jim said there hadn't been much change and left with Emily to go home and sleep. Cathy promised to keep them posted.

Over the next couple of days, all their friends took turns staying with Sophie. Whenever the hospital allowed visitors, someone was by Sophie's side. Then it was Cathy's turn again. She was sitting next to Sophie, holding her hand and telling her how the boys made sure every time they prayed—before meals, before bed, and in-between—to pray for Sophie. "I think even little Nikki is saying prayers for you."

Cathy had just finished telling Sophie about something cute Zack had done when she felt Sophie's hand move beneath hers. She looked closely at Sophie's eyes, and it looked like she was trying to open them. Cathy quickly pushed the nurse call button and a nurse arrived within minutes. "What's wrong?"

"Nothing's wrong. I think something great is happening. I think Sophie's trying to wake up." The nurse quickly ushered Cathy out of the room and promised to come get her when all was settled.

After what seemed to be a very long hour the nurse finally came out. "Someone's asking to see you."

Cathy hustled into Sophie's room and started to cry when she saw her friend looking at her with a weak smile on her face. "I thought we lost you. You gave us quite the scare."

Sophie looked serious and reached out to take Cathy's hand. "Cathy." Her words were slow but deliberate. "I heard you and Nikki come into my room when I was in a coma." Sophie had a sweet smile on her face. "Cathy, I heard Nikki talk."

"I know, she was cooing every time I said something."

"No, I mean I really heard Nikki talk. She told me that Jesus loves me and that she hasn't stopped praying for me since she's known me. She told me what she wants most in the whole world is for me to wake up and ask Jesus into my heart."

Cathy was speechless. She couldn't believe that Sophie understood Nikki's cooing. Sophie's words touched Cathy's heart deeply, giving her a glimpse into what she always believed was her daughter's heart.

Sophie continued. "Cathy, tell Nikki the first thing I did when I woke up was ask Jesus to come live in my heart." Sophie had tears in her eyes.

Cathy started to cry and whispered. "Thank you, Jesus. Sophie, Nikki's not the only one who's been praying all these years."

Sophie smiled. "I know."

* * *

Nikki was so wired up, she couldn't fall asleep. "Seefas, can you believe what mom said at dinner tonight? Sophie finally did it. She asked Jesus into her heart. And she heard me. She understood what I was saying to her. That is so cool." Nikki just kept talking; she could hardly contain her excitement. Cathy had been in twice to make sure everything was all right, and Zack kept laughing at Nikki being so animated. Usually Zack was asleep by this time, but Nikki was keeping him up.

Seefas laughed. "It really is an answer to prayer. There was a party in Heaven today."

"It will be so cool to be a part of that one day." Nikki's eyes shined.

"It is amazing to be part of." Seefas longed to be home but loved being Nikki's guardian angel. Soon he would be going to give an account of what he'd been doing on earth.

"Hey, I just thought of something. Do you think Sophie's husband, Kevin, was part of that celebration?" Nikki's eyes danced.

"You can count on it. He was probably leading the celebration, right behind Jesus."

Seefas loved the way Nikki thought through things.

"I wish I could tell Sophie that. It would make her so happy. Maybe Jesus can tell her for me."

* * *

Cathy had just made breakfast for the family, a treat they enjoyed on Saturdays when the kids were home and Gene was off work. "Sophie's come so far in her walk with the Lord," Cathy remarked as they sat down to eat. It had only been four months since Sophie's accident. She had recovered quickly, however, and wanted to jump right into getting involved at church. "She asked me last night if I would help her start a Bible study for her neighbors. It's so fun to see her excitement for the Lord."

"She's definitely a new person. Jim is so excited to see the change in her, but he's taking it slow. He doesn't want to rush into anything; he wants her to fall in love with the Lord first." Gene and Jim met regularly, and Jim really appreciated Gene's mentorship and the accountability their conversations provided.

"I think she's there. She wants everyone to know about Jesus." Just then the phone rang, and Cathy got up to answer it.

Gene knew instantly something was wrong because his wife had turned ghostly pale. Gene asked her what was wrong.

Cathy just sank into the dining room chair, thankful that her boys had just run upstairs to play. "Why don't you take Nikki up to play with the boys?"

Gene knew something was really wrong if Cathy even wanted their daughter out of earshot. When Gene got back down, Cathy had her head down on the table and was crying. He went over and stood behind her, putting his hands on her shoulders. "Sweetheart, what happened?"

Cathy looked up and said in a soft whimper, "It's my dad. That was Mom. During the night Dad had a stroke, and their neighbors Joe and Becki came over to help until the ambulance got there." Joe and Becki, a very sweet, young couple, lived next door to the Saterlees.

Gene was scared to ask. "Where is he now?"

"He's at Legacy Mount Hood." Cathy started to cry again. "Gene, he's not doing well. Mom said that he goes in and out of knowing who she is. The doctor's not hopeful that he'll recover from this."

Grant came home a few days later under hospice care. Cathy's siblings had told her to call if she felt they needed to come, so she made a call to each of them.

Over the next twenty-four hours all five of her siblings made it to Portland. They had to decide the best course of action for their dad, as well as consider what would be easiest on their mom. Cassie, Cathy's youngest sister, took the reins of caring for Grant. She was an X-ray technician and was used to working with people in the hospital. Grant couldn't do anything for himself; he needed help going to the bathroom, eating, and showering. Cassie was a big help, but she lived in Florida, and they needed someone who could be there twenty-four/seven. They talked about whether to place Grant in a home, which he had always been against, or have someone come stay at the house.

It all became overwhelming for Cathy, so she left the room and went in to see her dad. He was having a good day as far as recognizing them and seemed to have a little more energy. Grant was sitting in his favorite chair. Cathy sat on the floor and put her head on his lap. Grant stroked her hair. "What is it, Honey?"

"I just love you, that's all." Cathy had a hard time holding it together.

"I love you too. You're my darling girl."

Cathy just stayed that way, enjoying being by her dad and treasuring the time; she didn't know what tomorrow would bring. By the end of the day everyone was feeling a little more encouraged. They planned to call a nurse about coming to stay with Grant and May. Since Grant had a little more energy that day, Cathy went home and Craig drove home to Stayton. Chad, Cheryl, Charlie, and Cassie, who came from out of state, stayed at their parents' home.

The next morning, Cathy was planning on going with her family to see Nate and Lynn. Lynn had just given birth to a baby boy the night before. They named him Evan Andrew. Just as they were walking out the door, the phone rang. Cathy answered it. Her eyes were red, and Gene knew that the news wasn't good.

"It's Dad. He hasn't regained consciousness at all this morning. Hospice is there and said that he most likely only has a few hours." Cathy couldn't believe she was saying this.

"Should the kids and I go with you?" Gene and Cathy had talked with the kids earlier that week about how Papa wasn't doing well, and he could be going to see Jesus soon. The kids had wanted to go see Papa for a little bit every day.

"No, you guys go ahead and go over to your brother's. I'll call when I feel you need to come. I know the kids will want to say good-bye."

Cathy got to her parents' and everyone was gathered around Grant's hospital bed in the family room. They were still waiting for Craig to arrive, but he was on his way. "How's he doing?"

May was being so strong. It brought peace to Cathy. "He has times when he's in pain, then it subsides. The nurse gave him some pain medication, which has helped, but Dad hasn't woken up at all today."

It was especially hard to see Grant unable to do anything on his own; he was a retired Marine and was used to his independence. The family had agreed that if Grant was going to be this way, they hoped God would take him home soon. But now that it was happening, Cathy wasn't sure she meant it.

When Craig and his family finally arrived, Cathy called Gene about coming over. Everyone took turns talking to Grant. It seemed like he was fighting to stay with them, as one by one everyone told him it was okay to let go. They told him they loved him and would miss him terribly. That seemed to relax Grant. The kids took turns saying their good-byes. Then Cathy placed Nikki next to her Papa on his bed, and Grant let out his final breath. Everyone was quiet and sad, and then Nikki started giggling.

May looked shocked and blurted out that Nikki just talked.

Gene picked Nikki up and Cathy went over by her mom. "Mom, what did she say?"

May looked at Cathy. "As clear as day, I heard her say, 'Bye, Papa.'" Cathy was not surprised, especially after Sophie had heard Nikki talk. Cathy had always been sure that Nikki could see her angel, and now Cathy was convinced that her dad was the one who made Nikki laugh and that Nikki had seen him going up to Heaven.

This brought peace to everyone. Just a few minutes before, Cheryl had been asking where the angels were, and now May looked at her. "Cheryl, they were here. We got to see them through Nikki's eyes."

Gene took the kids home and Cathy called Annie's husband, Eddie, her childhood friend. Eddie worked for a funeral home and had told them that he would take care of the arrangements.

The next day, when they were all gathered at May's discussing the memorial service, Zack was looking around the house. He finally came up to his mom. "Mommy, where's Papa?"

Cathy got tears in her eyes. "Honey, remember Papa went to be with Jesus?"

Zack looked at her with a confused look on his face. "I know that. But, where is Papa's body?" Cathy was amazed at the understanding of her four year old.

She went on to explain to him that they would be having a memorial service, and then they would go to bury Papa's body.

The family decided that Dean, Cheryl's husband, at the service would sing "I Can Only Imagine," a song about what we will do when we are face to face with our Lord. Josh piped up, "I know what Papa will do."

Cathy laughed. "You do? What's that?"

Then Josh stood as still as he could, brought his right hand up and saluted. Everyone laughed. Cathy hugged him. "I bet you're right."

* * *

The memorial service was beautiful. Many of Grant's friends from all over the world came. They watched the slideshow Annie had put together of Grant's life, people shared stories about how Grant had impacted their lives.

Then they made their way over to a small graveyard in the country, where Grant and May had purchased plots long ago. It was a beautiful spot and so peaceful. The graveside service was touching. A military unit played taps, then folded the American flag and presented it to May. Cathy imagined how much her dad would have enjoyed the service. What a wonderful way to honor a truly remarkable man.

* * *

After a long day, everyone was tucked snuggly in bed, and Cathy was able to crash. Her last thoughts before falling asleep were of her growing up years and how her dad had played such a vital role in her life. She was going to miss him very much. She was so thankful for the closeness that each of her kids had with her dad; she knew they'd always remember him.

In the other room, Nikki was reminiscing with Seefas about her Papa. "I'm going to miss Papa so much. I was his princess."

"Yes, you were. You and your Papa had a great connection."

"Seefas, do you think that is why I was able to see Papa go up to Heaven with his angel?"

"That could be. You're able to see me, so I guess it makes sense that you could see your Papa."

"I'll never forget that. It was incredible being able to see Papa very much alive when his lifeless body lay next to me. Then he leaned over and tickled me and told me he loved me." Nikki's eyes got misty.

"It was a touching scene to witness. I've never seen anything like it."

"I'm so glad that Granda heard me talk to Papa. It seemed to help everybody."

"It gave everybody a glimpse of your Papa. It's also different when someone who loves the Lord dies because their family has a peace that they will see him once again in Heaven."

"I can't imagine what it's like for people who don't have that peace. It makes me sad for them. Seefas, why don't we spend some time praying for people who don't know the Lord?"

For the next hour, two voices were lifted up to the Lord in prayer.

CHAPTER FORTY

Josh's and Nikki's birthdays were here again. Josh was turning nine and Nikki seven. Cathy couldn't believe how fast the years had gone by. She always spent time on this day reflecting on their lives.

This year was marked by both sad and exciting events in the Ellertons' lives. The hardest part of this day was celebrating it without her dad. Cathy missed him so much. Some days when she would walk into her parents' house, she half expected to see Grant sitting in his chair.

"Mom, we need to go. Remember we need to stop by and pick up Granda." Josh, like always, couldn't wait to get to his party. May had always relied on Grant to do the driving. She was slowly learning to drive again, but when Cathy had offered to pick her up for the party, May didn't hesitate in accepting the offer.

The Ellertons were the first to arrive at the park and wasted no time in getting things set up for the party. They were expecting more people than usual this year; it seemed like everybody was in town.

The guests started arriving. Jill's dad, Ryan, and his family were first to arrive. Gene had led Ryan to the Lord about seven years ago, shortly after Nikki was born. Cathy greeted them as they walked up. "Hi, there. Is Jill joining us today?"

Ryan laughed. "She's coming. She and Paul will be here a few minutes late."

Cathy smiled. She knew that the two of them were getting close. "They've been spending a lot of time together lately."

Ryan smiled. "He's a good kid. They're pretty serious, and I'm expecting Paul to ask me anytime for Jill's hand in marriage."

Cathy laughed. "Wow, that is serious." As Gene and Ryan began talking about work, Cathy moved on to greet their next guests.

Cathy saw Lisa, her husband, Greg, and their kids walking toward them. Cathy ran up and gave Lisa a hug. "I don't see you enough now that Nikki's getting her therapy at school. I miss you my friend."

"I know. We need to make an effort to get together."

Lisa leaned over and kissed Nikki on the forehead. "And, how's my favorite girl?" Nikki giggled in response. Turning back to Cathy, she said, "Jessica told me that she saw you guys at Loved Ones at church. She mentioned that Nikki loved the worship time."

"She did; it was very sweet watching her. It's so great seeing Jessica involved with things like that."

Lisa nodded. "I know; she was the last of us to come to the Lord, and I think she's more involved than the rest of us."

Cathy laughed. "That's great."

Gina arrived with Lindsey, and they took Nikki over to swing.

At that moment, Cathy looked out to the parking lot and saw Adam unloading a stroller from the car while Val was pulling out a car seat. Val had called her last night saying they'd just gotten the baby and were going to bring him today to show him off. Cathy ran over to greet them. "Val. Let me see him." Cathy looked in at the little guy all bundled up in his car seat. "He's beautiful. Hi, little Benjamin."

Val beamed with pride. "He is beautiful, isn't he?" Cathy loved that Val was already the proud mama of this little guy.

"How is he doing?"

"He's doing well. We're going to have to start taking him to doctor's appointments to have him all checked out." Cathy was very familiar with this routine, as they'd had to do the exact same thing with Nikki. "Hey, there's my mom."

Tanya was walking over toward them.

"How's she taking to being a grandma?"

"You'll see," Val laughed.

Tanya walked up, smiled at Cathy, then leaned down into the car seat. "And how's the most handsome grandson a grandma could have?" Tanya picked up the car seat and gave the tiny guy lots of kisses.

Cathy laughed and leaned over to Val. "I'd say she loves it."

The party was in full swing, and Cathy couldn't help noticing that neither Sophie nor Jim was there yet. "Gene, have you heard from Jim? He isn't here yet."

Gene looked around. "I talked to him yesterday, and he said he's coming. I'm sure he'll be here."

"Hey, Cathy and Gene," Emily said, as she and Amanda ran by. "We're heading over to say hi to Nikki and the boys."

"Nice to see you girls. Hey, Emily, I take it your dad's here." Cathy looked around.

"Yeah, he and Sophie are unloading presents from the car. I think between the two of them, they bought out the store." Emily laughed and kept on running.

It didn't escape Cathy that Emily had said her dad *and* Sophie. Cathy smiled and went looking for them. She saw them at the car getting gifts out of the trunk and looking like two lovestruck teenagers. Cathy thought aloud to herself. "It's about time."

Jim and Sophie noticed Cathy heading their way, and Cathy was sure she saw them both blush. "Hey, you two. What did you do, buy out the store?"

They laughed. "We were having so much fun, I think we got a tad carried away."

"Ya think?" Cathy laughed. "You're going to spoil my kids."

As Jim and Sophie headed over to pile their gifts next to the others, Jim laughed. "A little spoiling never hurt anyone."

Gene had started grilling the meat and everyone was in their own little conversations. Cathy looked around her and felt so blessed to have such wonderful people in her life. She was honored that God had placed such a wonderful little girl in her life, and that through Nikki, their lives were rich with friendships.

* * *

That night when all was quiet around the Ellerton home, Seefas was telling Nikki that the time had come for him to give an account to the Lord about what was going on here on earth.

"How long are you going to be gone?" Nikki looked worried. "I will miss you tons."

Seefas laughed. "To you, it will seem like no time at all. Time here on earth is different than time in Heaven. But don't worry, another angel will come and watch over you until I return."

"Another angel? Will I be able to see him too?"

"Only the Lord knows. But you know that even when I can't be here, Jesus always is."

"Oh, Seefas. I can't wait to see Jesus one day. Oh, that reminds me. When you go up to Heaven, please give my papa a great big hug, and tell him I love him and miss him so much."

"I will do that. Now you should go to sleep, and I will be back before you know it."

"But, I'm not a bit . . ." Nikki said with a great big yawn, ". . . sleepy."

Seefas laughed. "Close your eyes and I'll sing you to sleep."

Nikki soon fell fast asleep. A couple of hours later she opened her eyes, as she often did, but instead of seeing Seefas, there was a different angel standing guard over her. In a very sleepy voice, Nikki asked. "What's your name?"

* * *

Seefas's heart soared; he was home again. Every time he came back, he was overwhelmed by the beauty that surrounded him and the songs being lifted to the King. As he was taking in his surroundings, he noticed a young man standing by a beautiful waterfall. The man looked like he was about to slide down the waterfall. As Seefas got closer, he realized that the young man was Grant Saterlee.

Grant turned around and when he saw Seefas, he ran up to him and threw his arms around his massive shoulders. "Seefas, so good to meet you. Thank you for taking such good care of my beautiful granddaughter. How is she?"

Seefas was overcome with emotion. He felt honored to finally meet this remarkable man, a man who'd done great things for God's kingdom when he was on earth. "She's great. She told me when I saw you to give you a big hug and tell you she loves you."

"She's amazing. Tell her I love her immensely. I still can't believe the whole time that you could understand her and carry on a conversation with her. I guess I'm not surprised; we all suspected that. As I was being led up here to Heaven by my guardian angel and had a chance to interact with Nikki, I got a glimpse of how Nikki sees the world."

"You left a great legacy for your family. You should be proud."

"I'm proud of all of them. I know that they're all right, and I will see them all up here one day. You know my grandson, Zack, used to ask if you could slide down waterfalls in Heaven. I'm thinking about giving it a shot."

Seefas laughed. "Go for it."

Laughing too, Grant turned around and jumped into the water. As Seefas was walking away, he looked back and saw Grant sliding down the waterfall.

Seefas's heart leapt as he approached the glassy sea that was so radiant, reflecting every color in the rainbow. He got in line with all the angels who were there to report to the Lord. This time, standing here was much different than the last. Then, he'd been waiting to receive a new assignment; now, he was reporting on all the wonderful activities taking place in Nikki's life and giving an account of his work.

As he neared the Lord, the longing grew deeper. Being next to his King was the greatest feeling there was. At last it was his turn, and as he approached, he fell to his knees in worship.

"Seefas, I'm so proud of the work that you are doing with my precious Nikki. What have you learned while being with her?"

"When You first told me about her, I didn't understand. I couldn't fathom how a little girl could have such an impact on the world without uttering a word. She has touched more lives with her contentment and joy than I could ever imagine. It's unspoken love."

"That's right. It's easy for people to get in trouble using their words. It's their actions that impact the world the most. Nikki has indeed mastered this."

"My Lord, her love for You is greater than I have seen in any person I have guarded."

"The same love is inside every person; others just have a harder time letting it out. Your time with her has just begun. There are many years to come, and she will need your strength, Seefas."

"I will be there. It is an honor to be Your servant and be guardian to such a beautiful little girl, on the inside and out."

"Many great things are ahead. Go, learn, and be on your guard."

Seefas bowed before the Lord, took another look around the place his heart yearned for, and left, ready to see what the years ahead would bring.

ACKNOWLEDGMENTS

When my daughter was born, I struggled with accepting her for who God made her to be. I decided to sit down and write; I prayed that the Lord would speak to me through my writing and show me how to love my girl well. I want to thank Him for showing up in a big way; there were many times that I would stop to read what I had wrote and it was like the Lord was speaking directly to me. He taught me how to see my daughter through His eyes, and I fell head over heels in love with who He made her to be.

I want to thank my kids: Josh, Nikki, and Zack. They are the inspiration in a lot of what takes place in this book. We have gone through a lot over the years, but with the help of the Lord we have all grown stronger because of it. The three of them are now young adults and are my biggest supporters. I couldn't be prouder of them.

The completion of this book wouldn't have been possible without the magnificent team at Deep River Books. I want to thank Andy Carmichael, who was always available to answer my questions and was supportive through the whole process. And, of course, my editor, Michael Degan, who made my book shine.

I'm grateful for my friend, Tonya Walmer, who took the time to read through my manuscript and do the initial editing of it before sending it to the publisher. She showed me that my book could touch countless lives.

I also want to take this opportunity to thank my kids' grandfather, Dave Bressel, who sent out a letter asking for prayer when we first found out that Nikki wasn't growing normally inside the womb. Because of his letter we had people praying all over the world.

ABOUT THE AUTHOR

Danielle Shryock grew up as a child of missionary parents. After her dad retired from the Marines, her parents felt the Lord calling them to the mission field; less than a month later, they were in the Philippines with their four children. While there, they brought two more kids into their family. Danielle has lived in four countries and twenty different homes, and attended nine schools. She graduated with her bachelor's degree in psychology. After graduating, she kept herself busy being a full-time mom to her three children. When her kids were young, she found herself a single mom. Fourteen years later she can look back and see how God blessed them in countless ways and is so thankful that all her children are walking with the Lord. Danielle works in children's ministry at Good Shepherd Church in Boring, Oregon.

www.DanielleShryock.com